The
Serpent's
Tooth
A Murder Mystery

The
Serpent's Tooth
A Murder Mystery

GWEN MOORE AND PAT BRITT

Published by
Turtle Press
Port Townsend, WA

The Serpent's Tooth
by Gwen Moore and Pat Britt

Published by

Turtle Press
P. O. Box 158
Port Townsend, WA 98368
(360) 385-3626

Book design by
Ruth Marcus, Sequim, WA

Back cover photographs by
Joe Englander, Port Townsend, WA

ISBN 978-0-9651963-2-1

—

This book is dedicated to the late
CHARLES EDWARD SHAW,
for many years Curator of Reptiles
and Assistant Director of the San Diego Zoo,
who in 1958 invited the authors
into his Reptile House
and its library
to discuss
what he called
"herpetological mayhem."

—

PROLOGUE

Madelyn Rivers brushed aside the fishnet curtain and scanned the crowded restaurant. Charles would be here, rehearsing his role. Thank God they weren't married. There was no judge to confront, no attorney, only Charles. In an hour she'd be free. There he was, by the window, saluting her with his drink. She took a deep breath and walked toward him.

"Mady! You look marvelous." His eyes ran knowingly over her body. "You've lost weight. Could it be—?"

He pulled her to him. For a moment she wanted to bury her face in the familiar tweed jacket. But the scent of English Leather tainted with gin evoked memories of his drunken rages.

She stepped back. "Please don't."

"Sorry. It's a hard habit to break." He helped her into her chair and squeezed her shoulders. "I came early to get our table. Your seagulls are putting on a show. They're glad we're together again."

"We're together because I have something to say—"

"I'm all ears. But first, a toast for old time's sake."

"I have to work this afternoon—"

"Come on, love, a glass of wine can't hurt. Waitress, a glass of white wine for the lady, and another martini for me."

He cupped her chin in his hand and turned her face toward him.

"Not that I need anything when I have you—you and those eyes. How I've missed those beautiful brown eyes."

She pushed his hand away.

"Sorry, darling. I keep forgetting I'm not allowed to touch."

"It's over, Charles."

"Whoa. Drinks first, remember? It's been three weeks. I want to hear about you."

"There's nothing to report." She felt his eyes caressing her face.

"Tell me about the zoo. How are all the creepy crawlies?"

"You don't give a damn about reptiles."

"You shut me out of that part of your life."

"You've never shown the slightest interest."

"When I ask about the zoo, you clam up. You're doing it now."

"I suppose you want to hear all about the Komodo dragon trade."

"Komodo dragons. They breathe fire, don't they?" She glared at him, and he raised his hand. "Testing. Just testing. So what's a dragon worth in the zoo world?"

"Fred's in Indonesia finding out. First he has to convince the authorities that we can handle dragons. They're ten feet long and have all sorts of special requirements."

"Well, love, if anyone can make them flourish, you can. You are one hell of a lady—talented, beautiful, and very sexy."

"Forget the bullshit!" She felt nothing for him. Meeting his eyes, she looked away quickly. Except desire. Oh God, yes. The chemistry was still there.

"Did Gerty greet you with open arms?"

"Yes, as a matter of fact, she did. I enjoy living in her house. It's full of animals and people."

"Gertrude and her little band of misfits." He chuckled.

"Those misfits are my friends."

"How well I know. But I see that was a bad topic. We could talk about my job, but there's not much to say. I've been too busy missing one Madelyn Rivers. I feel like half a person without her. When are you coming back, Mady?"

"I'm not. That's what I wanted to tell you. You can keep the couch. I just want my desk and the lamp."

"You can't just leave."

"I already have."

"You said you wanted time to think."

"I'm not coming back, Charles. I'll borrow Larry's van Sunday morning—"

"So that's it. Larry Cooper's calling the shots now."

"He has nothing to do with it. Larry's my boss and my friend."

"He's in love with you. And he's a no-good, lying—"

"Please not again."

He paused. "Sorry. There's something about Cooper that makes me crazy. That's the last time, I promise. I love you, I need you, baby." He reached out and took her hand. "One more chance, that's all I ask. For the good times in Ensenada, making love on the beach. We could go back there."

"It's too late for that."

"Nothing's changed, Mad. I'll prove it to you."

Her heart sank.

"Here are our drinks. A toast, love. To us."

She hesitated. "To the good times."

"Oh, sweetheart, don't make me beg. You're my life—"

"And you were mine. Once. To those times, to the good times, Charles." She clinked her glass against his.

"Thank you, my love. Speaking of good times, I have tickets for the opera Saturday. We'll go to the Silver Fox first."

"The zoo art show is Saturday. Larry wants me there."

"It's always Cooper, isn't it?"

"The art show is part of my job."

"And the other part is shacking up with that fart."

"You rotten bastard—"

"He treats you like a big shot and you eat it up. I tell it like it is and you leave me. Waitress, another martini."

"Can't you even make it through lunch without getting drunk?"

"I am not drunk." He leaned back with one arm over his chair, pointing at a man seated in the window booth. "Tell the lady I'm not drunk."

"You're disgusting."

"No. You're disgusting." Now the waving finger was pointing at her. "One of your snakes would be more fun in bed than that slimy Cooper."

"I've had enough of your sick fantasies. There is nothing between Larry and me."

"No, s'pose not. Take someone sexier than you to turn him on." She sat frozen as Charles stumbled to his feet. His hand tightened on her arm like a vise.

"Let go of me!"

He leered down at her. "You need a real man, not that asshole zoo wimp."

"You egotistical, son-of-a-bitch—"

"You can't leave me." He wiped his face with his sleeve. "No one else would have you. You'll come back for more. You need my—"

In a fury, Madelyn pulled free of his hand, seized his glass and threw the drink in his face. Her chair crashed to the floor as she stood up. Backing away, she felt the silence in the dining room. Charles was teetering by the table, his face a deep red. He lunged toward her, but stopped when a burly waiter appeared beside him.

"Go back to your zoo, you God-damned snake-whore. Go wrap yourself up in cobras. I hope they kill you."

She fled from the restaurant.

CHAPTER ONE

Morley Stevens poked at the mountain of paper on his desk. A slick magazine slid onto the floor, followed by a cascade of books, file folders and scraps of paper. He knelt awkwardly. "It has to be here somewhere."

"Oh, hell! Where's my pipe!"

Morley glared at the raven atop the bookcase. "Shut up, Caruso, and help me find that envelope. I can't make my pitch without the cage dimensions." He glanced at his watch. "It's almost nine. I'll be late for Cooper's meeting again, and that won't help, either."

The bird cocked his head as if listening intently.

"Without those figures, I'll never persuade Cooper that we need a lammergeyer flight cage. He'll say 'They're just oversized vultures. Use one of the eagle cages'."

Caruso flapped across the room and perched on the edge of the desk. "Oh hell! Where's my pipe?" he repeated.

"Just shut your beak, Caruso. You should be... What's that you're standing on? The envelope. Well done!" He stroked the smooth feathers. "I think you're underemployed." Opening a desk drawer, he pulled out several peanuts and a piece of apple. "Here you go, old friend. Don't let any strangers in."

Morley shut the door and headed toward the Administration Building, choosing the meandering path through the trees at the top of the bluff. The fresh scent of damp eucalyptus lifted his spirits. The zoo had all the ingredients for a world class organization. It just needed a breeding pair of lammergeyers to put it over the top. But Cooper was such a toad—

He paused at the top of the bird-of-prey cage. Getting this gigantic wire dome built had been a real battle, and it had been well worth it. It was the size of half a football field, and 100 feet high at the tallest point. The birds had hiding places and plenty of room to soar. But it wouldn't work for the lammergeyers.

At the top of the steps, he stopped to look into the high outcropping of rocks where the eagles had built their nest. He could see the two eggs, still intact, but what was that flash of light near the nest? He was late, but he'd better make sure it wasn't anything that could hurt the birds.

As he pulled a small pair of binoculars from his jacket pocket, he noticed movement at the top of the cage. The white-shouldered vultures should have been in their favorite dead tree, sitting within gossip range as they tasted the morning air. Instead, all five were circling.

"Morley!" Madelyn was coming down the steps toward him. "Have you spotted a hatchling? Male or female?"

"Pretty hard to tell while they're in the shell. Look up there, Mad. What do you make of that?"

She tilted her head back, eyes on the vultures. They were hovering, wings outspread like shrouds. "I've never seen them do that."

"Look! Over by that bush." He pointed to a thicket near the bottom of the cage.

"All I see is a scrubby manzanita…"

"Not the plant. Underneath it and slightly to the left. Someone's in there."

She took the glasses and focused on a half-concealed form. "You're right. Let's get closer."

Madelyn raced down the steep stairs, leaving Morley behind. She paused at the landing and raised the binoculars again.

Morley joined her, and took the glasses. "I'm going to wring his neck. He's trying to steal birds right out from under my nose," he grumbled.

"That's no bird thief, Morley. And forget the glasses. We'll have a better view from the bottom."

Madelyn ran down to the shrubbery at the base of the cage.

"Hurry! I can see a man's suit—" Her voice trailed off. "With a man in it."

"You there, in the cage," Morley shouted. "What the devil do you think you're doing?"

"He's not moving. I think—"

"He's hurt."

"Quick! Where are your keys?" She held out her hand, not taking her eyes off the still form under the bush.

"My keys." Morley fumbled through his pockets. "Must have left them in the office. Bit disorganized this morning."

"We've got to get in there. He might have fallen. Or he might be—"

"Yes. Look at the vultures."

"I'll call security and 911." She reached for her phone. "Damn. I must have left it on the desk. Give me yours."

"Mine isn't even working. Caruso dropped it in the toilet a couple of weeks ago. I'll stay here. You go find security. And don't run! We don't want to attract a crowd."

Wearily, Morley climbed back up to the landing, hoping the man had moved. But another glance toward the bush was convincing. He wasn't going anywhere. Ever. Sighing, he turned and leaned against the cage. This was going to be a rotten day. He was missing his chance to sell the lammergeyers, and Cooper would blame the whole thing on him.

"Dr. Stevens! Dr. Stevens, wait for us!" A short, heavyset woman in a magenta sack was struggling up the stairs, followed by a horde of children. "All right, boys and girls. Come and meet Dr. Stevens."

"There must be some mistake. I—"

"You said today would be perfect for telling the children about your captive breeding program."

Oh God! He had said that, thinking today would never come. But here she was in his face.

"Children, say good morning to Dr. Stevens."

"Good morning," they shouted in chorus as they gathered around him.

A small girl with yellow curls tugged at his pant leg. "Where are the baby birds?"

"What are those crows doing up there?" a freckle-faced youth asked.

"Hey, Miss Suttersby." A solemn kid with large round glasses was standing at the cage door, pointing toward the body. "There's a dead man in the cage."

Before Morley could stop them, the shrieking children surged forward, trampling the geraniums next to the wire.

"Mrs. Subtlety—"

"Miss Suttersby."

"Suttersby. As you can see, we have a problem, and I must ask you to get these children out of here."

"Hey, Morley! What's going on?"

Morley scanned the crowd and spotted one of his keepers. "Let him through!"

The young man elbowed his way to Morley's side. "I heard something funny's going on in the bird cage."

"There is a body in there, and I need your keys to get in."

The keeper produced his key, and Morley entered the cage. A hush fell. Maybe the birds would calm down now. But he'd have to work fast.

Pulling the branches aside, Morley bent over the body. He looked at the half-hidden face. The man was certainly dead. And he—Oh God—no! It was Charles Brooks!

A sudden movement caught his eye. A large, brownish snake was slithering along the ground just inside the cage and in front of the gathering crowd. Several spectators had noticed it too, and were struggling to move back.

He was halfway to the cage door when someone shouted: "Duck, Morley. Duck!"

Hitting the ground, he felt a rush of air. The giant Andean condor had swooped within an inch of his head. Morley scrambled to his feet and rushed out the gate, locking it carefully behind him. He stood for a moment, leaning against the wire, catching his breath.

The children were still there.

"Is the man dead?"

"Did the bird bite you?"

"How'd the snake get in there?"

"Miss Suttersby!" Morley shouted.

"Be quiet, children. Dr. Stevens is busy. When will you be ready to speak with the children, Dr. Stevens?"

"Isn't that what I've been doing?"

Morley was relieved to spot one of the security guards. "Move all these people out of here. We must have access to the cage."

He found Madelyn on her knees, close to the wire.

"Morley, it's the taipan. It has to be ours. There isn't another within a thousand miles."

He knelt beside her. "There are more important things in the world than your taipan, Mad—"

"I don't think so. The paramedics are coming, and the police. We can't let anyone in there with that guy loose. He's one of our most dangerous snakes, and he's angry. He could kill that man. That is, if he's not already—"

Helping Madelyn to her feet, Morley took a deep breath.

"He's dead. There's nothing we can do for him."

"You're sure?"

"Very sure. And there's something…Stop! Somebody get that kid!"

A security guard was already grabbing a small boy, who was climbing the cage.

"I'll get my snake hook and bag from the Reptile House."

"No. You're the snake expert, and the taipan's on the move. One of the keepers can get your gear."

She had to be told it was Charles. But not until the snake was under control. And not when there was a mob standing around watching. He'd tell her later, when they were alone.

"You okay?" Morley asked as he handed Madelyn a snake hook and a canvas bag.

"Why wouldn't I be?"

"You're shaking."

"It's just—all these people."

"Well, be careful."

She paused at the edge of the crowd. This was ridiculous. She'd handled hundreds of poisonous snakes. The only danger was overconfidence, and that certainly wasn't a problem today.

A paramedic waiting at the cage door stood aside.

"Shouldn't take me long," she told him.

"Don't hurry on our account," he replied.

As she closed the gate behind her, the fog lifted and she found herself in a blaze of sunlight. The crowd was quiet, waiting for the show to begin.

She inched forward, watching the taipan. A puffy, unappetizing snake, he undulated in the direction of a log. More than anything else, he resembled a vastly overgrown and rather dirty maggot. How arrogant of a maggot, to so disturb the universe of the zoo.

She focused on the snake's movements. She had to catch him before he became entangled in the underbrush—or, worse, disappeared. If he slid forward, she could get her hook around him and lift him into the bag. As she edged closer, he made a sudden lunge and wrapped himself around a bush. Catching a coil with her hook, Madelyn pulled him loose and, almost before she knew it, had closed the bag over his writhing body.

By the time she reached the door, the attention of the crowd had shifted to a shouted dialogue between the small boy, who had climbed up the cage again, and a fat guard who was trying to coax him down. She had been upstaged.

Seizing the opportunity, she headed for the calm and security of the Reptile House.

CHAPTER TWO

Madelyn loosened the top of the canvas bag and waited for the taipan to emerge onto the floor of his cage. He struck at her arm before slithering toward his rock. She locked the cage and sank into a nearby chair. She had to think. Someone—probably the dead man—had moved the taipan to the bird cage. Had he taken only one snake? Or were there others wandering around in there—or someplace else? She shuddered at the thought of the king cobra going for the ducks in the petting zoo. She and Ed would have to check the entire collection.

But she didn't want to move. The sweet, damp warmth of the Reptile House was reassuring. She took a deep breath and savored the aroma—a blend of wood chips after a summer rain and...snake. Only the night lights above the cage doors were on, and it was restful in the semidarkness.

Too restful. Resolutely, Madelyn rose and switched on the overhead lights. Ed must not be in yet. She'd have to do her own snake check.

She turned to the display cages that lined the outer wall. The easiest way to check the snakes was to go outside and walk along with the visitors. But she wasn't ready to answer the inevitable questions.

She peered into the king cobra's den and let out her breath. He was there. Next door, the tiger snakes were coiled in a ball as if nothing had happened. But what had happened? Perhaps the dead man was a disgruntled employee—like the keeper Morley had fired last month. Maybe he'd put the taipan in the cage, thinking it would kill some of the birds, or at least make trouble. But the snake had killed him, instead. That would explain everything. They'd know soon enough.

Thirty minutes later, Madelyn had checked all the displays. That left the hundreds of small cages and glass jars that filled the offices and spilled into the central courtyard. For those she would need Ed's help. She pushed an empty cage out of her way and walked across the courtyard to her office. Snakes were everywhere—the three puff adder babies for the Woodland Park Zoo, the rainbow boa that had arrived last week. Her desk had become the designated staging area.

Kicking off her shoes, she sat down and tried to relax. Larry would know if they'd identified the victim. She considered texting him, but instead sat staring at a baby emerald tree boa in a small jar beside the computer. The snake had twined like a vine around a tiny branch, its red skin hot against dark gray bark.

The sound of footsteps in the courtyard made her pulse race. How silly. That would be Ed. "Hi, Ed. I'm in my office. I suppose you know all about—Oh, it's you, Larry." His familiar round shouldered frame seemed diminished. "I was going to text you. Have you heard anything about the dead man?"

"He's been dead a number of hours. The police think he was murdered. There were no visible signs of violence—no gunshot wounds, no blood. So they're talking about snake venom."

"That fits my disgruntled employee theory."

"So you don't know. . . I'm sorry. That was no disgruntled employee, Mad. It was Charles. Charles Brooks."

"Charles? That body ... Charles is dead? It can't be..."

"It's Charles. I saw him myself. I'm sorry, Mad."

"But the cage.... Charles wouldn't have been in the zoo, let alone the cage."

"Mad, I saw his body."

"It can't be him. I'll go..."

She started toward the door. Cooper blocked her way, placing his hands on her shoulders. "There's nothing you can do. The cage is cordoned off, and the place is swarming with people. Listen, Mad, the police are talking murder."

"They think the snake—my snake—killed Charles?"

"Yes. You must decide what you're going to tell them."

"What do you mean?"

"You're being naive if you think they'll ignore the obvious."

"If it was murder, the snake didn't kill Charles. You'd have to be crazy to use that taipan as a murder weapon. He's much too dangerous if you don't know how to handle him."

"Exactly. You are the expert. And you and Charles—"

"I won't listen to this."

"You need an alibi for last night. We were supposed to meet for dinner and I—"

"You're not suggesting we lie!"

"I'm suggesting we stick together. You are in great danger, Mad. Do you understand?"

"You think I killed him."

"That's not what I said."

"It's what you meant. What's wrong, Larry? Is the murder going to hurt attendance?"

"Stop it."

"It was inconsiderate of me to kill Charles in your zoo."

"I didn't— I wasn't—" He hunched his shoulders in a gesture of defeat. "Forget it. I'll be in my office if you need me." He turned and started out the door.

"Wait," Madelyn held out her hand. "I'm sorry. I should thank you for coming."

"No need. But there is one thing. Don't tell the police I was here."

"Are you out of your mind?"

"I don't want to create problems for you."

"I have nothing to hide."

"Fine. Play Girl Scout. I hope it's fun, because prison won't be."

The door slammed behind him. Madelyn sank back into her chair and looked at the baby snake in the jar. Charles was dead. She had wished for her freedom so many times, but not like this. She didn't want to believe it. Charles was dead. Killed by a snake from her collection. She was the obvious suspect. Half of San Pablo had heard them quarrel. How could she ever explain? Her lover and her snake.

"You say Dr. Rivers just happened to be with you when you spotted the body?"

"Yes." Morley brushed Caruso off the corner of the desk. "Can't you see I'm busy? I'll feed you later. Sorry, John." He forced himself to meet the detective's eyes. "There's nothing strange about that. We were both going to Cooper's meeting—"

"And is that the route she would normally take from the Reptile House to the Administration Building?"

"Well— I don't know. You'll have to ask her."

"Right. And you pointed out the body to her?"

"Yes. We weren't sure it was a body."

"Why didn't you go in and check?"

Morley shifted in his chair. "I couldn't find my keys."

"So Rivers went to get help."

"That's right. Then one of my keepers came and I used his key to get in."

"That's when you realized it was Brooks, and that he was dead?"

"Yes. Sit down, John. That pacing is making me nervous."

Harris lowered his tall frame onto the side chair and tilted back against the wall. It was a familiar pose. He often sat like that when he stopped by to discuss a case. But this was different.

Lieutenant Harris of the San Pablo Police was here on official business.

"Rivers came back after you noticed the snake?"

"Right."

"How come you didn't tell her about Brooks?"

"There was too much happening. And I'm no good at things like that. Besides, Mad needed her wits about her when she went in after the snake."

"So you don't say anything to her. She goes in, catches the snake a few feet from the body, and still doesn't notice that the body's dressed in her lover's sports jacket?"

"She was concentrating on the taipan. Do you have any idea how hard it is to pick up an eight foot poisonous snake when he's angry?"

"YOU knew it was Brooks."

"I was staring him in the face. Mad was fifteen feet away, and her entire attention was on the taipan. She couldn't have recognized him."

"And I say again, a woman who's been living with a man will recognize him at that range, alive or dead."

"He was under a bush. Have you been there, John? Have you seen the body?"

"Put it this way. I would have recognized you under that bush. And I'm assuming she knew Brooks one hell of a lot better than I know you. I haven't met Dr. Rivers yet, but—"

"You must have met her at Gert's."

"I've only been invited a couple of times, and Dr. Rivers was not there."

"Really? Well, uh, you know Mad's living there again? She moved out on Brooks three weeks ago."

"They quarreled?"

"They were always fighting. I mean—"

"Face it, Morley, your friend's in trouble."

"That's ridiculous. I've known Mad for years. There's no way she would kill anyone—"

"This from the man who always suspects the little old lady in tennis shoes?"

"It's different when real people are involved."

Harris raised an eyebrow. "They're always real."

"I mean innocent people. Mad's no murderer."

"You surprise me, Morley. You know that nice people can kill."

"She's different. Wait until you talk to her. You'll see."

"Guess it's time to go do that." Harris walked to the door. "Well, Morley, you've been telling me you wanted to be in on a case from the beginning. I'll be interested to see how you like it." He left without looking back.

Morley pounded the desk with his fist.

"He thinks she killed him!"

Caruso sidestepped his way along the top of the bookcase toward Morley. Head cocked, he tried his rasping, Stevens-like voice: "Charles Brooks. Charles Brooks was her lover."

"Caruso, go to your cage." Morley stared at the phone. He hated to bother Gert at work. She'd been in crisis mode for the last month with that acceptance test. Still, computer programmers were always in crisis mode, and it couldn't be helped.

"Good morning. This is THE END."

"Gertrude Gypsom, please."

"Ms. Gypsom isn't in today. Can someone else help you?"

"No, no thanks." He hung up. "They worked all night, Caruso. I can't convince her it doesn't help to get that tired."

The raven nodded sympathetically. "Charles Brooks."

"Hush. I'm going to have to wake her up."

Gertrude's hello ended in a yawn. Morley paused, imagining her grey eyes, the impatient toss of her head as she waited for his response.

"Gert, it's me. Sorry to wake you—"

"Hi, darling. I'm so glad you're back. How was the trip?"

"Worthwhile, I think. We have the offer of some breeding lammergeyers— But I'll tell you about that later. Right now—"

"First, you have to congratulate me. We passed the acceptance test last night. Cyril and I made that system do cartwheels. It's being shipped today, and I'm going to sleep for a week."

"That's marvelous, but—"

"I've missed you, Morley. We've hardly had any time together all month. But tonight we'll make up for it, right, darling?"

"Gert— I have to tell you— Charles is dead."

"Charles Brooks?"

"Yes."

"Oh, dear God! Does Mad know?"

"Yes. No. She doesn't know it's Charles, but she knows someone's dead. She's the one who spotted the body."

"What happened? A car crash?"

"No. A snake. At least, that's what it looks like. We found his body in the bird-of-prey cage. Locked in with the taipan."

"Morley, this is a joke, right?"

"I'm afraid not. And John thinks the snake might be the murder weapon—"

"Charles was murdered?"

"That's about it."

"Does John suspect Mad?"

"I'm afraid so."

"And she doesn't even know Charles is dead? I can't take this in. I'm coming down."

"You'd better stay put. Harris' men are crawling all over the zoo and the press will be here."

"But Mad needs me."

"There's nothing you could do."

"Then I'll call her. Morley, you should have told her it was Charles."

"Well, I didn't. You don't know what it's like down here. My birds are getting policemen instead of breakfast. If this keeps up, the eagles may abandon their eggs. That would mean starting all over—"

"Then you should help the police finish in the cage. And while you're doing that, you can keep your eyes open for clues."

"I'd only be in the way."

"Mad needs somebody on her side. You can at least find out what they're doing. John won't mind."

"I suppose not."

"Call me if you hear anything. And be careful, darling."

"Of what?"

"Christ, I don't know. Whatever."

Morley sighed deeply. She wanted clues. For that he would need a container. Glancing around the office, he spotted his lunch bag. The plastic sandwich box was perfect. But he had to do something with the sandwich. Well, he wasn't hungry, and Caruso was.

The bird, who had watched attentively as Morley placed the sandwich on the floor of the cage, said "Charles Brooks. Charles Brooks."

"Unfortunately not, Caruso. Roast beef will have to do." Morley picked up the box and his magnifying glass and dropped them, along with his pipe, into his sagging jacket pocket. Thus armed, he nodded formally to the bird, and marched out the door.

Gertrude hung up the phone and pulled the comforter around her. She was cold, and Madelyn had obviously shut off both her phones.

Was this happening or was she dreaming? Or drunk? They'd had too much wine with dinner last night. But she didn't feel even vaguely high. It must be a dream. She just needed to wake up. But how? Maybe the alarm clock. She grabbed it and ran it ahead until it screeched loudly. For a moment she thought she was waking up.

But nothing had changed. Charles was still dead and she still had to deal with it. She might as well get dressed. "Up, Kanga." She tossed the Siamese cat onto the floor. "We have work to do."

Grabbing her old black caftan from the back of the rocking chair, she hurried into the bathroom. "Charles is dead," she told her reflection in the mirror. "And your hair looks like yesterday's linguine."

She splashed cold water on her face and pulled the shapeless garment over her head. John would be around to ask questions. He would want to know all about Mad. Charles had wreaked havoc, even in death. And this time his boyish charm wouldn't help.

Gertrude headed for the stairs. She needed a plan. No, she needed coffee. Coffee first. Then decisions. She was on the third step when her foot hit something small and furry. "Kanga!" she screamed as she fell forward. She groped for the banister and felt her fingers slide off the polished oak. The enormous gown gave her an odd buoyancy as she bumped and tumbled her way to the bottom.

John Harris walked along the row of cages, looking at the occupants. Hand-painted signs, with delicate, enamel portraits, described each snake's habitat and life history. Classy. King cobra, tiger snake—

He stopped at the next cage. TAIPAN—Australia. The large brown snake inched along the sand toward the window, eyes fixed on him. It was unnerving to make eye contact with a murder weapon. A gun was a lot more civilized. But how had the murderer managed it? The outside of the cage looked secure, with fixed, heavy glass. However the snake had been moved, it must have been an inside job.

"Got it! Beautiful shot, Lieutenant, and I do thank you so much."

The jaunty tenor was unmistakable. Harley Knopstead.

"Just one more, that's it. Perfect! You wouldn't believe the pix I've taken this morning. The vultures, a body and a snake, and then a snake woman performing in arena three. We haven't had a show like this since Potts was found dead on the roller coaster back in '04. I'll never forget that shot of you with his head—"

"The Chief still hasn't forgiven me for that. You almost ruined my career."

"But Lieutenant, you're the one who picked up the head—"

"Why me? Why not take someone else's picture for once?"

"You're photogenic. Hey, is it true the snake lady did in her lover?"

"Somebody talks too much."

"So it's true."

"I didn't say that. What caption are you going to run with that picture?"

"How about 'Policeman Eyes Murderer'?" An infectious grin lighted Harley's face as he brushed a lock of red hair off his forehead. "Or 'Interrogation of the Murder Weapon.' Which would you prefer?"

"I'd prefer you didn't run it."

"Ask me something I can do, Lieutenant."

"Beat it. I have work to do."

"I'm out of here. Rumor has it the next act is an elephant shooting poisoned darts out of his trunk."

Harris headed for the Reptile House entrance and leaned on the doorbell.

CHAPTER THREE

A lion was screaming. Gertrude opened her eyes. Again the scream. "Kanga! Did I trip over you? What's wrong, sweetie?" The regal brown and cream cat was crouched halfway up the stairs. Gertrude struggled to her knees. "I'm sorry, Kanga. Come and make up—" The Siamese backed and talked her way down the steps. Gertrude reached toward her, but Kanga retreated to her private window under the stairs where she pawed at the glass. "All right, already, I'll open it." She lowered herself to the floor gingerly and crawled slowly into the tiny space, convenient for Kanga, not so much for her. Her ankle was throbbing. She gritted her teeth and tried the window. It didn't budge. Finally she shifted her weight onto her legs and pushed with both hands. The window shot up and the cat burst past her to freedom. Gertrude was lowering herself to floor when her hand hit something cold. It was a flat piece of metal with a handle. Another bit of construction mess. This trowel must be a gift from the wallboard guys. She'd stick it in the box of stuff she was saving for Gus. He might be a great contractor, but that kitchen remodel had been the worst experience of her life. Until now—

Oh God, Charles. She grabbed the banister and pulled herself to her feet, suppressing a squeal as she tried to put weight on her ankle. She could deal with the headache and dizziness, but the ankle...

She limped across the hall and paused to throw the small trowel into the box by the kitchen door. Then she leaned against the wall for a moment, watching the ocean. Ruffled by the wintry wind, it segued between blue and green. The beauty went on as if Charles had never existed.

She swallowed two aspirin and was pouring a cup of coffee when the phone rang. Maybe it was Madelyn.

"Dr. Rivers?"

"No, she's not here."

"This is Harley Knopstead, San Pablo Star News. When do you expect her?"

Reporters already. "I have no idea when she'll get home, and I wouldn't tell you if I did. She has a right to her privacy."

"I don't see the snake as a big privacy issue, myself."

"The snake?"

"Yeah. I have some questions about the taipan—"

"She doesn't have time for that. Call someone else at the Reptile House. Call Ed Piper. He knows all about snakes."

"That's no good. You see, I have this shot of Dr. Rivers with the snake and…"

"Someone at the Reptile House can help you. I can't."

"But she's… Of course! Lieutenant Harris was headed for the Reptile House. That's where she is."

"If you knew that, why did you call here?"

"To find out where she is. And I did. Please tell Dr. Rivers I'll call later. That's Knopstead, Star News."

"Idiot!"

But if Harris was grilling Mad, that meant trouble.

Gertrude picked up her phone and hobbled to the closest chair.

She winced at the pain as she lifted her ankle and propped it on the table. It would be such a relief to crawl back in bed and forget the whole thing. But she couldn't do that. Mad needed her friends now. The problem was to figure out what they could do.

Gertrude sipped her coffee and looked out at the ocean. Only twenty-four hours ago her biggest concern in the world had been finding the last bug in the computer system. With Cyril's help, it hadn't even taken long. His methodical approach kept her from getting lost in her intuitive leaps. And he was marvelous in a crisis. But he was exhausted. And Christine had seemed tired during their late night dinner. Still, this was an emergency. It would require a nice loud landline.

Gertrude was disappointed to get a recorded message. "Keep it short. Especially you, GG."

"You don't want me wasting your valuable time, is that it, Cyril? Well, here it is in one short sentence. Charles Brooks was killed last night in the bird-of-prey cage by one of Mad's snakes and the police think she did it. Oh, and just in case you've forgotten my voice, this is GG." She hung up.

He had his nerve, making fun of her. But that could wait 'til tonight… Tonight! He'd made her forget why she called. Wearily she hit redial and listened to the message.

"I don't want to hear your stupid message. I wouldn't be calling back if you hadn't annoyed me in the first place. What I'm trying to tell you is that Madelyn is in real trouble. The police and the reporters and everybody are after her. We've got to do something, but I haven't figured out what. It hurts to admit it, but I need your brain. Every once in a while you see things more clearly than I do." She'd done it again.

She dialed and waited. "So all right. Just shut up. Madelyn needs your help. Please, come here tonight—at seven thirty—so we can talk about what to do."

She hung up and shifted her weight. Touching her ankle gingerly, she realized it was swelling. Hopping to the refrigerator, she dumped ice cubes into a plastic bag. But when she started back to the chair, the ice fell noisily onto the tile floor. Everything was out of control. She eased herself down, wrapped up the nearest ice cubes in a dishtowel and placed it on her ankle. Charles might be dead, but he still had power. She shivered. The house could be so cold this time of year. She'd turn up the heat.

But first she'd better pull herself together and call the others about the meeting.

Madelyn shivered as she listened to the voices outside.

The press had arrived. The newscasts would be full of it—the cage, the bird, the snake, Charles… Charles and her, with carefully worded references to their relationship. Her life had become public property.

She froze at the screech of the bell. The detective at last. She walked toward the door, trying to breathe normally.

"Dr. Rivers? Lieutenant Harris, San Pablo Police."

So this was Morley's great detective. He had the look of a runner— the loose stance, spare frame, gaunt face— and his eyes had the cold clarity of a microscope. Her scrutiny was being returned. A tingling sensation ran down her backbone and settled in a knot at the base of her spine. She must be on her guard with this man. He could destroy her life.

"Come in, Lieutenant. Shall we go to my office? I—"

Ed Piper burst through the open door. "What the hell is going on?"

"There's been a murder. This is Lieutenant Harris. My assistant, Ed Piper."

Harris offered his hand, but Piper didn't respond. He pulled a handkerchief from the pocket of his khaki jumpsuit and wiped his brow. "I heard Morley Stevens was found dead in the turtle pond."

"Not Morley. Charles Brooks was found in the bird-of-prey cage."

"In the bird-of-prey— That's. . .it's impossible."

"Mr. Piper," Harris said, "I'll be talking to Dr. Rivers for the next half hour or so. Then I'd like a few minutes of your time."

"I'll be in my office. But what should I do about those reporters outside?"

"That's up to you, Mr. Piper. I would suggest you watch out for a tall, red-haired photographer. He'll quote you out of context."

"That's the one. He wanted to take my picture. Can you imagine how Hilda's family would react to that? It's bad enough that I work in a zoo."

Harris turned to Madelyn, his eyebrow arched.

"He's concerned about his fiancée's family," she said. "The Smithsons. They own the castle up by the observatory."

"I'm sorry the murder is inconvenient for you, Mr. Piper. We do our best. Just cooperate. We'll get out of your life as quickly as possible."

"Well, I don't think it's right—"

"Now, Dr. Rivers, if we could proceed—"

Stepping over a small tortoise, Harris followed her down the hall. She was a surprise. From Morley's description, he had pictured a forbidding scientist— hair in a bun, no-nonsense bifocals. Instead, she turned out to be a slim-hipped brunette with large, disconcerting eyes. She seemed ill-at-ease, but that wasn't surprising. The advantage was his, even if it was her Reptile House.

He stifled a yelp of pain as his shoulder collided with something hard. A loud crash muffled his apology. An aluminum stepladder lay spread-eagled on the concrete floor. What a klutz! "Can I stash it for you?"

"I'm ashamed to say I don't know where it belongs." Rivers folded the legs together and leaned the ladder against the wall. "Disorganization is a way of life around here." She put her hand on his arm and pulled him out of the path of a young woman who hurried past with a cage full of fat rats.

Maybe it was Rivers' advantage after all. Harris was relieved to be led into a small office. It was cluttered, but at least he wouldn't step on anyone in here.

"Sorry, Lieutenant. Just toss those books on the floor, and sit down."

Settling cautiously into a decrepit chair, Harris opened his notebook. It was hard to concentrate. The zoo atmosphere was distracting, and Rivers— appealing. Clearing his throat, he said, "I understand you and Morley Stevens discovered the body."

She nodded. "At first we thought he—Charles—was alive."

"Did you recognize Mr. Brooks?"

"No. I just found out who it was a few minutes ago. Larry Cooper— he's the Zoo Director— told me."

"He came here?"

"Yes. Charles was my lover. Larry didn't want me to hear about his death from a stranger."

"Thoughtful of him." So Cooper's crisis had been a ruse to give him time. Deliberate deceit or well-intentioned meddling?

"When did you last see Brooks alive?"

"We had lunch— correction, a nasty fight— at Frank's Fish Tank yesterday." Her voice was flat, as if the sound had been forced through a wringer.

"What did you fight about?"

"The works. My job, my commitments, his drunken jealousy..." She bit her lip.

"Where were you last night?"

"Monday is the night I have dinner with Larry, but—"

"You're seeing both Cooper and Brooks?"

"You mean you think Larry— Oh no, Lieutenant. Larry is a friend and colleague. Nothing more. We've been meeting for dinner since I came to the zoo. Charles sometimes comes— came— along, but the reptile talk bored him."

"Brooks was jealous?"

"Only when he was drunk. Like at lunch. He knew..." She picked up a small yellow and black plastic snake. "He had no reason to be jealous."

So she had a partial alibi for Monday night. "Where did you go for dinner?"

"But we didn't go. Ironic, isn't it? I canceled dinner the one night it mattered. I had a terrible headache after that scene with

Charles. I came back here and talked to Morley for a little while. Then I went home." She paused. "Poor Morley got the brunt of my anger. He can tell you about that."

Harris nodded. Stevens hadn't mentioned seeing Rivers.

"What time did you leave the zoo?"

"About two."

"Did you stop anywhere on your way home?"

"No. I drove directly home. Then I called Larry to cancel dinner and went to sleep."

"Perhaps one of your neighbors saw you go in?"

"I doubt it. The house is perched on a hill, back from the street, and the driveway is screened with bushes."

"Did you see anyone during the evening?"

"Just my cat. GG— Gertrude Gypsom— she owns the house where I'm staying—"

Harris nodded. "I know GG."

"She worked late last night and was still asleep when I left this morning."

"So you argued with your jealous lover a few hours before he was found dead in the zoo, close to one of your own snakes, and you have no witnesses to your movements from two p.m. yesterday until this morning?"

"You make it sound ominous, but that's how it was. This morning I overslept. I was hurrying to make the nine o'clock staff meeting when I met Morley. The vultures were circling in the bird-of-prey cage, and we saw the body."

"What happened next?"

"I went for help. Miss MacMillan called 911, and I got the security guards to come. By the time I got back to the cage, Morley had spotted the snake. I caught it and brought it back here. Then Larry came down to tell me about Charles. After that I just sat here, waiting for you."

"How long had you known Brooks?"

She bent the toy snake back and forth between her fingers. "We met at one of GG's parties about a year and a half ago. He had been hired as a programmer at her company—END Computing. He only stayed three months. His father died and he inherited a business."

"What kind of business was that?"

"An importing company in Japsom City. Brooks Imports, I think. I really don't know anything about it. Charles didn't go there often— maybe once a week. He said it sort of ran itself. And he did have enough income to give up his programming job."

"When did you start seeing Brooks regularly?"

"Right after the party. He seemed interested in my work, and I thought he was wonderful. Brilliant, sensitive, curious... I moved into his apartment a couple of months after that. Everything was fine until he started drinking again."

"He was an alcoholic?"

"A recovering alcoholic. He'd been sober for ten months and four days when I met him. He'd been a binge drinker, escaping from his loneliness—at least that's what he told me. Everyone liked him— Everyone except GG. She said he had bad vibes. But that didn't stop me. First I was fascinated, then I felt sorry for him. I thought he needed me."

"When did he start drinking?"

"About a month after I moved in. One night he came home drunk, and tore the place apart. I fled and spent the night in a motel. I made plans to move back to GG's but he arrived at the zoo with a room full of flowers and a tender apology. And that's how it was. The apologies, the gifts, the binges, the threats. My attempts to help only made matters worse, but I couldn't stop trying. Why is it so obvious, now that it doesn't matter?" Two large tears trailed slowly down her face.

"So you left him?"

"Yes. I moved back to GG's three weeks ago. Then I finally got up my courage to end it. I told him that at lunch. That's why he was so angry." The plastic snake broke with a loud crack. Rivers sat for a moment staring at the pieces, then threw them on the desk and put her hands over her face. "It all sounds stupid, even to me. If I can't believe it, who will?" She fumbled for a Kleenex and wiped the tears from her eyes. "But you want to know if I killed him. I should have made that clear. No, despite all indications to the contrary, I did not kill Charles Brooks."

Harris stifled an urge to reach out to her. Those expressive eyes conveyed an intelligence and intensity that was unmistakable. Still, Brooks could have forced her over the edge. A cheery ringtone startled him.

She blew her nose and checked her phone.. "Sorry, it's from Fred Mahoney. He's in Indonesia negotiating a trade for the zoo. It's the middle of the night over there, so it must be important."

"Take your time. I'll go talk to Mr. Piper." He headed out the door.

Fred was bursting with news. It was probably better not to mention Charles' death. There was nothing Fred could do to help.

"So we're going to get our Komodo dragons?" she asked.

"We're close. I told the Minister of Tourism that you're so crazy about lizards you keep one in the kitchen. He was properly impressed."

"You're supposed to show him the pictures of the new enclosure, not talk about me."

"Trust me, Mad. I know how to sell."

"I do trust you. And I'm excited. Imagine what this will do for our endangered species breeding program."

"But before you start celebrating, you should know that your love objects are contingent on freeing up a female white tiger. Can you swing that?"

"Our friends in cat canyon won't like it. But we don't have a Zoo Director who's soft on reptiles for nothing. I'll talk to Larry and FAX you the details."

"Great. I've been out, drinking for my zoo, and I'm beat."

"I admire your dedication. And thanks."

Without pausing to think, Madelyn called Larry, who said he'd be right over. She had to push this through before John Harris made mincemeat of her life. She turned to her notes. They'd been working on the trade for several months and she didn't remember any mention of white tigers. She wanted to be prepared to make her case, but fragments of the conversation next door distracted her.

"What if the body had been found somewhere else? Would the snake bite have been detected?" Harris had saved his technical questions for Ed. That was how it was going to be.

"Ask the medical examiner." Ed's high-pitched voice was in sharp contrast to Harris' resonant baritone.

"My guess is he'll say it was detectable," Harris replied. "But we know about the snake and he's looking for it. Snake bites are pretty rare, and he isn't a herpetologist. You probably know more about venom than he does."

"I can't say for sure, but I don't think he would detect the bite if he weren't looking for it. The taipan is an elapid, and elapids have a generally neurotoxic venom. Like cobras. The venom attacks the brain and the nerve centers. That means there is relatively little sign of injury in the bite area."

"What about the fang marks?"

"They wouldn't be noticeable, and they could be covered by a superficial blow. No, I think a medical examiner who wasn't looking for a snake bite would conclude that the victim had died a natural death."

Madelyn jumped at the sound of the door shutting. "Larry! You startled me!"

"And you startled me. That was a fast recovery. When I left here, you were pale as a ghost—"

"I've been talking to Lieutenant Harris. And then—"

"The old sympathy ploy. I told you not to fall for that, Madelyn."

"The Lieutenant was impeccably suspicious. Listen, we don't have time to argue. Fred says we can have the dragons if we come up with a female white tiger."

"But that's not the trade we've been discussing—"

"I know, but that's the trade that will work. We may not have a chance like this again—"

Madelyn had little difficulty persuading him. She listened with satisfaction as he cajoled the Curator of Mammals into a reluctant agreement.

"I'm really grateful, Larry. This is important to me."

He didn't respond. He was standing at the side table, his back to her. Suddenly he turned to confront her. "You told Harris about your fights with Charles, didn't you?"

"Yes. It was awful. But by the time the trial is over, I suppose I'll be used to telling all."

"Trial? There's not going to be a trial, Madelyn. Not unless you let your guilt push you into one."

"What's that supposed to mean?"

"Use your head. If he could spend a couple of days with you, Harris would know you're incapable of murder. But he doesn't have that kind of time, and he's not into subtleties. He'll listen to you and to everyone else, and he'll draw some down-to-earth, unemotional conclusions. And if you tell him everything you know—"

"Like everything I told you the other night—"

"Last night."

"The night of the murder. If I tell him all that, heaven only knows what he'll make of it, because you're having second thoughts yourself."

"No. Listen, Madelyn, I'm your friend. Harris is not. Don't treat him like one. That's all I'm saying."

"If I want advice, I'll hire an attorney."

"I suggest you do that. I don't care if you hate my guts, but I'm going to get this said. You couldn't help Charles and you had stopped loving him. So you've been driven by guilt. You admitted as much last night. You let it build up until you were at the breaking point."

"And then I went crazy and killed him?"

"Stop putting words in my mouth. Now you feel guilty because you're glad he's dead. Admit it!"

"You have no right to say that." She rose to her feet.

Their eyes locked in waves of accusation.

"Don't I? Stop playing martyr, Madelyn. He wasn't worth it."

"I won't lie."

"I'm not asking you to lie. Just use a little discretion. You even told ME more than you should have."

"Obviously!"

He stepped back toward the door. "I give up. Tell him whatever you like. But he won't hear any of it from me."

She nodded in greeting as Harris appeared in the doorway.

Following her glance, Larry glowered at the detective and stalked out.

"You don't miss much, do you, Lieutenant?" She thought she detected a gleam of amusement in Harris' eyes. "Shall we continue?"

"Not now. Mr. Piper is going to show me around and I need to follow up some other leads. I'll catch up with you later."

She watched him leave and sank wearily into her chair.

Charles had always told her Larry was in love with her. And now he did seem to be jealous. Of Lieutenant Harris? Or Charles? It was all unfathomable.

Madelyn allowed her mind to drift while she contemplated the little tree snake in the jar on her desk. So unconsciously graceful, yet intensely self-concerned in the instinctive manner of the newly hatched. She stared at the snake a long time, sure she was detecting signs that he was about to trade in his infant-red suit for the familiar green of the adult emerald tree boa. The change in color occurred quickly, and she had never been on hand to observe it. Maybe if she sat here quietly she would see it happen...

CHAPTER FOUR

Harris paused at the dusty corridor window. Through the trees, he could see Cooper hurrying stiffly up the path toward Administration. That was one worried man.

Moving on, he peered through the wire viewing hole of each cage. On the visitors' side, the solid glass wall had cut off the sounds and smells. Here, he felt much closer to the snakes.

He read the hand-lettered sign on the taipan's cage:

DISTRIBUTION: Northern Australia
LENGTH: approximately 8 feet
FOOD: large rats
VENOM: neurotoxic/hemotoxic
ANTIVENIN: taipan specific—compartment 2A
CAUTION: NASTY DISPOSITION

Looking down at the quiet brown coils, he felt a little sick. He was used to guns and knives, but to be attacked by a snake? He didn't like this murderer.

"So you found your friend."

"Friend's a little strong, Mr. Piper. How often do you handle him?"

"As seldom as possible. Familiarity breeds contempt, so we approach these guys with respect."

"Is it a big deal to move him?"

"Not really. We have good access. Here, I'll show you."

Harris backed away, and Ed stopped moving. "Don't worry. I won't open the taipan's cage. He's excited, and he's large enough to reach the opening easily. But the rattlesnake next door is docile. This catch slides back, you pull the handle, and then you pick him up with your snake hook. Shall I bring him out for you?"

"I think I get the picture. What a beauty." Harris stood transfixed as the mottled reddish body moved into loose, undulating coils, tail vibrating, creating a buzzing noise. The head swayed, daring him to move closer.

A flash startled him. It was Knopstead, on the visitors' side. The photographer waved. Harris drew back and watched Piper secure the latches.

"The cages aren't locked?"

"No. We rely on the outside door to keep out troublemakers."

"Then anyone with access to the Reptile House could have taken the taipan."

"Right. But in defense of our policy, we've never had a problem before today."

"Could the taipan have been gone long without your noticing?"

"Two or three hours, I suppose. But we check the cages at least once a day to be sure no one's sick or unhappy. And our regular visitors are observant. An empty taipan cage would prompt questions."

They moved into the inner patio. Harris stopped at a temporary pen containing an assortment of tortoises, sitting in a pile of salad, nibbling contentedly. "They're pretty active for November. Why aren't they hibernating?"

"Didn't you notice it's summer in this Reptile House? We keep the entire building at eighty degrees with eleven hours of daylight year round. That's a compromise temperature. The new Desert World will be different—if we ever get it built. We'll have separate temperature, humidity, and lighting settings for each exhibit. Then the tortoises will be able to hibernate as they do in the wild, while the tropical snakes bask in eighty degrees. They're all more likely to breed under natural conditions."

"Interesting. Who's the artist?" Harris motioned toward the easel set up in the corner of the patio.

"Christine Featherworth. She's working on the new exhibit signs. We let her leave her stuff here."

"Does she have a key to the building?"

"Sure. That way she can come and go as she pleases."

"That gives me an excuse to meet her. I like her animal portraits."

"Really? I'm not keen on them myself. Here's my office."

Piper motioned him into a side chair. "So what else can I tell you, Lieutenant? I'm anxious to get this thing cleared up."

"I appreciate that." Harris noted the photo of an unattractive blond prominently displayed on the shelf behind the desk. The fiancee. Plain and expensive. No wonder Piper was worried. "Tell me about your job."

"I'm Assistant Curator of Reptiles. I handle the day-to-day care of the collection."

"How does that differ from Dr. Rivers' job?"

"She worries about the future—raising money for the Desert World and getting new exhibits. And she arranges trades with other zoos, goes to conferences, that kind of thing."

"How did you get to be Assistant Curator?"

"I studied biology. At Ferndale State College, Iowa. From there I went to the Hudson Bay Zoo. I was there four years, and I've been here for two."

"What was your position at Hudson Bay?"

"Curator of Reptiles. But it was a small zoo, and that made the job a dead-end. So I was delighted to come to work for Madelyn."

"How well did you know Charles Brooks?"

"Hardly at all. He came around often enough, but we never said more than hello to each other."

"He came to see Dr. Rivers? He wasn't officially involved in the snake business, was he?"

"Aside from being a bit of a snake in the grass himself, no."

Harris was surprised into a chuckle. "Tell me about Dr. Rivers' relationship with Brooks."

Piper shifted in his ancient desk chair. "Oh, no, I really don't think it's my—"

"Mr. Piper, this is a case of cold-blooded murder."

"But I don't know—"

"You must have seen something."

"No, really. Except I have noticed that she's been unhappy. Even yesterday—"

"Please go on."

"She seemed miserable all morning. And then she went home early."

"But that wasn't the first time you sensed trouble?"

"She's been depressed. They quarreled. I couldn't help hearing them. The acoustics—"

Harris nodded. "Did she do or say anything that struck you as unusual?"

"Why all this interest in Dr. Rivers? You surely don't think she—"

"I don't think anything yet. I'm just trying to find out what happened."

"Well, I can't tell you what's been bothering her. It might have been the sick cobra, for all I know. She's been down here at night several times to check on him."

"Was Brooks in the zoo yesterday?"

"No. He called, but Mady wasn't here."

"What time was that?"

"Afternoon. Three, maybe."

"Tell me about your zoo keys."

Piper removed the key holder from the belt of his uniform. "This one's for the Reptile House, and this opens the service gate out back. That's all I have."

"And where were you last night?"

"I left here about six and was home by six-thirty. Mother fixed dinner, and then the Corbetts—Frank and Edna Corbett— came over to play bridge. They arrived about eight-thirty, and we played until after one."

"You live with your mother?"

"Yes."

"Did you notice anything strange when you arrived at the zoo this morning?"

"The television people, the crowds— Normally I get here around 8, but today I had a dentist appointment. I had just arrived when I met you in the hall."

"Tell me, Mr. Piper, how do you learn to handle poisonous snakes?"

"It's pretty much a hands-on thing. Someone shows you, and you start to get a feel for it. Then it's just a matter of time until you can handle any snake—unless it's extremely large, in which case you need help."

"Who on the staff is capable of handling the taipan?"

"Well, there's Madelyn, Larry Cooper, and me. We have one keeper who's good with snakes, but he's in Panama, on vacation."

Harris made a note. "Can a snake be forced to bite?"

"No, but you could create a situation where there's a high probability. You'd have to be sure the victim was close enough to the snake—"

"How close is that?"

"That would depend on the size of the snake. With the taipan, probably a range of—oh, three feet."

Harris smiled. "Wouldn't it be bizarre if the snake were the murderer? Suppose he escaped, met Brooks in the hall, and didn't like his looks. So he bit him."

"Sounds like the perfect crime. I guess there aren't many laws on the books about prosecuting snakes."

"No. Well, thank you for your time. I'll check back with you later."

Harris let himself out of the Reptile House and joined the crowd of visitors on the eucalyptus-clad path outside. He was looking forward to an interview with Larry Cooper.

A media event was in progress in the reception area of the Spanish-style Administration Building. Harris made his way around a disbanding TV crew and spotted Cooper across the room. He was posing for Knopstead.

"Call me if you have any questions." Cooper shook Knopstead's hand before turning to another reporter.

"Lieutenant!"

"Knopstead! You're bothering someone else. What a pleasant surprise."

"Oh, it's you I'm after, Lieutenant. But the Reptile House was boring, so I came on ahead."

"You knew I'd turn up here?"

"Sure. You always check with the CEO early in the game."

"Really? And then what?"

"Then you eat with Sergeant McDuff. Breakfast, lunch, or dinner. That's when you come up with a plan of attack."

"You're observant. With all that wisdom stored up, you must have a pretty good idea who killed Brooks."

"Oh, no. I don't worry about details like that. I just try to keep abreast of your investigation."

"What a waste of a good mind."

"So I'm off. Got to upload these pix now so I can catch you and the Sergeant at Frank's." Knopstead hurried off into the crowd.

Shaking his head, Harris waded through a group of newsmen who had collared a jump-suited keeper. Cooper was standing in a doorway, listening attentively to an attractive woman with carefully arranged frosted hair. Her softly tailored suit looked out of place in the zoo. Her voice was raised, and Harris could hear her easily over the din.

"…and how was I to know who she was?"

"Listen, Peggy, it was a comedy of errors, and I—"

"I don't see anything funny about it."

"I said that badly. It was an unfortunate situation, and I take complete responsibility for your misunderstanding with Dr. Rivers. I should have introduced the two of you." Cooper's head jerked to one side as he recognized Harris. "But I see I have a visitor. Won't you come in, Lieutenant?"

"Thanks. But first I'd like to talk to your assistant." He glanced at his notes. "Ms. MacMillan?"

"Of course. This is Peggy MacMillan. Lieutenant Harris. I'll be in my office."

Peggy MacMillan looked carefully at Harris' identification before raising her hazel eyes to his face. "What's this supposed to mean?"

"You are aware that a man was found dead here in the zoo this morning?" She nodded. "I am trying to establish exactly what happened. Dr. Rivers came to you for help?"

"Yes. She told me this incredible—"

"Do you remember exactly what she said to you?"

"She said there was a man in the bird cage and that she had to have a key. I'm not in charge of keys. If she works here, she should know that."

"That's all she said?"

"No. She asked me to call the police." She paused. "I asked for the paramedics as well."

"So you believed her enough to place the call, but not enough to give her a key?"

"Well, she was screaming at me. I was confused—"

"I understand you're new here. Why did you choose to work in a zoo?"

"I needed a challenge. I like animals."

"Just one more question. We're asking everyone about their activities after five last night. Did you by any chance work late?"

"No. I had a four o'clock doctor's appointment. Then I went home, had some soup, and was in bed by nine."

"Well, if you think of anything important, please give me a call." Handing her a card, he took his leave.

Something didn't ring true. Cooper's conciliatory tone seemed inappropriate and MacMillan's appearance and air of authority even more so. And Cooper had clearly lied about her earlier—he'd said he had to get back to his office because his new assistant couldn't be left to handle things by herself. She seemed more than competent.

Harris paused at the entrance to Cooper's large, high-beamed office. The ambience was unexpected. Everything from the heavy oak furnishings to the enormous mural of the San Diego Mission, seemed to date from ranchero days.

"Come in, Lieutenant."

"Thanks." Harris sat down opposite the desk. Cooper had finessed him three times this morning. Now it was his turn.

"Is that a zoo map I see in your IN basket?"

"Hot off the press. This one shows the entire two hundred eighty-six acres. As you can see from the slogan," he pointed to the words

CELEBRATE LIFE AT THE SAN PABLO ZOO

printed in large letters at the top. "This is for our publicity campaign. It starts next week, only now we don't need it. The zoo is setting an attendance record today."

Harris opened the map. "Show me where we are."

Cooper pointed to the lower left corner. "Here's Administration. The main gate is directly across from us. The three service gates are clearly marked, and this is the connecting loop road. There are service roads throughout the zoo, all marked in red. The paved walks for visitors are shown in black, and the rougher trails as broken lines."

"Thanks. Now tell me about keys. How are they distributed?"

"Full time employees have keys to the buildings they work in and to the nearest outside gate. There are parking areas at each gate, and most people like to avoid the main entrance. People who have offices have door keys. And curators and keepers have the appropriate cage keys."

"What about support staff, cafeteria workers?"

"They come through the main gate. So do the volunteers. There's a guard on duty there all day every day. During off hours, they ring the bell and one of the security guards lets them in. But you ought to talk to Miss Thomas down the hall. She has the final word on keys."

"Right. Tell me a little about your organization. I know Dr. Rivers is a curator. Do all the curators report to you?"

"Yes. They each run what amounts to a separate department—mammals, birds, and reptiles. And I report to the Board of Directors."

"How long have you known Dr. Rivers?"

"She came looking for a job when I was heading up Reptiles. It's been. . .yes, ten years. We didn't have any openings, but she stuck around and enticed our Indian rock python to start eating. Mady had some special experience with that species, and her advice saved the snake's life. Then she put together her own collecting trip. Somehow she persuaded the Mexican government to let her export beaded lizards, and she came back with three breeding pairs."

"So you hired her on the strength of that?"

"Yes. She worked for me for about two years. Then the Zoo Director died suddenly and—"

"A natural death?"

"Heart attack. I was offered his job, and Mady was the obvious choice to replace me."

"How long have you known Charles Brooks?"

"I hardly knew him at all. You'll have to talk to Mady."

"But you were acquainted with him?"

"We'd been introduced." Cooper was staring out the window.

"Then how is it that you denied knowing the victim this morning?"

"I couldn't see him under that bush."

"Stevens identified him in your presence. Yet you still told me you didn't know him. Why?"

"Well, I think I can explain that, Lieutenant." Cooper's eyes shifted to the window again. What was he looking at? Cue cards? "Or maybe I can't, I don't know. Why does one make foolish statements? To be quite frank with you—"

"That would be a refreshing change, Dr. Cooper."

"I was so upset when I realized it was Charles, I couldn't think of anything but protecting Mady. I was afraid you'd keep me answering questions if I admitted I knew him. I wanted to warn her."

"Warn her about what? Why did she need protection?"

"I didn't want you landing on her with a bunch of questions before she had a chance to—to think things over."

"What would she need to think over? If she's telling the truth, it'll be the same whenever we talk to her."

"You don't understand."

"No, I don't."

"Lieutenant, I could have come up with a much more convincing explanation. It sounds stupid because it's true."

"Good try, but no. Sounding stupid does not make a story true. But then, maybe you thought your explanation was good enough for. . . How did you put it? . . .a simple man?"

"Unsubtle, not simple." Cooper's cheeks were flushed.

"Yes, of course. Unsubtle. The truth is, you wanted to get your stories straight before I talked to you. You're in love with her."

"Nonsense, Lieutenant. Mady is my colleague and I value her friendship. She cared deeply about Brooks. She would not have been involved with two men at the same time."

"That must have made it worse. She chose Brooks over you."

"My relationship with Dr. Rivers is not relevant to this investigation."

"You don't see jealousy as a viable motive?"

"Me, jealous of Brooks? That's not worthy of you, Lieutenant. I admit I was worried about Mady. Brooks had started drinking again. Everyone knew that. But she loved him, and she's my friend. End of story."

"Where were you last night?"

"I left the zoo at five, ate dinner out, and went home to bed. I read for a while and was asleep a little after nine."

"Where did you eat?"

"An Italian place on the highway. La something."

"Did you see anyone you knew?"

"No."

"Where, exactly, is this restaurant?"

"Out near the airport."

Harris rose to leave. "Can you think of any other zoo employees who can handle poisonous snakes?"

Cooper consulted the window again before replying, "Not right off hand. Sorry."

"Thanks so much for your cooperation."

Harris' mood was not improved by his talk with Miss Thomas. She confirmed what Cooper had already told him. The only people with bird cage keys were the bird men, and the same was true of the other departments. Each employee had a key to the entrance gate or to one of the three service gates, whichever was most convenient. The curators had duplicate sets of keys for their own areas.

"Nobody—with the exception of Dr. Cooper—has keys to everything."

"Are you telling me that Dr. Cooper, and ONLY Dr. Cooper, has keys to both the Reptile House and the bird cage?"

"Well, he is the director, you know."

"What about the letters and numbers I've seen stamped on the zoo keys. What do they stand for?"

"All the keys are stamped with SPZ. Next is a department code: B for birds, M for mammals, R for reptiles, A for Administration, V for veterinary, etc. That's followed by an office or cage number. The bird-of-prey cage has a special code: BFC. And the service gate keys are G with the gate number."

"Tell me about your spare keys. Are they all accounted for?"

She stood and checked her key board. "Yes. I can account for every one of them. I'm extremely careful about security. I've always been afraid of an incident just like this. Mark my words, Lieutenant, it'll be the lion next time."

"It's good to know you have the lion's key under control. Now, Miss Thomas, for the record, where were you last night?"

"I left early. Straight home to bed with a headache."

"This place creates them. Thank you, Miss Thomas."

As he walked toward bird mesa, Harris wondered who the hell had been running the zoo when all those people decided to go home to bed early. Come to think of it, that was what he had done, himself. That must prove something, but he wasn't at all sure what.

CHAPTER FIVE

"Good morning, Dr. Stevens." Sergeant McDuff smiled pleasantly as he closed the door to the bird-of-prey cage. "You'll be wanting us out of here."

Morley nodded. "All this confusion is tough on the birds." McDuff's cheerfulness annoyed him.

"Come on, gang. You finished in there, Johnny?"

"Be right with you, sir."

A heavily laden photographer brushed past Morley and pushed the door open.

"And where do you think you're going, Knopstead?"

"Hi, there, Dr. Stevens. I just wanted an interior shot." The flash erupted eerily against the rocks.

"Get that—that thing out of here."

"Sorry. But the readers will want to see the scene of the crime. And what a crime this is. That snake lady might as well have left a lipstick confession on the sidewalk."

"You're not going to print inflammatory garbage like that—"

"Hey, don't get mad at me. I just take the pictures. But it is an open and shut case, isn't it, Sergeant?"

"Let's just say we're pursuing a lead," McDuff growled. "On second thought, let's just say nothing while you get the hell out of here."

"I'm gone. But keep me in mind when you arrest her."

"Knopstead, if you print any of that I'll have your job," Morley shouted as the photographer disappeared down the stairs. "What kind of investigation are you running, McDuff? He's going to print accusations against Dr. Rivers."

"So what's new? He's going to print what he's going to print. Besides, it'll all come out soon enough."

"Madelyn couldn't possibly have killed Brooks. She—"

"Oh, I am sorry. I'd forgotten she's your friend. That's always a shock."

"Hey, McDuff, you comin' or not?"

"Right away. Thank your staff for me, they've been great."

Morley clenched his teeth as the cube-shaped officer struggled up the steps. Shutting the gate with a bang, he headed for the manzanita bush where Brooks had been found. He knelt in the gravel. The low-growing vegetation had been trampled, and the indentations from Brooks' body were still clear. Otherwise, nothing. Maybe something had fallen out of Brooks' pocket—or the murderer's.

He'd find it if it meant going over every inch of dirt in the cage. Handful by handful, he sifted through the gravel. He had crawled forward to peer behind the bush when a sparkle caught his eye. His fingers closed over a sharp pin. He held it up and shook off the loose dirt. It was a platinum snake, partially coiled, head weaving gracefully upward. There was only one such pin. He had seen it a hundred times. Gert had commissioned a friend to make it—a Christmas present for Mad.

He wrapped the pin carefully in his handkerchief and stowed it in his pocket, then walked slowly to the door. He hadn't expected to find incriminating evidence. He needed to talk to Gert.

Morley locked the cage door and turned toward the steps. It was a maneuver he'd made thousands of times, but he was thinking about the pin, and he stumbled off the path.

"Look out!"

Startled by McDuff's angry shout. Morley stopped abruptly, but he had already blundered into a puddle of plaster.

"Damn it, Stevens, you've ruined the cast. Get out of here." McDuff hustled him back to the stairs.

"Sorry about that." Morley walked to the fence, looking for something to scrape the plaster off his favorite loafers. Behind him, he heard footsteps, and a voice calling to McDuff.

"You were right, Sergeant. I followed the footprints right to the Reptile House door. They were erratic the whole way, so Brooks must have staggered all the way down the hill. . ."

". . . after the snake bit him," McDuff concluded. "So he was in Dr. Rivers' Reptile House when he was attacked."

Morley turned angrily to McDuff. "You're talking circumstantial evidence, Sergeant." He wanted to punch the self-satisfied expression off that ruddy face.

"Stevens, I'll thank you to keep your nose out of our conversation—"

McDuff was interrupted by a shout from above. A young officer was calling from the top of the steps.

"Sergeant McDuff, come quick!"

McDuff started up the steps. Morley hesitated and then followed them.

The young man led them to the service gate behind the Reptile House. "Here," he said, "you see those tracks? It didn't rain until late yesterday afternoon, and it looks like those tread marks match Dr. Rivers' tires. I think she was here last night, Sergeant."

"Get the lab results before you think too much... Stevens, what are you doing here?"

"Keeping abreast of the investigation. Your people have been busy. But that mud puddle has been there for at least a month. So she parked there yesterday."

"Not the mud puddle—the tracks just in front of it. You can't tell me there's been mud there for a month. That's fresh."

"Whatever. It's all circumstantial. She could have been set up."

"Not bloody likely. And there's motive—" Sorry to be the one to disillusion you about your friend. But these things happen."

Morley walked slowly toward his office. Mad's pin was burning a hole in his pocket. Maybe Brooks had been carrying it for some reason. And, if the explanation was that simple, why bother John with it at all?

But that would be suppressing evidence. Besides, Mad was innocent, and new information could speed up the investigation.

Morley knocked tentatively on his own office door and was relieved when no one answered. He wasn't ready to deal with John.

Harris was fighting his way upstream through the crowd on the bird-of-prey cage stairs when a fat lady in a flowered muumuu forced him against the wire. What were all these fools expecting to see? The police had finished long ago, and the birds were in hiding.

Why the cage? The snake was at least a lethal weapon. But using the cage was not only grotesque, it seemed pointless and inconvenient.

Hearing a thundering sound, he twisted toward the cage in time to see an Andean condor land nearby. The immense bird daintily picked up a cigarette package in its beak and carried it back to a nest high above. He hoped it hadn't been dropped by one of his men. Looking high in the cage, he could see a second glint of light. In the eagles' nest? Morley would never forgive him if the birds got hold of something harmful.

The fat lady tried to move, lost her balance, and fell heavily against him. Clinging to the wire, he struggled to prevent her from sending both of them down the steps. A flash went off as he regained his footing.

"Knopstead!" Shaking his fist at the photographer, he apologized to the frantic woman.

"Watch where you're going," she admonished him as he made his way slowly through the mass of people toward Stevens' office.

It would be nice to sit and relax for a minute. And there were a couple of things he needed to discuss with his old friend. He knocked softly before entering.

"Ah, John. Yes, come in. Here, use my chair. You look done in." Stevens smiled but avoided his eyes.

"Thanks. But that side chair looks a bit small for you."

"No, I insist. This will convince me I need to go on a diet. You talked to Mad?"

"Yes. And Piper and Cooper and MacMillan and Thomas— And I don't know any more than when I started. God, what a day."

"Look, John, I know you have calls to make, so I'll just get out of your way—"

"Not so fast. I need to talk to you."

"We could do that later."

"You have an appointment?"

"No, I thought you needed some time to yourself."

"What I need is to pick your brain about the zoo. Morley, this case is about access. Keys. Tell me about your keys."

"My keys? Well, let's have a look." Stevens pulled a key ring from his pocket. "Car, house, service gate—the one behind the Reptile House—and my office."

"Where's your key to the bird-of-prey cage?"

"It's on another ring—with the keys to the storage sheds and the aviaries out on the west side. Speaking of which, have you seen our new monkey-eating eagles out there? We're hoping to breed them."

"Monkey-eating? You're not sacrificing those cute little guys out on the mesa, I hope?"

"The monkey guy would never forgive me if I started raiding his collection. But if those birds ever got loose—"

"Morley, we were talking about keys. Could someone have taken your bird-of-prey cage key without your knowledge?"

"Possibly. I wouldn't notice unless I needed it."

"But this morning you couldn't open the cage door—"

"I didn't have that key ring with me."

"Where is it?"

"I'm not sure. It should be in my jacket pocket. But it wasn't there this morning, and I haven't had a chance to look for it. The backup set is in the top drawer. Have a look."

Harris pulled it open. "There's no key ring here."

"That's strange. Someone must have borrowed it."

"It's hard to believe you could have misplaced two sets of keys."

"Oh, I remember now. When I travel, I always leave a set with one of the other curators. I forgot to retrieve them yesterday."

"And that other curator was Dr. Rivers?"

"Why, yes. How did you know? Mad is my backup. She's extremely knowledgeable about birds. I rely on her to straighten me out from time to time."

"Now, for the record, where were you yesterday evening?"

"You know I was away at a conference? Yes, well, I arrived back here about one, and worked all afternoon. It must have been around seven when I walked down to the pizza place for dinner. I was back here by eight. And then I finished going through my mail."

"When you returned to the zoo, what route did you take?"

"I didn't have my key to the service gate, so I went to the front gate and rang the bell. One of the security guards—Horatio Jones—let me in. Then I walked past Administration and up the hill—"

"Here." Harris pulled Cooper's map from his pocket. "Show me on this."

"CELEBRATION OF LIFE! That's a laugh. He should have called it CELEBRATION OF DEATH. At least it's a nice map. Now this is where I came in." Stevens pointed with his pen to the main gate. "I crossed the road, and turned off at the top of the bird cage. Everything was pretty much as usual. But when I left around eleven, I remember thinking how dark it was. The moon was hidden, and I stumbled on a rock in the path."

"But you didn't notice anything unusual?"

"No."

"Think for a minute. Retrace your steps in your mind."

Morley paused. "There was something odd. When I was leaving, I saw a man on the road—I'm sure it was a man—somewhere near the entrance."

"Show me exactly where you were."

Stevens poked at the map. "Here, by the polar bears."

"Did you recognize him?"

"I thought it was one of the security guards, and I wondered why he was wearing a business suit instead of his uniform."

"Did you speak to him?"

"I was just about to when I realized he was carrying something heavy. Yes, that's it. I thought if I startled him, he might drop it."

"What was it?"

"It was a trash can—a white one. That struck me as odd, because all the other zoo cans are green."

"You're sure it was a trash can?"

"It was a large white cylinder—a trash-can-shaped cylinder. That's the best I can do for you."

"Which way was he walking?"

"Away from me. I was standing near the bird-of-prey cage, and he was walking the other way, now that I think of it."

"That's why we try not to hurry interviews, Morley. It takes time to recreate the details."

"And this has certainly been worth your valuable time. The white trash can puts the whole thing in perspective, I'm sure."

"You never know. Who else has bird cage keys?"

"My staff—the assistant curator and two keepers. They hang out in the storage area, if you want to talk to them. And Peggy

MacMillan— That's it! My second set of keys."

"Miss MacMillan has your keys?"

"Yes. She borrowed them for a friend."

"This is the same Peggy MacMillan who has worked here only a few days and who didn't know Dr. Rivers before this morning?"

"Yes. Her friend's an ornithologist, and he was supposed to be here last week. I was leaving town, and she wanted to show him the bird-of-prey cage."

"Surely you don't allow tours in there."

"For visiting ornithologists, we do. I know, a lapse of security and all that. But she seemed so eager, and Miss Thomas had turned her down."

"I'll bet. So has this ornithologist been here?"

"Not to my knowledge."

"Is he well known?"

"According to Peggy, he's an expert on birds of prey, but I've never heard of him. I meant to Google him. I don't read the journals the way I should. But I thought I might run into him at the vulture conference."

"You had a meeting with the birds?"

"No, no. It's an annual get-together for experts on carrion eating birds. We call it the vulture conference because we're vulture *aficionados*. We want to improve the vulture image."

"Maybe Cooper would give you the name of his PR man. That's all you know about this mysterious visitor?"

"He may have come and gone while I was in New York. I asked one of the keepers to show him around if he turned up."

"So we've accounted for your keys. Why didn't Dr. Rivers give them back to you this morning? For that matter, why didn't she unlock the cage?"

"I suppose they were in her office. It didn't occur to me to ask."

"So there you were, working away near the scene of the crime. No alibi. And yet you managed to get rid of both sets of keys."

Morley grinned. "I thought you'd like that touch."

"How well did you know Brooks?"

"Not well at all. I talked to him several times at Gert's, and he seemed intelligent. I suspect he was a dabbler. He played a little piano, Gert says he was a so-so software developer, he'd traveled with his father— But he never seemed to really DO anything."

"But you didn't find him objectionable?"

"Not until Gert told me he was treating Mad badly." He bit hard into his pipe stem. "But whatever your so-called experts say, Madelyn Rivers is not your killer."

"Aren't you being a bit premature? No one has accused her."

"You obviously haven't talked to your own Sergeant McDuff lately."

"No. So you've been poking around. Did you find anything we'd overlooked?"

"Well, since you ask—" Stevens pulled his handkerchief from his pocket and carefully folded it back to reveal the glittering pin. "I think this is Mad's."

Harris peered at it closely. "A snake? Where did you find it?"

"In the cage. By Brooks' manzanita bush. I was sifting through the gravel. The pin was right on the surface."

"McDuff's men shouldn't have missed this."

"They were pretty busy. It's overkill, John. Mad's being set up. Or maybe she dropped it there this morning."

"Was she wearing it this morning?"

"I have no idea. You'll have to ask her."

Harris listened to Steven's account of the footprints and tire tracks. The keys, her car—He hadn't realized how much he wanted to believe Rivers was innocent. With an effort, he kept his voice flat. "Now you ARE being premature."

"I'm just reacting to McDuff. He's ready to go for a conviction."

"He was just talking."

"Well, that kind of talk makes me nervous."

"Give us a chance. I don't need you going off the deep end. All the footprints tell us is that Brooks was in the Reptile House—"

"Objection. The footprints were outside the building, not in it."

"Stop being so jumpy. The investigation is just beginning. Maybe they'll find some fingerprints. And you have a right to be proud of yourself, finding this pin."

"I'm not proud, John. I didn't have the guts to tell Mad who it was under that bush. I let her go in there and chase that snake around the cage with Brooks lying dead practically at her feet. I haven't done a thing to help her, and now your people are jumping to conclusions."

"It's much too early for conclusions—"

"You say that, but all this circumstantial stuff looks bad. I keep thinking how she must feel."

A rasping voice from overhead startled him. "My words fly up, my thoughts remain below; words without thoughts never to Heaven go."

"Caruso, someday you're going to go too far. But John, I am concerned about Mad."

"It's a damn shame that innocent people get put through this kind of a wringer. But getting emotionally involved won't help. A detective has to have even less soul than a news photographer. Well, maybe not that little. Anyway, if you're sure you don't mind my using your office, I need some privacy to make some calls. Unless there's something else you want to tell me."

"How can you say that after I gave you Mad's snake pin? Stop putting me down." Stevens heaved himself up from the side chair and moved to the doorway. "I'll be on my way."

Good. He needed some time to himself. Morley's office was perfect.

CHAPTER SIX

"Listen, Scot, it's a setup," Harris shouted over the din in Frank's Fish Tank. "Someone's out to frame Rivers. Someone who knows enough to make it convincing."

"Bullshit. If she's half as bright as you say she is, she's capable of killing Brooks and making it look like a setup."

"She DIDN'T kill him." Harris stopped short as the raucous background music faded, leaving his angry statement hanging in the air. Embarrassed, he pushed his plate away and pulled out his notepad.

"You're leaving halibut?" McDuff eyed him quizzically. "That's got to be a first."

"I'm not hungry. This case is getting to me."

"So it seems."

"How can you sit there deliberately unwrapping your third pat of butter as if nothing's wrong?"

"Don't lose your perspective, John. Take away the zoo, and this is nothing more than your everyday crime of passion."

"Oh yeah? And when did you last encounter a murder weapon with wanderlust? Not to mention MacMillan's vanishing ornithologist, and Stevens' trash can. And the alibis. Except for that wimp, Ed Piper, everyone in the entire zoo spent the evening alone."

"Sounds like you had a tough morning." McDuff settled back in his chair as the waitress took his plate. "Black coffee, please, with banana cream pie on the side."

"I saved some for you," she replied with a wink.

"Thanks, Jess. Well, John, I had some luck. The tire treads were—"

"Morley told me."

"Then he probably also mentioned the footprints going from

57

the Reptile House down the hill to the cage. We'll have a good case to present before long."

Harris stared at him icily. "It's not that simple."

"I think it is. Why don't we summarize what we know?"

"Okay. I'll take notes. Shoot."

"We know Brooks was murdered—"

Harris raised an eyebrow. "Not so fast, Scot."

"Oh, come on. You can't believe that a well-dressed man strolled into the bird-of-prey cage accompanied by a taipan and died a natural death. And it won't wash as a suicide. No one would use a snake to kill himself. Pills, a gun, a car, water—any of them would be easier."

"No, probably not a suicide. Unless—"

"Unless what?"

"Brooks and Rivers had a bitter fight. Here." Harris looked around the dining room, wondering where they had been sitting. "He might have staged a suicide to get even by incriminating her."

"Could he have handled the taipan?"

"You don't have to know much about snakes if you want to get bitten."

"But he couldn't have locked himself in the bird-of-prey cage. He wouldn't be able to reach the lock from inside. The wire mesh is too fine."

"The security guard might have locked it." Harris made a note. "I'm discounting the suicide angle, but we can't ignore it completely. We're assuming that the taipan and Brooks entered the cage at the same time. But they could have arrived separately."

"Sure, John. Maybe the snake has his own key."

"And he probably could have reached the lock. No, but how's this? Brooks is attacked, or frightened. He runs down the hill to the cage. The attacker finds him, out cold, by the cage door. He tries the door, it's unlocked—or the attacker has a key, either way will do—and he hides the body inside to get it out of the way. All this activity annoys the snake, and he turns on Brooks. Which makes the taipan the murderer."

"Life imprisonment wouldn't be much punishment for a guy living in a zoo exhibit."

"Yeah. Or maybe the taipan was an innocent bystander. Say Brooks was in the throes of a heart attack. He staggers down the hill looking for help. The cage door is open, he blunders in and dies. Coincidentally, the snake has chosen this exact night for his big adventure—"

Scot chuckled. "But seriously, we both know this is a clear case of murder."

"If it's such a simple case, why the snake? Why the cage?"

"The murderer might have wanted the birds to mutilate the body beyond recognition."

"No. Brooks' wallet was full of ID."

"Then maybe she wanted the body disfigured. Given time, those birds would have had quite a feast."

"But Scot, wouldn't a ghoul like that do his own mutilating?"

"So we're back to 'why the cage'. I don't know. Your turn."

Harris noticed an enormous fish staring at him from the tank behind McDuff's head. The fish looked as if he, too, were waiting for an answer. "The murderer wanted to obscure the cause of death. Of course, that still leaves us assuming that the snake sneaked down to the cage under his own power."

"It's about that key." McDuff grinned. "But now you're talking. Because it's obvious—"

"Maybe the snake bit Brooks in the Reptile House, and then the snake pursued him down the hill. They ran into the cage together while the murderer went on home."

"Simplicity itself. Or maybe Brooks fled after the attack, and the killer wasn't sure he'd been bitten. So she chased him, snake in hand."

Harris shook his head. "You'd have to be crazy to chase your victim around the zoo with THAT snake clutched to your chest."

"That depends on your skill—"

"And it still doesn't explain why the body was in the cage."

"Oh, but it does, John. The murderer finds Brooks by the cage, dead. She wants to get the body out of the way, but can't move it far with an eight foot taipan on her hands. She opens the cage door, and *voila*."

"I wonder if it's possible to hold a taipan in one hand while opening a door with the other." Harris made a note. "Anyway, he throws in the snake and then stashes the body. Not quite according to plan, but still neat and secure. But would he really take time to stow the body under a bush?"

"We're talking cool, man. But Rivers—"

"Getting back to my theory, I see a flaw," Harris interrupted. "If the murderer didn't want it known that he was using a snake, the zoo was a dumb place for the murder. It would have been better to take the snake anywhere else."

"But you're assuming the murder was planned. As a spontaneous gesture, it wasn't half bad. And I happen to believe it was spontaneous, and Rivers—"

"But why a snake? And if Brooks ran down the hill after the attack, why didn't anyone hear his screams of agony? Stevens didn't hear a thing."

"Maybe Stevens left the zoo before it happened." Scot paused. "Or maybe you can't hear outside noises in his office. The walls are pretty thick."

"I'll check acoustics, and we'll need a better estimate on time of death. Stevens left at eleven. But the security guard should have heard something, regardless. Speaking of which, Stevens' man with a trash can obviously wasn't a guard. But it could have been our murderer."

"Carrying the body around the zoo in a can looking for a convenient dumping spot?" McDuff grunted. "Not bloody likely."

"He could have used the can to transport the snake—"

McDuff was staring across the room. "Hey, John, isn't that Larry Cooper over near the window?"

"This is a zoo hangout. The next nearest restaurant is twenty minutes away." Harris craned his head around and spotted two familiar faces at a small table behind him. "I see he's with Peggy MacMillan. Standard new employee lunch, or a special session for plotting the next murder?"

McDuff was still staring across the room. "That's Knopstead behind Cooper."

"He told me he'd be here."

"Did he tell you he'd be spying on Cooper and MacMillan? He's not watching us, he's watching them. But forget them! Our murderer needed keys to three zoo locks, could handle the snake, enticed Brooks to the zoo at night without arousing his suspicion, and maneuvered the body and the snake into the bird-of-prey cage. That's limiting, suspect-wise."

"Too limiting. Let's turn it around. The murderer might have assumed we'll miss him on round one if we are concentrating on access. Who emphasized a lack of keys?"

"Stevens. I can't wait to give him the news."

"Let's do a quick rundown of suspects." Without waiting for a reply, Harris started making notes.

DR. LARRY COOPER. Zoo Director. Lying. Handles snakes. Has all necessary keys. Knew Brooks. In love with Rivers. No alibi.

ED PIPER. Asst. Curator of Reptiles. Has snake keys. Handles snakes. Knew Brooks. Good alibi if it checks out.

MORLEY STEVENS. Curator of Birds. Missing two sets of keys. Snake handling? No alibi. Was at zoo. Close friend of Rivers. Knew Brooks.

"I can't believe you're including Stevens."
"He found the body. No special treatment here." Harris continued writing.

DR. MADELYN RIVERS. Curator of Reptiles. Fighting with Brooks who was her lover. Had all necessary keys. Can handle snakes. Apparently no alibi. Question Gertrude Gypsom.

PEGGY MACMILLAN. Cooper's Assistant. New at zoo. Had borrowed Morley's keys, telling him unlikely story. Check it further and question her. Could she handle taipan? No alibi given. No known connection with any of them.

"Are you sure?" Scot looked pointedly at the table across the room.
"Right. I'll note that. And there are a couple more names."

GENEVIEVE THOMAS. Security Administrator. Has all keys. Seems unlikely.

CHRISTINE FEATHERWORTH. Artist. Has access to Reptile House. Can she handle snakes? Alibi? River's friend. Question her.

"And that about does it, until we learn more about Brooks. Meanwhile, we can tidy up some of the loose ends." Harris was pleased with his list. It suggested a format for the investigation.

"Well, back to the real world."

"Speaking of which, isn't it about time to review the details of the case against Rivers?"

"We are not ready to build a case against anybody."

"Hold on, John. She had easy access, and she could probably rustle up a key to the bird cage."

"Actually, she had Stevens'—"

"She could handle the snake, those tire marks matched her car, and it would have been natural for her to meet Brooks at the zoo."

"If she had planned to murder Brooks, the zoo was the last place she would have chosen."

"Maybe she planned to take him away."

"She's not strong enough to lug a dead man around, and she would certainly have been aware of that. Secondly—"

"All right, all right. It wasn't Rivers. Sorry I made such a crude suggestion. But listen to me, John Harris. It's not like you to get emotionally involved, and you'd better watch your step." McDuff stood up and straightened his suit. "I'm headed for the morgue to check personal effects and talk to the M.E. Then on to Brooks' place. "

Harris grumbled a farewell. Damn Scot, anyway. No one should be that sure of himself.

Still fuming, he backed recklessly out of the parking space, narrowly missing a fence. Better calm down. Wrecking his car wouldn't help anything. He had planned to interview GG next, but now he was in a rotten mood. Well, she'd cheer him up if anyone could, and she might know something that would help.

CHAPTER SEVEN

Gertrude dropped the knife and turned to the sink. It wasn't a deep cut, but it was bleeding profusely. She stuck her hand under the tap just as a tan head appeared out of the murky water.

"I'm sorry, Thorndyke. I know you don't like to be disturbed while you're bathing. And there's the phone." She shoved an alligator-shaped pot holder over her hand and grabbed it.

"Gus here."

"Gus! I thought you were going to stop by."

"I did. Yesterday. You weren't home. I read about Madelyn. She's no murderer. Anyone would know that right away. Can I talk to her?"

"She's resting. Listen, Gus, when you installed the faucets in the kitch—"

"Well, tell her old Gus is on her side."

"Thanks. The taps in the kitchen sink are backwards. I'm afraid someone will get scalded. You must fix it."

"I could do it tonight. It'd be after dinner—"

"That's fine. And there's a box of stuff in the kitchen that belongs to you and yours. I've never seen so many stray tools."

"We felt right at home. See you around eight."

"There's the doorbell. I must run. Thanks, Gus." Her ankle was worse. She stopped at the kitchen door and yelled, "Come in."

"It's locked," was the muffled response.

She limped to the door and peered through the fisheye lens. John Harris, looking grim. Slowly she unlocked the door and pulled it open. "Hello, John. Come in."

"Thanks. I guess you know why I'm here."

"Charles."

He nodded.

"We can go in the study, but first let me finish what I'm doing."

He followed her into the kitchen. "What happened to your ankle?"

"I fell down the stairs, if you must know. Now where was I?" She stared at the hunk of cheese on the counter.

"I don't suppose the cheese is related to the injured finger?" John asked.

"How'd you know about my finger?"

"The blood dripping from the alligator's mouth was a small clue."

She looked down and wrapped the pot holder more securely around her hand.

"Who's coming to the party?"

"Larry, Cyril, Christine, Morley— But it's not a party."

"A wake then?"

"No, a meeting. John, we have to help Mad. They—" She paused and looked directly at him. "You think she did it."

"Who told you that?"

"Morley."

"You're all so busy listening to rumors you don't have time to ask me what I really think."

"I'm asking, John. Do you think Mad killed Charles?"

"I don't know. It'll be time enough to worry about suspects when we have the facts pinned down. Now you go put some disinfectant on that finger and I'll deal with the cheese."

"But John—"

"Go!"

When Gertrude returned to the kitchen, he had the cheese cut and neatly arranged on a platter.

"I didn't know you could cook."

"Divorced men learn all kinds of amazing things about themselves." He covered the cheese and stashed the plate in the refrigerator, then walked to the window. "Your remodel is a great success."

"I really use this view."

"You use it?"

"Yes. Like a pacifier. At times like this." She pulled the protective folds of the caftan around her. "I asked Morley one time how a relaxed guy like you could be a detective. He told me you were entirely different on a case."

"Am I?"

"You betcha'. You're giving me cold chills."

"Who told you about Brooks' death?"

"Morley. He called this morning."

"What did he say?"

"That you'd be coming around to ask questions."

"Is that all?"

"He told me to be careful because you think Mad is guilty. Was that a breach of protocol? No one briefed me on the rules."

"There are no rules."

"I almost wish there were. I don't want to say anything that would hurt Mad."

"If Dr. Rivers is innocent, the truth can only help her."

"I'd like to believe that."

"You've been here alone all day?" John picked up the dirty knife and turned to the sink.

"Be careful with that knife! Thorndyke's in there," Gertrude shouted.

"Thorndyke? Ah yes. The golden-eyed monster who's glowering at me from the depths. Has he taken up residence there?"

"He's not a monster, he's a tegu lizard, and he's bathing. But I think he may want out now." She struggled to her feet.

John held up his hand. "Stay where you are. I can handle Thorndyke. Where does he belong?"

"John, I don't think you should pick him up. He has long claws—"

But she was too late. Thorndyke hated being handled by strangers, and he had scratched John's cheek before plopping back into the water.

"Here, let me take him." Gertrude hopped to the sink and retrieved the lizard. As she put him back into his cage next to the refrigerator, she asked, "Do you want to try my disinfectant?"

"No, I washed my face. That'll do for now." He helped her back to her chair. "So, where were we?"

"You asked if I'd been here all day. I went out around one. I thought I might be able to help Mad at the zoo. But the place was a disaster area. I couldn't even park. So I came back here. I was alone until Larry brought Mad home about three-thirty. She looked terrible. What did you do to her, John? Her eyes had this animal fear—"

"Why do you assume it was me?"

"Sorry. And she had been fighting with Larry. I'm so angry with him. She needs her friends—"

"What were they arguing about?"

"I have no idea. I tried to divert them by talking about the meeting tonight. But that didn't help. Larry acted like it was an imposition to come, and Mad doesn't want us to do anything. But we can't sit idly by while the police—" She felt her cheeks flush.

"Did Dr. Cooper say anything else?"

"Not that I remember."

"But he was upset?"

"Extremely."

"So what did you do after he left?"

"Mad went up to bed, and then I came down here—"

"—to fix cheese. Okay. I need a little background information. How long has Dr. Rivers been living here?"

"Six years except for the time she spent with Brooks."

"Would you say you're her closest friend?"

"Yes. We go back to grad school."

"Believe me, I don't want to poke around randomly in her personal affairs. But I can't know in advance what will help. I just have to collect data and hope I'll trip over the answer."

"Now that's something a software developer can relate to."

John laughed and started to sit down. "What's this on the chair?"

"It looks like a level. Toss it in the box over there. Gus will be picking up the construction castoffs tonight." She felt much more at ease. This was hard for John. Bad enough to have someone you knew under suspicion. But he was bound to hear things he didn't want to hear. "How can I help?"

"Tell me about Brooks."

Harris had hoped Gertrude would come up with some new information. Instead, she verified what he had already heard.

"Did you see Dr. Rivers yesterday?"

"No, not since Sunday. I've been a zombie all month over this crash project."

"You worked late last night?"

"Yes. Cyril and I finished the acceptance test at nine-thirty. We wanted to celebrate, so we picked up Christine—that's Cyril's wife—after her class. She teaches pottery at the college. And we all went to dinner. It was after one when I got home."

"Where did you go?"

"La Viera. We drove down the highway and then came back by the ocean route. And, oh yes, we did stop by the house before we left. That must have been ten-thirty. I had to change my clothes. But you don't care about that."

"Why not?"

"Because Mad wasn't here."

"Where was she?"

"With Larry. Didn't she tell you?"

"You're quite certain she wasn't here?"

"Of course. I came in through the garage and turned on the light. Her car wasn't there. They usually take Larry's car, but I figured it was in the shop or something. Besides, the house was completely dark. She would have left a light on for me if she'd been home."

"Did you check her room?"

"Why would I do that when I knew she was with Larry? They must have gone to a show or something, because I heard her drive in just as I dozed off. I wanted to tell her about the project, but I was too tired to get the old bod out of bed."

"Then you heard nothing further? No doors closing or anything like that?" He snapped.

"No, just the sound of the car in the driveway. Why do you ask? She has a perfectly good alibi up to one a.m. Or was the murder after that?"

"We don't have the medical report yet, so we can't place the time of death."

"If only I'd talked to her when she came in. That would have given her a complete alibi. But if the murder was before one o'clock, she's clear?"

Harris didn't answer. Scot had been right. Rivers was lying. Her car tracks, the pin— He had behaved like an idiot long enough. He'd let those big brown eyes get to him. Well, he wouldn't do that again. Gertrude was staring at him.

"Is Dr. Rivers an unusually strong woman? Could she, say, lift a heavy weight?"

"I suppose so. Why? What did I say to make you angry?"

"I am not angry. Get Dr. Rivers for me. I have some questions to ask her."

"Now? Couldn't you wait until later? She's so tired."

He barked a command, and Gertrude hurried up the stairs. He was sick of lies. If Rivers was tired enough, she'd talk.

He studied her as she entered the room. Her face lighted up… as if she trusted him. Not a bad act, he'd give her points for that.

"Do you want me to stay?" Gertrude asked.

"It's up to you." She should know the truth. And that meant Stevens would hear. Well, that was tough shit! "I won't keep you long, Dr. Rivers. I realize you're tired. But I must ask you once more where you were last night."

"I told you. I was here, alone."

"But Mad, you couldn't have been here. Your car—"

"Later, GG. You'll have plenty of time to straighten out your stories after I leave. Dr. Rivers, do you still insist you canceled your dinner with Dr. Cooper?"

"Certainly. I went to sleep early. I told you that."

"Then why does GG think you weren't home at ten-thirty?"

Rivers looked convincingly startled. Maybe she was surprised that GG hadn't covered for her.

"What are you talking about? I WAS here—" She turned to Gertrude, an agonized look on her face.

"Your car was gone, Mad. And there weren't any lights—"

"I must have been asleep by four. Why would I turn the lights on at that hour?"

"If that's true, Dr. Rivers, why wasn't your car here when GG stopped by?"

"What are you talking about? I drove home and parked it in the garage. And it was there this morning."

"But the garage was empty, really. It wasn't there when I turned on the light. Cyril and Christine both saw it. I mean, didn't see it. We were wondering where you guys had gone after dinner—Oh dear God! I didn't have to provide two extra witnesses." Gertrude buried her face in her hands.

"Now listen to me carefully, Dr. Rivers. We know you weren't here last night. Even your closest friend doesn't believe you. Are you shielding someone else? Is that why Dr. Cooper was encouraging you to lie?"

Rivers' mouth dropped open. She looked away from him. When she finally spoke, her eyes were flashing, her voice firm.

"Lieutenant, I WAS here last night. I didn't lie to you before, and I'm not lying to you now. I left my car in the garage yesterday afternoon, at about two-thirty. I don't know how to prove it to you, but it's the truth. Ask Larry. At least he knows I wasn't with him."

"I can guess what Dr. Cooper's answer would be. Look, Dr. Rivers, we also know you drove to the zoo last night. The tracks we found in the fresh mud by the Reptile House service gate match the treads on your tires."

"I don't care if you found my footprints. I wasn't there."

"And there's one more thing." He pulled out the snake pin, still nestled in Morley's handkerchief, and handed it to her.

"But— That's mine. Where did you get it?"

"Have you worn it recently?"

"I have to think— I wore it to a meeting about two weeks ago— But maybe this isn't mine. Let me check upstairs."

He nodded his assent and she rushed from the room. Gertrude started to speak, but Harris quelled her with a glance. He walked to the corner table and looked through a stack of books. Rivers was still moving back in. He picked up *Snakes of the World* and was thumbing through it when she walked slowly back into the room.

"It's gone." She sounded hopeless.

"I'm not surprised. Morley found this in the bird-of-prey cage. Close to Brooks' body."

"Morley gave you the pin?" Gertrude asked angrily.

"Stay out of this, GG."

"What are you leading up to, Lieutenant? Are you accusing me of murdering Charles?"

So it was going to be righteous indignation this time. Well, he was ready for her. She had fine eyes. But now he knew they lied. "We aren't accusing anyone at this point, Dr. Rivers. We're simply following up on the evidence."

"All right! Hide in your offiicial position! I don't care about you or anyone else in this whole filthy mess." She glared at Gertrude. "I didn't go anywhere last night. I didn't drive my car. I didn't meet Charles and I didn't kill him. Do you understand? I didn't kill him."

She was crying as she fled from the room. Another stellar performance. She really had missed her calling.

Gertrude was staring at him. "This can't be happening. What have I done?"

"Believe me, GG, it's better this way. If you'd lied to protect her, it would all have come out sooner or later."

"It's impossible to do the right thing, no matter how hard you try."

Nodding, Harris left her alone with her thoughts.

CHAPTER EIGHT

Harris hit the brakes hard. Please, God, not another dead end. No, there was the mailbox, right at the edge of the cliff. How like Cooper to live where no one could find him. Harris slammed the car door and hurried up the walk to a rustic bungalow. There was no response to his ring, but the lights were on and he could hear muffled voices. Probably a TV. He rang the bell twice more, then raised his fist to pound on the door. It swung open.

Startled, he lowered his arm. "Wasn't sure your bell was working."

"The bell's fine. I'm not eager to see anyone." Cooper was wearing pajamas and a robe.

"I have a few questions. Mind if I come in?"

The living room didn't make a statement—just like its owner. Harris glanced at the TV. The anchorman was describing the grisly discovery at the zoo. As the picture of Stevens in front of the bird-of-prey cage appeared, Cooper hurried to turn off the sound.

"It's a great story," Harris said. "Think what you're doing for those reporters."

"And publicists. Ours keeps calling. He wants me to appear on the 'Today' show."

"Will you?"

"No way. We need publicity, but not that kind."

"Cheer up. Maybe one of your employees will do it for you."

"No one on my staff would—"

Harris' eyes strayed to the screen and Stevens' dramatic gesture toward the manzanita bush.

"I'm surrounded by imbeciles," Cooper said, zapping off the picture. "So what's on your mind, Lieutenant? I have some calls to make."

"This shouldn't take long." Harris sat down at the dining table. "I want to know where you were last night."

"I told you. I had dinner at an Italian restaurant on the highway. Then I came home and went to bed. Think you can hang onto that for a while or should I write it down?"

"You were not with Dr. Rivers?"

"Of course not. What the hell are you suggesting?"

"I'm not suggesting anything. But since Dr. Rivers has a serious alibi problem—"

"Nonsense. What's wrong with going to bed early? Must everyone have an eyewitness?"

"Not everyone. But when three people, including Gertrude Gypsom, say Dr. Rivers' car was not in her garage at ten-thirty last night, and when GG further insists Dr. Rivers did not arrive home until after one a.m., an eyewitness would be useful."

"Well, I can't help you. Maybe she begged off dinner because she had a better offer, and trapped herself in a lie trying to save my feelings." Cooper grimaced. "I wouldn't know, Lieutenant. She certainly didn't confide in me."

"And you're sure you didn't see her last night?"

"Goddamn it, I told you. I did not see Dr. Rivers last night. If we had an alibi like that, we'd tell you. What do you take us for, a couple of idiots?"

Admitting there might be some truth in that, Harris asked a few more questions, and finally gave up. Cooper had won again.

By the time Harris reached his condo, he was in a foul mood. He hadn't run all week, and he felt stiff and flabby. Maybe it would help to take the stairs.

He emerged, panting, on the ninth floor, feeling more like himself. All he needed was a little quiet reflection.

"Hi there, Lieutenant." Knopstead emerged from the shadows. "That's quite a climb. You sure do stay in great shape for an old man."

"Knopstead! Of the things I don't need tonight, you are at the top of the list. Get out of here."

"Hey, I'm just doing my job. Sergeant McDuff won't tell me about the Medical Examiner's report without your okay, and I'm here to get it."

"Well, you can't have it. I haven't seen the report and I don't know when it will be available."

"But my deadline—"

"Why does a photographer need to see the report, anyway?"

"They fired Smith. I'm doing double duty."

"Well, I can't help you. You can see the report after I've read it. Tomorrow." Harris slammed the door and switched on the lights. That damned kid drove him nuts.

He wandered into his cupboard-sized kitchen. He wasn't really hungry. Maybe a ham sandwich and a can of beer. Or just the beer.

And some music— Hoping Beethoven would change his mood, he turned on the Bose. But after a few bars he realized that was no good, either. He was simply trying to tune out his own thoughts.

Standing at the floor-to-ceiling window, he watched the lights below. Viewed like this, the city lost its ugliness. The garish signs became soft pools of color, the noisy freeways rivers of silently flowing light. The air was clear, and the whole world seemed close enough to touch, beckoning in an outburst of joy. But tonight he wanted more than a light show. He wanted answers. His eyes moved back and forth across the panorama. He was as bad as Cooper, reading his cue cards. The answer wasn't out there.

Scot was right. He had become emotionally involved. He felt protective of Rivers, concerned for her welfare. Her

75

openness appealed to him. But there was something more. An inner fire—he wasn't sure what to call it—had caught his imagination. He moved away from the window and sat heavily on the couch.

Was she open—or a persuasive liar? He dealt in facts, but he had learned to pay attention to gut reactions. Still, there was substantial hard evidence against her, and she had motive and opportunity. She was extremely attractive, and he couldn't allow himself to be swayed by that. Resolutely he turned on his phone. Twenty-five messages, mainly from McDuff.

His call got a quick response: "I've been calling you all afternoon. Did you have your phone turned off?"

"It's been a busy day. Sorry, Scot. What's happening?"

"We shook down Brooks' apartment. Someone got there first. No big mess, just everything a little bit askew, and wiped clean. By the way, he did have a zoo key—for a service gate. But more important, there's a concealed drawer in the desk. It was full of newspaper clippings and tape cassettes. I made a quick check of the clippings. They're from small-town Southern California newspapers, all reports of local scandals. We haven't listened to the tapes yet, but it looks like blackmail."

"Blackmail! Now we're getting somewhere. Make a complete search of the place, and get the tapes converted right away."

There's a safe-deposit box. Shall I get that opened in the morning?"

"Yes, and get George Pierce on it. Give him the tapes and clippings to catalog. And he can start digging into Brooks' telephone records and bank statements."

"George is tied up on that embezzlement case. How about Simon?"

"I want Pierce. We need a first rate bean counter if we're going to untangle a blackmail operation. Tell the Chief I'm calling in my chips. Did you get anything on Brooks' business?

He apparently inherited an outfit called Brooks Imports from his father."

"We have an address. That's about all."

"Put Pierce on that, too. Also look for a will and/or an attorney. What else?"

"We talked to one of Brooks' neighbors, a Marsha Stebbins. Seems reliable and sharp. She's old and not too active, so she spends a lot of time watching the street. She said a glamour puss with frosted hair has been coming around lately. That doesn't sound like Rivers. Would you believe MacMillan?"

"Interesting thought," Harris said. "We'd better show Stebbins a picture of MacMillan. I'll do that tomorrow. How about the autopsy report?"

"Markleson says the cause of death was 'snake bite and resulting shock. The site of the bite was the outside of the right leg, five inches above the patella. . .' And he goes on '...edema of the surrounding tissues due to—' I can't read the next words, but he does say that death was clearly caused by snake bite."

"All very well. But he already knew about the taipan."

"Didn't Piper tell you they might have missed it otherwise?"

"Right. And that means a murderer who was knowledgeable about snakes might have thought the venom would go undetected. That could have been the reason for using a snake in the first place."

"You lost me there, John."

"Never mind. I'll stop by Markleson's house tonight and go over it with him. Is there anything else in the report that's written in English?"

"Yeah. 'Other injuries: Blow on top of head possibly sufficient to produce unconsciousness.' Cautious blighter, Markleson. 'Also fairly extensive scrapes and bruises to arms and legs. Time of death: between ten p.m. and twelve-thirty a.m. Death followed bite by probably no more than an hour.' And here we have another effusion of technicalities."

"Thanks, Scot. Anything else I should know?"

"That's not enough?"

Harris chuckled. "It'll do until morning. Tomorrow I want you to go to the zoo personnel office and see if you can get anything on MacMillan. I'm sure she's lying about something. Oh, and don't forget to contact Hudson Bay about Piper."

"Anything else for my spare time?"

"Get a feel for the zoo. Our murderer has some connection with the place. And I'd like a blackmail report at noon, tomorrow. In my office."

"Right. Did you catch up with Cooper?"

"Yes. He's so defensive I can't even tell what he's lying about. But he is lying."

"At least he's consistent. Say, John, I'd like to apologize for what I said at lunch."

"Forget it, Scot. It'll be a sad day for me when you don't speak your mind."

So Brooks' murderer might be a blackmail victim, perhaps not even connected with the zoo. Harris felt decidedly better as he set out for Dr. Markleson's house.

Sam Markleson was standing in the doorway as Harris started up the front walk. "Well, John, this is a pleasant surprise. I was expecting a phone call. Come on in."

Markleson led him to an untidy study, filled to overflowing with heavy furniture. "I don't mind telling you, I'm finding this case fascinating. You know—or perhaps you don't—that I'm sort of an amateur herpetologist. Nothing this challenging has come my way in all my years as a pathologist."

"Glad we were able to please somebody. Listen, Sam, if the body had been found without the snake, would you have detected the venom?"

"Almost certainly yes. Let me explain. There are two main families of dangerously poisonous snakes: the vipers—like rattle-snakes—and the elapids—like cobras and our friend, the taipan. And there are two types of venom: neurotoxic and hemotoxic. A primarily neurotoxic venom will cause comparatively little damage in the area of the bite. The pain of the bite is slight, and the main effect is on the brain and nervous system. It paralyzes the nerves running to the eyes, ears, nape of neck, and respiratory muscles. Death usually occurs within—oh, from two to eight hours. Now a hemotoxin, on the other hand, results in severe local symptoms: the wound becomes discolored and the area extremely swollen. The hemotoxic venom destroys the endothelium—you know, the membrane lining of the blood vessels."

"I'll take your word for it."

"The destruction of the lining results in seepage of blood through the vessel walls and into the surrounding tissues. That's what causes swelling. Further, the lining itself becomes rough, leading to blood clotting and subsequent blockage of the blood vessels.

"Now most of the elapids have a primarily neurotoxic poison—say 95% neurotoxic, 5% hemotoxic. If this snake had been some other elapid—a coral snake, for instance—then I wouldn't be so sure about spotting the bite. But the taipan is an exception. His venom is about 60% neurotoxic and 40% hemotoxic. That's only an approximation, as I say. But you see the point, don't you?"

"You mean that we're going to get both kinds of damage?"

"Yes. The hemotoxic properties of the venom are sufficient to cause the local and blood vessel symptoms I've described. In this case, the fang marks are clear and unmistakable, and there is a lot of local swelling and discoloration. That's typical of snake bites and, in my opinion, it would be remarkable if it were overlooked."

"Might the murderer have assumed the bite would go undetected because taipans are elapids?"

"Could be, John. It would depend on how much he knew about taipans. I'm interested in venom, but most of what I know about taipan venom comes from working on this case."

"It's an important point. Being able to handle the taipan really narrows the list of potential suspects—and it would help to know if he thought we'd find out."

"Right. But don't pin too much on known snake-handling abilities. There are large numbers of non-professional snake lovers out there. I'd rather not, but I could probably handle our friend myself."

"Still, he's big and nasty. Moving on, your report says death occurred within an hour of the bite. Didn't you just say the toxin takes at least two hours?"

"In this case, death was probably due to shock. I don't think the victim could have been alive for more than an hour, because blood vessel damage had not spread far enough. The poison moves through the system rather slowly unless a major vein or artery is struck—and in this case no important blood vessel was immediately involved. The symptoms were still confined to the upper leg."

"Well, that's all clear enough. Thanks, Sam."

Harris took his leave and headed for the zoo.

After a frustrating thirty minutes spent trying to rouse someone, Harris wondered if the night security guard might be deaf. But Horatio Jones, who finally showed up on his regular rounds, proved immediately that his hearing was acute.

"That howl there," the old man pointed toward the sound, "that's the jaguar. Not often up at this hour."

"Yes, Mr. Jones. That's interesting. Now could I ask you—"

"He's hungry, that one. They changed his feed schedule, and he don't like it."

"Quite understandable. Mr. Jones, I need your help. We are investigating a murder, as you know. And since you were one of the few people in the zoo last night, I have to ask if you noticed anything unusual during the evening."

"No. Things were pretty usual. Didn't see no lights in the Reptile House. I recall goin' past there just after I seen Dr. Cooper."

"Dr. Cooper was in the zoo last night?"

"Sure was. Nothin' new about that. He comes to hear them animals. Same as me. He was here late. After midnight."

"Did you speak to him?"

"No, I keep to myself, and he keeps to hisself."

So Cooper didn't know he'd been seen. "Where was he?"

"Down near the big bird cage. You know, the one with all them buzzards, where they found the body."

"Tell me what you do on your rounds. Do you check the locks?"

"That's what I do, all right."

"And last night? Did you check all the locks?"

"Sure did. First I do the locks on the main gate, and then I goes to the service gates. Every ninety minutes."

"Did you by any chance check the lock on the big bird cage? The buzzard cage?"

"No. Can't do 'em all. Too many cage locks in the zoo."

"I don't suppose you locked anything that was open?"

"No, everything was just like it's s'posed to be."

"Did you see Dr. Stevens?"

"Sure did. I let him in. And later, I seen a light in his office, so I peeked in the window to be sure it was him in there."

"Thank you. If you think of anything else, Mr. Jones, let me know."

"Won't think of nothin'. Nothin' happened."

Jones locked the gate behind him.

As Harris climbed into his car, he heard the roar of a distant lion. The zoo was eerie at night. Wild and beautiful. He glanced back through the moonlit trees toward the flight cage. Its arches rose, black and silver against the sky. It had been a useful evening. Jones apparently hadn't locked the body into the cage by accident, and it was satisfying to have caught Cooper in another lie. Things were looking up for Madelyn. He could drive out to see her right now— But he wasn't sure how much he should tell her. For all he knew, she was involved in Brooks' blackmailing. No, she would have to wait—at least until tomorrow. Anyway, she was tired and so was he. He'd go home to bed.

CHAPTER NINE

"Vulture droppings! Who does John Harris think he is?"

"Hush, you'll wake Mad. Come in the living room." Gertrude took Morley's hand and led him inside.

"I can't believe it, Gert."

"What did you expect? You gave him the pin."

"You asked me to go down to the cage."

"To find evidence supporting her, not that pin."

"I had no choice. Once I'd seen it, I had to give it to John."

"I know. It's just. . .with friends like us…"

Morley kissed her lightly on the forehead and pulled her close, holding her against him so hard it hurt. But what a comforting hurt.

He pulled away. "I'll turn up the heat. Where is it you hide the thermostat?"

"In the second shelf of the bookcase. But this room takes hours to heat. Start a fire if you're cold."

"It's you who's cold. Don't you know you're shaking?"

"That's fear—or some other misery. Still, a fire would feel good. It's ready to light. Mad always—"

"Just sit tight for a moment." Morley moved to the fireplace and struck a match. The tinder flared, and the fire was soon blazing. He made a nest of large tan pillows nearby. "Okay. Come get warm."

She laughed as he tried to lift her off her feet and failed. "You'll hurt your back." She pulled him down onto the pillows and snuggled against him, savoring his nearness. The crackling of the fire soothed her. Gradually, the shaking stopped. He was supporting her against his chest, arm around her, hand lying lightly on her thigh. To her horror, she felt bubbles of pleasure rising, tickling her spine, bursting in her brain. How perverse. This was no time to turn on. She pushed herself upright and faced him.

"What are we going to do about Mad?"

"Stay calm. Listen, Gert, it's not all bad. Mad is asleep upstairs, and Charles was an asshole—not worth a moment's grief."

"But all this evidence—"

"I admit it's awkward, but we know she didn't kill him."

"John thinks she did."

"I don't believe that. John's a first-rate detective. He doesn't jump to conclusions. I trust him implicitly."

"I did, too, until today. He sounded...reasonable, kind...and then— Oh, Morley, it was like being a witness for the prosecution."

"John's been under a lot of pressure lately."

"Next you'll be blaming his midlife crisis. Listen, Morley, forget John Harris. We have to help Mad ourselves."

"And we will. I—" A cheery ringtone sounded from the kitchen. "I'll get it. Stevens...You what?...But Mad needs...Well then, be sure you get a good rest!" He slammed the phone down on the table.

"More good news?"

"Cooper's not coming. He says he's sick."

"What a jerk. Morley, will they all turn against her? Is that what happens?"

"Not a chance. Cooper's just being his insensitive self. We're better off without him. Mad's real friends will be here. You'll see." He stroked her face with his finger tips.

"You really think they'll come?"

"Any minute now. And what, my angel, are you going to do with them?"

"Figure out who murdered Charles."

"I think we amateurs had better stay out of this. We don't need any more snake pins."

"That was bad luck. There must be evidence out there to support her case, but the police won't find it."

"I don't know. I'm not convinced we can help."

"We have to try."

"Yes, I suppose you're right. And there's the bell. Your reinforcements have arrived."

Cyril Featherworth sized up the empty chairs. Most furniture was inadequate for his large frame, and tonight he yearned for comfort. If this weren't so important to GG, he'd never have come.

She smiled up at him. "You're tired, Cyril. Try the new one."

Gratefully, he sank into the voluminous chair.

"You look like a folded giraffe."

"Bent, folded and mutilated. This is one punched out giraffe."

"He's not exaggerating. I had trouble getting him up for lunch." Christine settled back into the couch and curled her legs under her in a single motion. Her sun bleached hair fell softly around her face.

"You're tired, too, Chrissy. You haven't been to bed before two all week."

"Why so late?" Gertrude asked.

"My art show's coming up next month, and I have four paintings to finish. The pressure is terrible. I guess I have stage fright."

Cyril reached over and took her hand. "You're almost ready, darling. It'll be wonderful." She smiled gratefully, and his heart turned over. God, she was beautiful!

"That's right, Christine," Gertrude said. "And before long you'll be famous!"

"Well, at least it's a step up from being the zoo's sign painter. I just need to stop worrying and start painting again. Anyway, enough of me. How is Mad? Is she joining us?"

"She decided not to," Gertrude replied. "It's been a tough day."

"But you told her we want to help?"

"Of course. She says we shouldn't bother, but that's Mad."

"Where's Larry?" Cyril asked.

"He's not coming," Gertrude replied.

"Larry should be here. I'm going to call him." Cyril started to get up, but felt Morley's hand on his shoulder.

"No, don't. Larry's help we can do without."

"That's all well and good, but what kind of help do you want?" Christine asked.

"We aren't sure yet," Gertrude said. "But we must come up with a plan tonight, because Mad's being railroaded. Someone's setting her up, and the police are buying it."

"I can't believe it," Christine said.

"Mad wouldn't hurt a flea," Cyril added.

"We know that," Morley said, "but John Harris doesn't. We've got to turn this around."

"But I don't see what we can do." Cyril tried to imagine them examining footprints and looking for hairs.

"There are two ways to approach it." Morley was leaning against the mantel, foot on the fender, studying his pipe intently. "We can work with the police and try to explain away the evidence against her, or we can go after the murderer ourselves."

"I don't know about the police," Christine said. "It sounds like they're off on the wrong foot."

"She's right." Gertrude's eyes flashed with anger. "John thinks he has it all figured out. He's not going to spend much more time on this case. It's up to us to find the evidence they've overlooked."

"Before we do that, Gert, we should review what the police think they know. Like the motive. John is apparently convinced Mad is the only person in the world with a reason to kill Charles Brooks."

"That's ridiculous!" Cyril exclaimed. "The binge drinking alone tells it all. Sure, he could be charming. But Mad can't have been the only one to see him out-of-control drunk."

"You may be right, but let's face it—none of us saw him like that. So where do we start looking?" Christine asked.

"He must have had other friends. Who knows anything about Brooks' contacts?" Morley shook his head. "I sure don't."

"I'm afraid Mad's the only one," Gertrude replied.

"We could ask around at END," Cyril suggested. "He did work there for a while. The last time I saw him, he said he was out of the computer business. His father had left him an importing firm."

"Does anyone know what it's called? I could check on it," Christine volunteered.

"You taking notes, Gert?"

"Right. And I'll talk to Mad in the morning. She'll know the name of the place."

Cyril set his notepad on the coffee table. "I must have missed something. Are you saying that Lieutenant Harris is building a case against Mad because she lived with Charles?"

"It's much worse than that. Didn't I tell you? Mad's car was missing last night."

"What do you mean?" Cyril asked.

"I mean, it wasn't in the garage when we pulled into the driveway on our way to dinner. Remember? That was about, what, ten-thirty?"

Cyril remembered: a light coming on in an empty garage. "Right, but wasn't she with Larry?"

"No. She'd cancelled dinner," GG explained. "She says she was here from about two-thirty on. And that she left the car in the garage when she got here. The person who took the car must have picked it up after dark, but no later than ten-fifteen."

"And we know it was back in place at one-thirty because Gert thought she heard Mad driving in. What time did you arrive here, Gert?" Morley asked.

"It was before one. If we'd been a little later, we would have seen the whole thing."

Cyril tried to imagine the scene. The car driving up and someone— Not Madelyn? "So what's the car got to do with the murder?" he asked.

"Its tread marks were found near the Reptile House service gate."

"So what?" Christine asked. "She always parks there."

Morley gave his pipe a last jab and put it in his pocket. "Unfortunately, the heavy rain last night produced a fresh crop of mud. That's where the tire tracks are. They're deep in that permanent mud puddle, but they're also in an area that was dry yesterday afternoon. Besides, they are right in front of the gate. She wouldn't normally park there. So I think we can safely assume that the murderer drove the car to the zoo."

Christine uncurled her legs and sat up straight. "It doesn't make sense. Why would the murderer risk stealing the car? Madelyn might have missed it and called the police."

"That's true. But maybe he didn't mean to keep it as long as he did. My guess is he got stuck in the mud. He'd planned to drive to the zoo, park the car in the mud where the tread marks would show, kill Brooks, and get the hell out. Instead, he had to dig the car out. It could have taken several hours."

"Is there evidence of that?" Cyril asked.

Morley looked embarrassed. "I don't know. I was so upset with McDuff, I didn't check the area as carefully as I should have. We'll have a look in the morning."

"How hard would it be to get a car out of there?"

"Sorry to bother you, GG, but I wanted you to know the faucets are okay now."

Everyone turned to stare at the paunchy middle-aged man in the door.

88

"Gus! Thank you!" Gertrude blew him a kiss.

"Tell Mad if there's anything she needs—"

"I will. Thanks, Gus."

"Who was that?" Cyril asked.

"The contractor. So, where were we?"

"Cyril was talking about Mad's car."

"I had a question, actually," Cyril said. "You have maintenance vehicles around the zoo, Morley. Is there a sturdy one everybody knows about that's equipped with a winch?"

"Possibly. But they're always locked away at night."

"I'd call the Auto Club," Gertrude said.

"That's ridiculous, GG. No murderer would risk that. The Auto Club keep records."

"Well, is anyone checking those records in case the murderer didn't think that through?"

"GG, a murderer would go to a lot of trouble to avoid involving outsiders. And there are a thousand ways to get a car unstuck."

"That may be, but I think the car was towed."

"It doesn't make sense. The chances of being traced are so much higher. Even if he called someone to help get it unstuck, he'd drive it home."

"I still say the car was towed."

"Why, GG?"

"Call it intuition."

"Gert, this is not the time for nonsense. We need facts."

"I don't know, Morley," Cyril said. "GG's intuition helped us locate several major system problems last week. I'll drink to her intuition any day." He held up his beer.

"Thanks, Cyril. I'm glad someone appreciates me."

Morley sighed. "Okay, let's make that an action item for you, Gert. But I don't think the Auto Club will tell you anything."

"If you're serious about this," Cyril said, "the local garages might be a better bet. But I don't know where you'd start. There are a lot of them."

"Her intuition will lead her to the right one," Morley suggested. "Now moving right along, what are we going to do about Peggy MacMillan?"

"For starters, you might want to tell us who she is," Christine said.

"She's Larry Cooper's new assistant. The thing is, she borrowed a bird-of-prey cage key from me. She said it was for a visiting ornithologist, but I'm beginning to think he doesn't exist."

"You mean you just handed her a key?" Christine asked. "I had to fight with Miss Thomas to get my keys."

"MacMillan is an employee."

"So am I, if only part-time."

"So I shouldn't have done it. Hawk shit! I hate all this security nonsense. And it's never mattered— Until today."

Cyril sat up. Everyone was getting touchy. He'd have to cheer them up somehow. "The point is, this is great news. MacMillan had the key the night of the murder. That makes her a prime suspect."

For a moment the only sound was Morley poking at his pipe again. "You're suggesting Peggy MacMillan killed Charles?" he asked finally. "I don't know—"

"Wait a minute!" Gertrude said. "Wasn't she in the papers last year? Don't you remember? There was a Peggy MacMillan holding a South American rattlesnake she'd brought to the zoo?"

"Yes! I was there!" Christine said. "There was a press conference in front of Administration. By the time Ed and Larry arrived, she had the snake around her shoulders."

"That can't be the same woman," Morley protested. "Mad would have remembered her. But when Mad asked for a key this morning, Peggy didn't know who she was. They'd never met."

"Mad wasn't at the zoo that day," Christine said. "Ed Piper was handling everything."

"So MacMillan met Cooper over a rattlesnake—" Morley said.

"—and managed to wangle a job. Now there's an action item. Write that down, Gert. Why did Larry hire MacMillan?"

"Forget the action list. She's our murderer."

"GG, your intuition just got fogged in."

"It's not my intuition, Cyril. It's simple logic. MacMillan lied to get the key to the cage, and she's an expert snake handler. What more do we need?"

"For starters, how about a connection between MacMillan and Brooks?" Morley asked. "But I must admit I think there may well be one."

"Why, Morley?" Cyril asked.

"There's something about the woman—"

"It's his intuition," Gertrude said.

"It is not. It's something much more basic than that. I don't know what she's up to, but I intend to find out."

"How?"

"I could ask questions, but that's the way Harris is proceeding. I think I'll follow her. She won't be expecting that."

"You're right there," Cyril said. "But I think we'd be better off waiting for the police."

"We don't have time for that," Gertrude replied. "Morley's right. And in the meantime we need to hire an attorney so we'll know how to proceed if Mad's arrested."

"GG, Mad hasn't been charged with anything. And, with any luck, she never will be," Morley responded.

"I still say we should think about it." Cyril felt a wave of—dread?

"All right, we'll think," Morley replied. "And unless there's something else urgent, that's about it for tonight."

Cyril reached over and snatched Gertrude's notebook. "Let me have a look at that action list. Just as I thought. Listen to this:

There was a vain rascal named Brooks,
Non grata in somebody's books.
So a viper engaged
Was with him encaged.
His subsequent death spoiled Brooks' looks."

"Sorry, Gert, it won't wash. It's clever enough, but taipans are elapids, not vipers."

"Well, you don't have to be so smug, Morley. I was rather proud of knowing what a viper was. Elapid, you say."

Cyril stood and reached for his wife's hand. "I'm exhausted. Take me home before I die."

Christine hesitated. "I do hope Mad's all right."

"Wait, before you leave," Gertrude said. "I have a fix."

"Do we have a choice?"

There was a vain rascal named Brooks,
Non grata in somebody's books.
So they got an elapid
Whose action was rapid.
The vultures then finished off Brooks."

"Time to go. It's getting worse!"

"I don't know, GG," Cyril said. "You're a much better poet than programmer."

"I love you, too, buddy. Why is everyone leaving so early?"

"Must be getting old. Here I am, half dead at eleven-thirty."

"Well, you're not alone," Christine said as she moved to the door. "Don't worry too much, GG. It's going to work out. And tell Mad we're behind her a hundred percent."

Morley shut the door behind them and put his arms around Gertrude. "If it didn't sound ridiculous, I'd tell you it was a great party."

"We have to try to keep people's spirits up. But Morley, I'm so frightened."

He pulled her close and kissed her softly on the lips. She buried her face in his jacket, fighting back the tears.

"I need you, Morley. Tonight I really need you." She felt her body relax as his arms tightened around her.

CHAPTER TEN

The waltz quickened. Madelyn leaned against Charles' arm as they whirled around and around, her long skirt billowing like a cloud. The band slid into a ballad and he drew her close.

Suddenly, his arms tightened like a vise. She couldn't move. "Charles, let go! You're hurting me!"

He tilted her head back and kissed her, his hand caressing her throat. Her fears dissolved in the sweetness of his lips. She was floating in his arms.

And then she was choking. Something was pulling tighter and tighter around her neck. Frantically, she reached up to free herself. Sharp teeth touched her hand. It was a snake, an enormous snake, its coils wound around her neck. As she fought against its grip, the writhing constrictor hardened into a silken rope. She screamed.

"Here, let me help you." Charles pulled the rope over her head and held it out to her. "It's a present. I made it myself." She reached for the rope and a hangman's noose fell out of his hand. Her screams covered his laughter.

"Mad! Mad! Wake up!"

"GG, is that you?"

"Yes, I'm right here. You were screaming."

"Charles was choking me. It was a hangman's noose. It must have been a warning—"

"Yuch! What a horror! But it was just a dream."

"It was so real, the rope—"

"They don't hang people anymore. It's some sort of injection."

"You are such a comfort." Madelyn sat up and swung her feet onto the floor.

"We should have expected Charles to come back and haunt you. What you need is to forget him and have a good strong cup of coffee."

"In a minute. Tell me about your meeting last night."

"Everyone thinks you're being set up. And Cyril says the murderer may have made a fatal mistake by moving your car."

"About the car. I owe you an apology. I know—"

"Forget it. We're all stressed out."

"But you're not planning to play detective are you?"

"No. We're just going to check out a couple of things. Don't worry. We'll be careful."

"I do appreciate the support. I'm just afraid you'll get carried away."

"Who, me?" Gertrude smiled. "I'll go make that coffee."

Madelyn moved to the window. The early morning sunlight was streaming in. She could feel it on her cheeks. If was a beautiful morning. And Charles could never frighten her again. He was dead.

"I can't get to the entrance, Morley." Gertrude slowed the Buick to a crawl as a group of mothers with small children meandered across the road. "I've never seen the zoo so busy."

"All these stupid fools, back to bother my birds. Let me off at the bus stop."

"It's a long walk to the gate."

"It'll do me good. You okay?" He squeezed her hand.

"I'm fine. What's the fastest way to Tommy's car place?"

"Tommy Lake's? Did he find you a Porsche?"

"This is not the time to buy a new car."

The Buick belched loudly.

"I don't know, Gert. That sounded like a death rattle to me."

"Well, it's not. I'm going to see Tommy because he owns a garage."

"And he has a computer freak for a son."

"Don't be so hard on Oliver."

"Oliver's hard on me. Look, Gert, if you talk to Tommy he'll tell Oliver and the next thing you know Oliver will be at the door asking questions."

"He'll have to take a number like everyone else. I'm sorry, Morley, but I'm going to Tommy's. It's easier to start the search with someone I know."

"So you're really going to do this. I thought that was a hypothetical discussion we were having last night."

"If you don't know by now, I'm not a hypothetical person. Damn this car! She stalled again."

"Tell Tommy to find you that Porsche before it's too late."

He ambled off through the crowd. What a sweet man. It had been so comforting, lying in his arms in the firelight. She was in love with a bird-loving mammal. Did that make her a penguin?

Harris eyed the stunning blonde appreciatively. "How do you do, Ms. Featherworth? Thanks for seeing me on such short notice."

"I should thank you. It's much more convenient, having you come to my apartment."

"No problem. I had to pass here anyway."

She led him into the living room and indicated the couch. The room was airy but cluttered. One entire wall was devoted to electronic equipment, and four humongous speakers dominated the corners. A TV screen covered another wall.

"I see you're interested in Cyril's toys."

"More amazed than interested."

"I told Cyril we'd have to move if he keeps this up. Between my paintings and his acquisitions—"

"Is that yours?" Harris nodded toward a large abstract above the couch.

"Yes. It's Cyril's favorite." She shut the door into the hallway before sitting down. "I hope you don't want to talk to him now. He was so tired this morning, I couldn't wake him."

"Not today, no."

"I should be at the zoo, but I couldn't face it. I decided to wait a couple more days."

Harris reached over and stroked the two Siamese cats curled companionably on the couch. "Were you fond of the victim, then?"

"Oh, no, I hardly knew him. But the Reptile House feels creepy." She pulled her sweater around her shoulders. "I guess I'll find work space somewhere else in the zoo."

"I'm interviewing everyone who might have relevant zoo keys. Let's cover that first. Which keys did they give you?"

"The service gate nearest the Reptile House and the Reptile House door. That way, I can go in and work when I feel like it, and it's easy to take in materials. The lot is close."

"Fine. Now for the record, may I see the keys?"

"If I can find them." She fumbled in her large handbag and pulled out a key ring attached to an enameled brass hippo. Two of the keys were stamped SPZ, one with G3, the other, R1. Right. Before handing the keys back, he examined the hippo more closely. It was blue, with a wreath of green riverweed around its shoulders. An appealing creature.

"Do you like it, Lieutenant? That's one of my sidelines. It helps me cope with my failure as a serious artist." Her smile was rueful.

"It's well done." He handed it back to her. "And I'm impressed with your zoo signs."

"I'm glad someone noticed them," she replied.

He considered asking her about a lion painting. But that would have to wait until he was finished with this case. After all, she was a possible, though unlikely, suspect. She had some of the needed keys, and knew the people.

"So this shouldn't take long. What can you tell me about Charles Brooks?"

"As I said, I didn't know him well. He worked with Cyril and GG at END for a while. And Mad brought him to parties at the beginning. He seemed like a nice guy, and I was sorry when they stopped coming around. I heard he had a drinking problem, but I never saw any evidence of that."

"When did you first meet him?"

"It must have been about a year-and-a-half ago, just after he went to work for END. Charles and GG joined us for dinner one night. They'd been working late, and everyone was tired. Something about him seemed to irritate GG and they argued all evening. That's the only time I had a real conversation with him. After that, we said 'hello' at parties, and then he dropped out."

"Another routine question: can you handle snakes?"

"Well, I've handled small, non-poisonous ones, but the taipan? No way." She grimaced.

"And one final question. Purely routine. Can you tell me how you spent Monday evening?"

"Certainly. I teach a pottery class at the college on Mondays. It starts at seven. I meant to leave the zoo early so I wouldn't have to rush. But I was over in the small primate house, trying to get some good sketches of the golden lion tamarin, and my watch had stopped. It must have been six-thirty by the time I noticed. I dashed home, fed the cats, and was a couple of minutes late. Not that it mattered. The class started work without me. I taught until ten. I usually go out for a beer with some of the students, but Cyril and GG came in just before ten. They wanted to celebrate finishing their crash project at END— You've heard about that?"

Harris nodded.

"Anyway, I agreed to go to dinner with them. We followed GG home—she wanted to change—and then drove to La Viera. We must have lingered, watching the surf, until after midnight.

Then we dropped GG off and were home by two. That's all I remember until ten o'clock yesterday morning, when I finally made it out of bed."

"Did you go to the zoo yesterday?"

"After lunch. I didn't stay long."

"That seems clear enough. I appreciate your help."

Madelyn hurried up the path toward the Reptile House. The zoo hadn't changed. She savored the smell of eucalyptus, the crunch of dry leaves underfoot, the cries of the monkeys. But as she neared the building, the discordant sound of a milling crowd drowned out the zoo noises. Rounding the corner, she saw a television crew, photographers, and policemen, vying for position in front of the door.

She ducked behind the trees on the hillside path. She wasn't ready for that scene. There had to be some place where she could work for a few hours— Maybe Morley's office.

She threaded her way slowly through the crowd. She'd never seen so many people in the zoo. If only she could get to the Bird House without meeting a reporter.

Surprisingly, she met no one, and was soon ringing the bell.

"Madelyn. Come in." Morley threw the door open wide.

"I need a place to hide. There's a small riot in front of the Reptile House."

"I heard about that. Make yourself at home. I have great news. MacMillan's ornithologist doesn't exist. She lied to get her hands on my key. We still have to figure out how she got into the Reptile House. But, beyond that, our only problem is her motive."

"Is that all?"

"Yes. And I'm off to work on it." He pulled an old sweater over his head. "Caruso is feeling gregarious."

"We'll have a nice chat. Thanks, Morley."

Madelyn shut the door and settled down at Morley's desk. This might be her last chance to finish her paper for the herpetological society meeting in February. She wondered if she'd be there to present it. But there'd be time to worry about that later. Right now she needed to read it through and see if it made sense. She stared at the page, trying to concentrate, but the words seemed meaningless.

The coral snake of the United States (*Micrurusfulvius*, and *Micruroides euryxzanthus*, family *Elapidae*—

Elapids. Taipans were elapids, too. All this emphasis on snakes was beginning to wear her down. Turtles would have been easier, but this was a snake conference and the paper was due next week.

The page blurred. Cheery exchanges with Morley were a respite from the madness, but she really was trapped. The argument. The pin. The tire tracks. The empty garage. She could rage about her innocence, but no jury would believe her. Innocence was not enough. The web of evidence was too tight. Someone must have designed it to catch her. Someone who hated her. Charles? Maybe the dream really was a warning. Yes, Charles had been capable of that. But could he have pulled it off? She'd have to think about that. Later.

Resolutely, she pulled out her phone and set a reminder. She would work for an hour and then take a break.

The time passed quickly, and she'd made good progress. Relieved, she stood up and wandered over to the drapery rod where Caruso had stationed himself.

"How are you old friend?" she asked.

He eyed her curiously, but didn't respond.

"Vulture droppings?" she suggested.

He edged closer and launched into a monologue, moving quickly through his Shakespearean repertoire and mixing in a few choice Morleyisms. Madelyn laughed. Caruso was always a comedian.

Having exhausted his favorite speeches, he paused as if to recall something special for his appreciative audience. When he spoke again, it was in a different voice. She listened with mounting anger as he mimicked John Harris:

"The bird cage! The bird cage! Some broad killed her lover in the bird cage."

Impossible! John Harris wouldn't have said that. But Caruso couldn't have made it up. Trusting the Lieutenant had been a terrible mistake. She had told him—

The door swung open to admit Harris.

"Sorry. I should have rung. Morley said I could make some calls in here. It isn't easy to have a private conversation in this zoo."

"Maybe you can't."

"What do you mean?"

"You forgot Caruso. There are two things I want to say before I walk out that door. One, I did not kill my lover, and two, I do not appreciate being called a broad."

"A broad—"

Caruso interrupted: "The bird cage! The bird cage! Some broad killed her lover in the bird cage!"

"Oh, I am sorry." He stepped toward her. "I'd forgotten all about—"

"Obviously." She turned away.

"Look, Dr. Rivers, you weren't supposed to—"

"No, I suppose not." Picking up her papers, she started for the door.

"That's not what I meant. Mad—" He moved in front of her and put his hand on the knob. "—Dr. Rivers, that quote was out of context. Give me a chance."

"I'm waiting."

"It happened just after I got here yesterday. The Chief had heard crazy stories about multiple murders and wild animals on the loose. I told him the only animal loose out here was Knopstead, and I wasn't sure what would appear in the next edition of the paper, but it would probably be something like—well, what you heard. We had a bad connection and I had to repeat the punch line three times. Repetition gets Caruso's attention."

"He's a quick study."

Harris walked to the drapery rod and looked the raven in the eye. "Come on, Caruso. Tell her the rest of what I said. How about it, my friend? Please!"

The sight of the detective pleading with a bird was too much. Madelyn burst out laughing.

"That's a relief." He smiled broadly. "And while I'm doing apologies, I'm sorry about that scene at GG's. I said things I had no business saying."

"It was a bad day for all of us."

"I'm afraid I lost your confidence. I need your help—please, sit down for a moment. Did you have any idea that Brooks was a blackmailer?"

"A blackmailer? Surely not!"

"It's quite certain. I wondered if you could tell me anything—"

Charles—a blackmailer. She wanted to deny it, but couldn't. There had been something about him— Madelyn shuddered. She had lived with the man.

"Anything at all," Harris was saying.

"I'm sorry, Lieutenant. I'm having trouble taking it in."

"There's no hurry." His voice was warm, but when she looked up, his eyes were cold and attentive.

"So you think I knew?"

"Only indirectly. I think you can help us, but it means going back over the details—Brooks' friends, places he went. But first,

I'd like to go over what happened on the day of the murder, again."

"I already told you. I was as open as I know how to be."

"I appreciate your candor. But we might have missed something."

"After our fight at Frank's, I went back to the zoo for a while, left early, and fell asleep shortly after I got home. It must have been about six when Larry called. We talked until almost seven, then I slept for the rest of the night."

"You talked to Dr. Cooper for an hour?"

"Yes. I was so upset after that scene with Charles—I had to talk to someone."

Harris looked puzzled. So he didn't believe her.

"Dr. Cooper wasn't aware of your problems with Brooks?"

"I'm not sure. He probably suspected. But I didn't really talk to him about it until that night." She paused. "I'm sorry, Lieutenant. I don't really know anything I haven't already told you."

"You're doing fine. Listen, I know it's painful, but I'd like you to think about the time you spent with Brooks. Don't look for anything in particular; just review it in your mind. Make some notes. Sometimes our memories play tricks on us. When I interviewed the security guard—"

"Horatio?"

"Yes. He insisted nothing unusual had happened Monday night. But when I asked him to talk me through his rounds, he remembered seeing Dr. Cooper."

"Larry was in the zoo Monday night?" Larry couldn't have had anything to do with Charles' death. The murderer hated her enough to plant all that evidence. But Larry—

"What I'm trying to say, Dr. Rivers, is that you may know more about Brooks than you realize. I'm particularly interested in any contacts he may have had, phone calls, people turning up at the door. If anything occurs to you, please give me a call." He handed her his card. "It's amazing..."

She was trying to listen to him, but her thoughts kept returning to Larry. He had been in the zoo. He could have killed Charles. Larry had lied to her. She needed time to think it over.

"All right. I'll try. And now I'll be on my way so you can have some peace."

"Thanks, we'll talk later."

Madelyn opened the outside door and was momentarily blinded by a flash.

"Damn it, Knopstead," Harris shouted from behind her. "Get out of my sight before I arrest you."

She fled onto the tree lined path, and hurried back to the Reptile House.

CHAPTER ELEVEN

Gertrude felt a surge of excitement as she pulled up at the Evergreen Lake Garage. She'd find out what had happened to Mad's car if it took her a month. Thank heaven she knew Tommy Lake. Dealing with mechanics always made her feel like she'd stumbled into the men's locker room. Maybe Tommy already knew what Mad's car had been up to.

She pulled into a parking space and was getting out when a young man yelled, "Hey, lady, we don't do Buicks."

"It's too late, anyway," she replied.

"And this isn't a junk yard. You'll have to move it—"

"It's all right, Joe. The lady's a friend of mine."

"Sorry, boss."

"GG, how are you? We read about Madelyn." He buried her in a deep hug. "What can we do? Oliver is terribly upset. You know he's always had a bit of a crush on Mad."

I know. We're all trying to help. Tell Oliver we'll call him. But there is something you can do."

"What's that?"

"The killer used Mad's car the night of the murder. It got stuck in the mud. I think the murderer called someone to pull it out and tow it back to the house."

"That would take a really stupid murderer. Anyone with sense would get the car out of the mud on his own."

"It'd be stupid to spend hours mucking around when you could call a garage and get the hell out of there. That's what I think happened, but I need your help finding the guy who towed the car."

"Even if you're right, that's a pretty tall order. A lot of us close at six."

"Then we only have to find the people who stay open. How can I go about this? I feel like I'm looking for a needle—"

"—in a bachelor's apartment. GG, this isn't reasonable. Have the police check it out."

"They don't care. They think Mad killed him. Tommy, I must find the man who towed the car."

"Maybe Oliver can help—"

"We'll keep him in mind. Meanwhile, where should I look next?"

"Google's your friend. Try 'NIGHT GARAGES SAN PABLO.' And you'll be doing a lot of driving. Will that old monster of yours hold up?"

"No. I don't suppose you'll ever find a Porsche for me?"

He snapped his fingers. "I almost forgot. I saw one the other day, blue with a FOR SALE sign in the window. I called for the address, but never made it over there. I might still have that slip of paper..." He reached into his pocket. "Yes, here it is. Send Morley over to have a look."

"Why would I send Morley?"

"To be sure everything's on the up and up."

"Tommy, do you have a minute?" A mechanic was standing with an obviously distressed customer.

"Let me know what happens. I'll have a look at it for free if you're interested."

"Before you rush off, can I use your phone? I forgot my cell."

"Anytime, sweetheart." He blew her a kiss.

Gertrude hurried into his office and opened the phone book. She'd Google later, but meanwhile she could jot down addresses for a couple nearby garages. And there were several in Cyril's neighborhood. Fantastic. Quickly, she dialed his number and waited impatiently for the message to end.

"Cyril, I'm at Tommy Lake's garage. He didn't tow Mad's car, so I'm going to try night garages in this part of town. I was

106

wondering, if and when you ever wake up, if you could check the ones near you— Damn it, I'm out of time." She redialed and drummed her fingers as the familiar message droned on.

"Cyril, I'm sick to death of that message. It's content free, and you sound slick, like a puffed up car salesman. What is it, anyway? Fear of the microphone? I mean, it's only a cell phone. It's not like you're being broadcast—"

"No, but you are, sweetheart."

A hand reached around her to turn off a switch. It was Tommy. She set the phone down and picked up her purse.

"Broadcast?"

"The mike was on. The customers on the lot were most amused."

"But you weren't. Look, Tommy, I'm sorry. I'll get out of your way."

"No problem. It was worth the laugh."

"You're sure it's all right?"

"I'm sure. And just to prove it, I'm going to walk you to your car."

He was the perfect gentleman, handing her in and closing the door. Before she pulled out, she glanced at the address he had given her. Simmons Street. She could swing by there on her way to the first garage. The Porsche might even be parked in front. And this was certainly something she could handle on her own. Gentleman or not, Tommy had his nerve telling her to send Morley.

It was a short drive, and the car was parked in the driveway. She could at least look.

She was staring in the window when she heard a voice behind her. "You'll have to come back if you want to see the car. Hank's not here, and I don't have time."

The woman in the doorway was obviously pregnant. Two small children were hugging her knees. "This is exactly the car

I've been looking for. Is there any way I could take her for a drive?"

"No. I can't leave the kids. You'll have to come back—"

"What if I gave you—" Gertrude rummaged through her purse and pulled out her credit card holder. "Here, I could leave these with you while I take her out."

The woman hesitated.

"Look, if she runs okay, I'll make you a good offer."

"All right. I'll get the keys."

She returned a moment later and silently handed them to Gertrude.

"I won't be long." Gertrude climbed in and was soon on the street, shifting easily, enjoying the power, the smooth handling. She'd take a quick run on the freeway before going on with her search. Merging into the left lane, she put her foot down. The car responded as if it were alive—a magical animal, ready to take her anyplace in the world. She was flying—

The red lights strobed in her rear vision mirror. It wasn't until she rolled down the window that she heard the siren. She had been grounded.

John Harris walked slowly into the zoo's Administration Building. This investigation was getting to him. Especially Cooper. That man was a congenital liar. He must be protecting someone. Madelyn? Another employee? Or maybe himself. Well, it was time to find out.

Peggy MacMillan greeted him with a stony face. "Dr. Cooper is in conference." She moved in front of Harris, blocking the door. "Your investigation is bringing the entire zoo to a grinding halt. I hope it's worth it—"

"Sorry about that." He brushed past her and into the office. Cooper was alone, staring out the window.

108

"I'd like to ask you—" Harris began, but MacMillan interrupted.

"Dr. Cooper, this zoo is completely out of control. First the Rivers woman, then the photographer, and now this—this—"

"Detective?" Harris suggested. "Has our friendly red-headed photographer been making trouble again?"

"Trouble?" She pushed a manila folder into his stomach. "Didn't you see those ghastly pictures in the paper?"

"Sure. Three people requested my autograph."

"You and that snake. Now the photographer wants to get into the Reptile House. And the watchman caught him climbing over the fence into the camel yard before the zoo opened. I think he—"

"It's all right, Peggy. It won't happen again," Cooper said soothingly. "I had a chat with Mr. Knopstead just a few minutes ago. He won't be back."

"And you believed that?" She flounced out of the room, slamming the door.

Harris took the chair in front of Cooper's desk. "Dr. Cooper, there were a number of problems with what you told me about your activities Monday night. I'm sure you know withholding evidence is a serious matter in a murder investigation. I think it's time you told me what really happened."

"I went to dinner—"

"—at the little restaurant down the highway. The one without a name. What time did you arrive at this famous restaurant?"

"Around six. I must have been back home by seven."

"You called Dr. Rivers from your table? The conversation must have fascinated the other customers."

Cooper reacted with just the right degree of confusion. "I guess I was mixed up the first time I talked to you. I couldn't remember what I'd done, so I made up the business about dinner. Then I thought it might sound strange if I corrected my story."

"Nothing could possibly seem stranger than the misinformation you've been feeding us." Harris walked to the desk and leaned over to stare Cooper in the face. "What really happened?" He paused. "Okay. Let's start at the beginning. Where did you go when you left the zoo?"

"I got home about five-thirty." He paused as if retracing his movements. "It was probably six when I called Madelyn. She wanted to talk about Komodo dragons. She's trying to—"

Harris held up his hand. "I'm familiar with the Indonesian connection. Is that all you talked about? Dragons?"

"Yes. And then I ate a sandwich and went to bed."

"Dr. Rivers told me about the call."

"What we talked about is none of your business."

"I might agree if it hadn't been about Brooks. But let's continue. You did nothing else that evening? Just went to bed?"

"That's right."

"Didn't talk to anyone, go for a walk, take a drive?"

"None of the above." Cooper shook his head emphatically.

"You were seen in the zoo Monday night, near the bird-of-prey cage. I had hoped for your sake you would volunteer that information."

"You can't expect me to remember every detail."

Harris stifled an urge to punch him out. "You're lying, not forgetting. Whom are you protecting?"

"I'm not protecting anyone. I've answered your questions—"

"With lies! I ought to take you in for questioning, but I can't spare the time. And it would obviously take lots of that. Perhaps you'd be kind enough to tell me about that midnight stroll."

"I wanted to look in on the sick lion cubs. They're better, by the way. And then I walked for a while. I love the sounds of the zoo at night. And I wasn't alone. I saw Stevens, Horatio, and four people from the veterinary staff."

"So that justifies your lying about being there? Is that it?"

Cooper shrugged. "I was just a face in the crowd."

"And you didn't think we might like to know there was a crowd wandering around the zoo the night of the murder? You're in this up to your neck, Cooper." Harris grabbed the nearest door knob and yanked it open. But instead of the hallway, he found himself inside an enormous closet, overflowing with books and papers that only partially hid Harley Knopstead. Seizing him by the arm, Harris dragged him into the room. "Knopstead, what were you doing in there? Eavesdropping?"

"It wasn't deliberate, Lieutenant."

Cooper was staring coldly at the photographer. "I thought I told you to leave the zoo grounds."

"You did, sir, only I couldn't. I'm on assignment. You were coming, and I knew you didn't want to see me. So I ducked in here."

"This happens to be my office. I want you out of here, and out of the zoo."

"No appeal?"

"Out!"

"Sorry we can't do business."

Harris suppressed a smile. He'd been finessed again, but Knopstead had made up for it. How much had he actually overheard? Harris didn't want to think about what the Chief would say if any of this appeared in the Star News. And trying to stop Knopstead would be like setting off a charge of dynamite.

Harris stopped at Peggy MacMillan's desk. "Excuse me, Ms. MacMillan."

"Yes, Lieutenant?"

"I'd like to see your zoo keys—offices, service gates, cages, whatever."

"I don't have them with me, Lieutenant. I changed purses this morning." She smiled at him coyly.

"What's that key ring by the printer?"

Angrily, she handed it to him. He flipped the keys over one at a time. Most of them had the designation A, for Administration. None bore the Reptile House code, but that wasn't conclusive. She might have borrowed a key from Thomas on Cooper's behalf, and then returned it. Or she might have pinched one when Thomas wasn't looking. He recognized the B FC on Morley's bird-of-prey cage key, and a service gate key: G3.

"Gate number 3. Which one is that?"

"It's near the statue of Audubon."

Translation: behind the Reptile House. "I would have expected you to park across the street. That lot is closer to this building."

"I do. This isn't my key. It just turned up on my desk."

"You always put stray keys on your personal key ring?"

"Why not?" she replied coolly.

Harris walked out of the building and paused at the flamingo exhibit, hoping for a moment of tranquility. But his thoughts were full of MacMillan. Attractive, intelligent, and wrong for the job. It wasn't her clothes. Miss Thomas was a sharp dresser, too, and she hadn't bothered him. But MacMillan was different. Something didn't ring true. She was used to giving orders, not taking them.

Harris hurried into the station at eleven-forty. He'd have time to call out for a sandwich before the meeting. It was going to be a busy afternoon.

Glancing into the booking room as he headed toward his office, he was startled to see Gertrude Gypsom. Maybe she'd discovered something. Or, more likely, she just thought she had.

"Well, GG, this is an unexpected pleasure. What brings you here?"

"Your officers in your squad car. Auto theft, indeed, I was just—"

A uniformed patrolman entered the room. "I was looking for you, Lieutenant. When Ms. Gypsom told us she was involved in your investigation, we thought we'd better let you know. Though I don't know what speeding in a stolen car could have to do with bodies in the zoo."

"Nor do I. And stealing cars doesn't sound like Ms. Gypsom. What happened?"

"I was trying to buy it, not steal it—"

"She was doing ninety-five on the freeway. When we called it in, the car came up stolen. Her story's being typed, but it sounds weird."

"Her stories usually do. I'll vouch for her on auto theft—not on the speeding ticket, of course. You can go as soon as you sign the statement, GG. Meanwhile, come back to my office for a minute. There are a couple of points you may be able to help me with, since you're here."

He led her down the hall and opened the door. "Have a seat. Should I ask why you were trying to buy a stolen car?"

"Because I didn't know it was stolen. How could I? It didn't have a big red 'S' painted on its windshield, or anything." She seemed uncharacteristically succinct. Subdued, maybe.

"Never mind. What I really want is more information on Brooks. We're finding surprisingly little about him—his business, his interests, his personal life. Aside from Dr. Rivers, we haven't even identified any friends. Can you help us?"

"Funny you should ask. We talked about that last night. None of us knew much about him. Just that he worked at END for awhile and then inherited both money and a business from his father. Madelyn probably knows more."

"He was apparently a blackmailer. That's confidential for the moment, but I'm sure it will be public knowledge before long. Does that surprise you?"

"Not me. I always thought he was slime. But I never suspected blackmail. He must have been discreet about it. Most people thought he was Mr. Charm."

GG began to relax, and talked more freely, but she didn't really know much about Brooks—just that she hated him. McDuff rapped on the door, interrupting her tirade.

"Come in, Scot. Thanks for the information, GG. They're probably ready with your statement by now."

McDuff set an evidence box on Harris' desk: the contents of Brooks' pockets, neatly filed.

GG stood up. "Well, thanks for being a character witness. Hey, that's one of Christine's key rings." She pointed at an enameled brass figure of a seal in the box. "Did it belong to Charles? I suppose it was a present from Mad."

Of course. The cheerful seal was a relative of the hippo he'd seen at Ms. Featherworth's apartment.

"Probably. Take a look. See if you recognize anything else."

She poked through the keys. "Nothing much, I'm afraid. That's a zoo key, but you probably already know that." She picked up a newspaper clipping that had been tucked into Brooks' wallet. "Odd thing for him to be carrying around. It's about that animal dealer there's been so such a fuss about. That's more in Mad's line than Brooks'."

Harris glanced at the article. Blackmail? He vaguely remembered an expose about the man, Botticelli Brown. But this story painted him as an upstanding, though possibly eccentric, local citizen. The picture showed a youngish man with wild curly hair. Handsome, in a rough, craggy way.

Gertrude turned toward the door. "Thanks again, John. Do you think I can get my credit cards back?"

"I'd be surprised. I'd report them lost, ASAP, if I were you. And take care. Don't buy any watches from street vendors."

He watched her appreciatively as she dodged around solid George Pierce at the door.

"Okay, George, have a seat and let's get started. What do we have, so far."

"No doubt about the blackmail. Brooks kept business-like records. He had a spread sheet with cross references to the clippings and tapes. He also had a hard copy in his file. It's all in some kind of code, but the meaning is clear enough. I'm getting it all cataloged and looking at his bank deposits. Some stuff has been removed from the hard copy. Maybe that's what the guy who tossed Brooks' apartment was looking for."

"What do we know about the victims?"

"We haven't gone through them all, but there's one big surprise, so far," Pierce responded. "We found a file from an army court martial. A Lieutenant was on guard duty at a base out in the desert. A carload of local drunks came roaring in and he thought they were terrorists, or something. Anyway, the Lieutenant got spooked and fled. The court martial found extenuating circumstances—his father had died recently and there'd been some family problems. They gave him a general discharge. Nothing so awful in the end, but certainly not an impressive service record. God knows where Brooks got the file, but the Lieutenant's name was Edward W. Piper. It must be the same guy."

"Piper! That story would be a deadly blow for him. His fiancee's family are real saber rattlers and any suggestion of cowardice would end his plan to marry money. But I can't see Piper as the murderer."

"I can't either. And there's his alibi. Still. . ."

"We'll confront him with it and see what we get. It might at least give us a different slant on Brooks. What else?"

"We're checking out the principals mentioned in the clippings and trying to find out whether they've had any contact with Brooks. So far, zip."

"How about Brooks' business?"

"Nothing but the name and address. Since it's in Japsom City, we sent a request for information to the department there. We should be hearing from them shortly."

"I'm going there tomorrow night to give a speech. I can follow up with them then if necessary. Meanwhile, keep me informed." Harris waited until the door was closed behind Pierce and McDuff and picked up the phone just as it rang.

"Harris."

"This is the Chief's office. He wants you down here, on the double."

Sighing, Harris picked up his notebook and headed down the hall. Lunch was looking increasingly like a non-event.

Harris maneuvered his red M.G. into the center lane of the freeway. He would have liked to cancel dinner at his sister's, but he'd put her off too many times lately. Cursing at a driver who had slithered in ahead of him, he slowed, falling easily into the rhythm of the traffic around him. He loved his car. Driving it—always with the top down—gave him a sense of oneness with the machine and the road. His ex had given him a personalized license plate—SNAIL—and he liked to joke about the speed and responsiveness of his SNAIL. Deftly, he evaded an ancient Ford that was cutting in too close from the right. Pure stupidity.

Just like MacMillan and Cooper with their barefaced lies. There seemed to be no purpose to what either of them said. And it was damned exasperating the way Cooper admitted the lies time after time. They'd been together at Frank's. Could they be accomplices? Cooper had a motive—jealousy—but how about MacMillan? Maybe blackmail? None of the evidence in Brooks' apartment seemed to fit MacMillan, but someone had beaten the police to the search. Could she get into Brook's computer? Maybe

Pierce's computer expert would turn up something.

Or she could have been Brooks' 'glamour puss' visitor. Stebbins, the neighbor, had been uncertain. The hair was right, but she wasn't sure about the face. She'd said she'd know if she saw the woman walk. McDuff could take Stebbins into the zoo to watch MacMillan. If Brooks was MacMillan's lover, that would shed a new light on her lies.

Stebbins had also said she'd seen someone who walked like Brooks' visitor get out of a tan station wagon about four a.m. Tuesday. It had been dark, and the woman had been wearing rain gear, but Stebbins had been sure it was the same person. The searcher?

He'd been on this case for two days now, and there weren't many hard facts. Markleson's report established that Brooks had been killed by the taipan no earlier than eight p.m. and no later than midnight. There were a lot of possible motives, including blackmail. The murderer had to be able to handle the taipan and to enter the zoo, the Reptile House and the bird-of-prey cage. Everything else—white trash cans, Cooper's lies, Rivers' car, Stebbins, MacMillan—might be so much noise.

Smoothly, Harris pulled around a brown BMW. This case was loony. GG being booked for car theft fit right in with the rest of the nonsense. What a free spirit—driving around town in a stolen car, doing ninety-five. Why she—

A piercing siren sounded behind him. He pulled to the shoulder of the freeway and stopped.

"Well, buddy," the officer said, "that's quite a snail you have there."

CHAPTER TWELVE

Morley shifted his weight away from a particularly aggressive thorn. His lookout post in the middle of the pyracantha hedge between MacMillan's house and driveway was directly under her living room window. Excellent for listening to what was going on inside. Terrible for his knee. He had always admired these bushes—the waxy green leaves, and, in winter, the scarlet berries. At a distance, they had seemed friendly. Intimacy had changed all that.

Here he was, half standing, half sitting, barefoot, miserable, and embarrassingly entangled in the shrubbery. Two hours in this position had permanently altered the shape of his spine. He moved his foot and discovered his leg was asleep. If MacMillan decided to leave now, he would be incapable of giving chase.

He must be out of his mind, tailing a colleague. But he'd been so sure she was a key player. And he hadn't stopped to consider what it would be like. Why, he'd even had trouble following her out of the parking lot. The stupid hat had kept falling into his eyes. Dark glasses would have been quite sufficient, but Gert had insisted on a hat big enough to float his head in. And the drive across town had been a disaster—a near collision with a bus, three run stop signs, and an indignant raven screaming in his ear. Caruso had had a point. It was a miracle he hadn't killed them both.

A phone rang inside, and he tore himself loose from the hedge and hurried to the window. He had hoped to hear what she said, but she had gone into the other room to talk. This was a complete waste of time.

Morley stepped on a particularly pesky branch and was climbing over it when it snapped under his weight. He lost his balance and barely managed to catch hold of another sturdy branch as thorns grabbed his hair. Pulling loose, he ripped his lip open.

He ached all over. Maybe it was time to give up. He hated admitting defeat, but it wasn't his fault nothing was happening. And getting out of the pyracantha was going to take forever. Maybe he'd better do it before Caruso started making a ruckus. It was one thing to leave Caruso in the car, but he'd wanted to make amends for the terrible drive, so he'd left the music playing. If only he hadn't taught the raven to run the automatic windows up and down.

Morley was moving back through the hedge when a car pulled up. He froze. He didn't want to be arrested for trespassing. The driver was walking up the path as if he owned the place. It was too dark to make out his features, but he was about six feet tall, and his hair was blond. Or grey. The street light reflected off the license plate: AKZ 843. Aha! He had a key. Time to creep back under the window.

Maybe he should put on his loafers. No. They made too much racket in the underbrush. Shoes in hand, Morley forced his way back through the hedge.

Hawk shit! He was stuck in the thorns again, and their voices would never carry this far. He'd have to rip himself free and get back to the window.

He finally reached his goal, with only a few more scratches. What did he think he was doing? He wasn't a Peeping Tom, but that was his assignment. Resolutely, he used the window sill to pull himself up and look inside. His quarries were out of sight, but he could make out their voices over the din of the TV.

". . .losing my nerve, Ted."

"Now, sweetheart, you're forgetting how much you've already accomplished. I mean, they don't hire just anybody at the zoo."

"Yeah? Well, maybe I like working at the zoo. Maybe that's the job I was meant to do. Maybe you can find someone else to do your dirty work for you."

"Hey, I'm not thinking of me, Peg. It's you. You have a lot invested in this project. If you quit now, it'll all be down the tubes."

Morley was stunned. This was supposed to be a game—a humiliating, uncomfortable game. But these people were really plotting something. At best, it was illegal, and he was way out of his league. Maybe he could call John. No, that wouldn't wash. He was here, John wasn't.

"I don't like using the zoo. It's not a good cover anymore, not since—"

"Listen to me, Peg. The whole plan is geared to the zoo. It was your idea—"

"Don't rub it in."

"No one will connect us with that murder."

"And just how do you know that?"

"Common sense. You can't back out now. There's too much at stake."

"That policeman—Harris—can see right through me. My nerves are shot. Doesn't that matter to you?"

So John made her nervous. Good. But what the hell were they doing? And why?

"Of course I care about you. That's why I don't want you to make a damned fool of yourself. You've been absolutely marvelous. No mistakes, no problems—"

"Oh, Ted, I wish I'd never gotten involved."

"So let's get it over with. Then we can forget it ever happened."

"But they're suspicious of me. Can't you get that through your thick head?"

"Who's suspicious? One policeman? He doesn't have anything on you. Sweetheart, this is worth a lot to both of us." His voice was gentle, pleading. "Don't you want to go to Tangiers with me?"

Tangiers. Good Lord! They were planning to flee the country.

"Oh, Ted, I—"

"And look, baby, you're not alone. I'll be right there with you."

"That's a good one. You're going to talk to Harris, is that it?"

"Hey, you can handle that two-bit detective. But if it's equality you want, how about lugging our cargo through the zoo?"

Cargo? Could they be talking about Brooks?

"That's about all you did." There was a pause before she went on, "All right. You win."

"I knew you'd come through, baby. That's why I love you so much. Let's. . ."

"No, Ted, not now. We have to make plans. What night do you think is best?"

"The moon's too bright. It'll have to be tomorrow night—or the night after that."

"No, I think we'd better wait until Sunday or Monday. Things will have calmed down at the zoo by then."

"We don't want too much calm. I'd like to take advantage of the confusion."

"Saturday at the earliest."

"Okay. That still gives us lots of time, baby—"

"Ted—"

So they weren't planning to do anything tonight—at least, nothing lethal. He'd better get back. Maybe there was still time.

Morley heard a rustle behind him. "Oh hell, where's my pipe?"

"Hush, Caruso, hush." He had to be close. "Come, Caruso, here on my arm," he whispered.

"Oh hell, where's my pipe?"

He reached out in the direction of the voice, but the raven only whistled in response. This wouldn't do. Morley started carefully retracing his route through the hedge. He was in the middle of the thorniest patch when Caruso landed hard on his shoulder. The sudden movement and the tight grip of the bird's claws were too much. He yelped in pain. Now he'd blown it. What a glorious end to his assignment—trapped in the hedge, screaming.

Sweat was running into his eyes, half blinding him as he struggled frantically to free himself. Maybe they'd already called the police.

"Some broad killed her lover—"

"Shut your beak." Morley tore his sleeve free, then scratched his hand as he tugged his pant leg away from another branch. Abandoning his loafers, he fought his way through the hedge and onto the sidewalk. He had just started to run when he heard a door open behind him.

"Who's there? What's going on out there?"

It was Ted, and, from the sound of his voice, this was the wrong time for a chat. Morley tucked Caruso under his arm and raced toward the car. Someone was chasing him, but he had a good head start. He felt Caruso getting ready to shout. Morley increased his speed as mighty cries of, "Fire! Fire!" rang in his ear. The bird was having the time of his life.

Morley and the raven tumbled into the car and were two blocks away before the pursuer rounded the corner.

"Stay calm, Caruso. Gert will know what to do."

"Some broad killed—" Caruso shouted from his perch on the back of the seat.

"Shut your beak! Gert has to be home. This is important stuff, and I need her help figuring out what it means."

"Vulture droppings!" The raven flapped his wings with contempt.

Morley swung into Gertrude's driveway. Cyril's orange Volvo wagon was parked in front. Good. They could use extra help. Morley started for the house, then turned around and held out his arm for Caruso.

"I'm not going to face Gert alone. You're as much to blame as I am."

The bird ran up his arm and onto his shoulder. Morley opened the front door and yelled, "Gert? Where are you? I'm here."

"My God, Morley—" She stood staring at him from the kitchen door.

"I'm sorry, Gert. I tried. We both tried, matter of fact, but we blew it."

She didn't respond.

"You needn't look so horrified. Everybody makes mistakes."

"Are you all right?" She touched his face. "What happened? You look absolutely awful."

Glancing down, he was surprised to see that what remained of his suit was covered with a remarkable combination of dirt, leaves, and spider webs, creating a collage with the blood from his multiple wounds. And he was still barefooted.

"We ran into some unexpected difficulties."

"Looks like they ran into you. Let's get you into the tub."

She took his hand and led him down the hall. "Here, Caruso."

She pointed to the top of the bathroom door, and the bird flapped up to the perch. "Now let's get those clothes off you. Morley, you've ruined your suit."

"It could have been worse. They could have caught me."

"Yes, I suppose so... They could have what? What happened?"

"I was right about MacMillan. I was in a thorny hedge, listening to her tell her boyfriend how she had hoodwinked Cooper into hiring her. And the boyfriend carried their 'cargo' in the zoo, the night of the murder. I can't get over it."

"I told you she was the murderer. Oh, this does call for a celebration."

"Actually, it made me feel a little sick. I'm not cut out to be a detective."

"Come, darling, your bath's ready. You did good."

He eased himself into the water. "Then why do I feel so bad?"

"Those cuts don't look deep enough to worry about. Just soak for a while. Your robe's behind the door, and the Bandaids are in the medicine cabinet. I'm going to make some hot tea."

"I saw Cyril's car. Where are the others?"

"Larry said he had plans tonight."

"What a jerk."

"We can't count on him. And Mad said she wasn't ready to face a meeting."

"So nobody's doing anything."

"I was working on a promising lead this afternoon. But it took forever to get away from the police station. Why, if John hadn't turned up, I'd be there yet."

"The police station?"

"It was about the Porsche."

"I see."

"Anyway, Cyril and Christine and I have been talking. But without you, the meeting didn't seem to get anywhere."

"That's flattering." He leaned back in the tub and smiled up at her. "Nice to be appreciated for a change. I'll be through here in no time, and then we'll sort it all out. Oh, Gert. How about some scotch instead of that tea? A double."

"What's the matter? Can't take it? You know the old saw, 'When the going gets tough—'"

" '—the tough get stuck in the pyracantha.' I know all about it, and I need a good, stiff drink."

Laughing, Gertrude disappeared. Morley sighed. He didn't really understand what he had overheard, and he had no idea what they should do next. Still, if his friends needed a leader, he'd try to keep their spirits up until Harris solved the crime. Naturally they wouldn't do any real detective work—not this motley crew. Meanwhile, he was going to relax in the soothing warm water.

He had just leaned his head back and closed his eyes when Caruso landed heavily on his arm, one claw digging into an open wound. Shrieking, Morley rose out of the tub while the raven flapped into the hall. Grabbing a towel, he decided to get on with it. He'd have no peace until this thing was settled. But how his own private raven had gotten into the employ of the enemy was beyond imagining.

CHAPTER THIRTEEN

Madelyn pushed her way through the cluster of children around the balloon man and walked toward the Administration Building. The murder was obviously still drawing well. She scanned the crowd and spotted Cyril, towering above the Boy Scouts at the entrance to the building. And there was Christine beside him.

"Cyril! Christine! Wait!" She hurried up the steps. "It's wonderful of you to come to this—this event of GG's. Where is she, anyway?"

"She and Morley are looking for Sergeant McDuff. He's the agenda."

"Hi, all." Gertrude shouted from just ahead. "Come join us."

"GG, what's going on?" Madelyn asked. "Your note mentioned Lieutenant Harris, not the Sergeant."

"Harris had a meeting with the Chief. He told Morley to talk to McDuff."

"That doesn't explain why I'm included."

"We thought you'd want to be in on this."

"Morley doesn't need help telling Sergeant McDuff he heard Peggy—"

"We must get started." Morley interrupted, taking Gertrude's arm.

"We can't. McDuff's disappeared."

"Not entirely." Madelyn nodded toward the H.R. office, where McDuff's plump behind was in plain view as he bent over the bottom drawer of a file cabinet.

"Sergeant. Good morning," Morley said.

"Good morning yourself, Dr. Stevens. Five of you, is it? Quite a delegation. Let's go in here." He opened the conference room door. "They're letting me use this today."

Madelyn settled into a comfortable leather chair and glanced at the others. They had fallen into an uneasy silence. Well, it wasn't her meeting. She concentrated on the zoo photos on the wall.

"Dr. Stevens, I don't have all day," McDuff said. "What's this important information?"

"It's hard to explain, Sergeant. You see, I got stuck in the hedge. A pyracantha hedge. Very thorny. And since I was barefoot, I—"

"Morley, you're starting in the wrong place," Gertrude said. "Tell him about Ms. MacMillan being the murderer."

Cyril leaned forward and tapped his pencil on the table. "That won't make any sense unless the Sergeant knows her job at the zoo was a cover."

"But the crucial thing is that they were talking about doing 'it' again," Christine said. "Only you missed the end, didn't you, Morley, when Caruso landed on your head."

McDuff looked utterly confused. "Hold on a minute here—"

"So I picked up my shoes—"

"And he heard her say—"

"But the bird—"

"So you see, she must have—"

"—they're probably planning the murder for tomorrow night."

"A murder? Shut up, all of you!" McDuff shouted. "Stevens, are you telling me you were spying on MacMillan and she threatened to kill someone?"

"Not exactly. They were talking about doing 'it' again, and it didn't seem much of a leap from there to the murder."

McDuff listened intently until Morley finally finished his story. "Why didn't you call me last night?" he yelled. "If what you say is true, you've set this investigation back twelve hours. They could have left the city by now. The country, for that matter. And, Dr. Stevens, you might have had the courtesy to tell me yesterday that MacMillan's ornithologist doesn't exist. I wasted two hours trying to locate him. Even if you don't give a damn about my time, you could at least have saved the taxpayers a few dollars."

Morley looked chagrined. "Oh. I—I am sorry."

"You people are impossible. Playing cops and robbers with a bunch of murderers, turning in false fire alarms—"

"We never—" Gertrude started to protest.

"I saw the report this morning. One of MacMillan's neighbors called the Fire Department last night because someone yelled 'Fire!'"

"Oh, Lord. That was Caruso."

"Caruso? Your pet crow?"

"Raven."

"If you care about that precious raven of yours, keep him out of my sight." McDuff walked to the door. "Now listen up. No more interference. I intend to find out what MacMillan's game is, and I do not want your help. But I do want that license number, Stevens."

Morley repeated it.

"Sergeant, I'm delighted you agree with us about Ms. MacMillan," Gertrude said.

"That was not agreement you heard." McDuff hurried off.

Madelyn looked around the table at her deflated friends.

"I really thought he'd be pleased," Gertrude said. "Now I don't know what to do with myself."

"That's a luxury Madelyn and I don't have," Morley replied. "We are off to a real-world meeting."

"And I have to find a new place to hang out," Christine pushed her chair back. "No offense, Mad, but the Reptile House has lost its charm."

"We'll miss you, Chrissy. Morley, we're late." Madelyn stood up and gathered her belongings. "GG, try not to get arrested today."

Morley opened the door and the three of them walked out into the hall.

"So," Cyril said, "end of meeting. Tell me, GG, where does the zoo hide its cafeteria? I can't go on without coffee."

"Can you make it across the hall or should I get you a wheel chair?" Gertrude led him into the coffee shop.

"So what's with all these animals?"

"We're commingling with them. The tables are in the middle of the exhibits, so you can eat and watch the animals at the same time. Do you prefer seals, polar bears, or tropical birds?"

"Whatever," Cyril replied.

"I say seals. They're so reassuringly impossible."

"What's reassuring about being impossible?"

"The design is flawed, but they still move with joy."

"I see what you mean. Seals it is. I'll be right back."

Cyril returned with coffee and sat staring at the cavorting animals. Gertrude cradled the hot cup in her hands. He was so quiet. "Is anything wrong?"

"It's the murder—" Cyril replied. "And I'll tell you what else. It's that lousy Cooper. He's been acting like a bum, and I want to know why. I'm going to follow him."

"Good for you!" Gertrude saluted him with her cup. "That's one problem solved. So now what are we going to do about Mad's car?"

"GG, there's more to this case than the whereabouts of Madelyn's car Monday night."

"But I feel guilty about it. I'm the one who told John it wasn't there."

"The missing car would have come up eventually. It's a good thing you told him early on. Otherwise he might have thought you were trying to hide something."

"That may be, but I'd still like to straighten it out. So far, all I've done is make trouble. Except for the Porsche."

"Do tell me how the Porsche is involved in the case."

"It's not involved. I'm going to buy it. Only first I have to persuade the real owner—or his insurance company—or whoever it is you have to deal with—to sell it to me."

"Wouldn't it be easier to buy one you hadn't stolen?"

"But that wouldn't be the same car."

"No." He sighed. "I suppose not."

She snapped her fingers. "I've got it. We'll advertise."

"For the Porsche?"

"No, for Madelyn."

"Is she lost already? And here I thought she'd gone off with Morley."

"You know perfectly well I meant Mad's car."

"I think you're going soft in the head. Her car's fine. It's sitting right outside in the parking lot. Would you feel better if we went out and spoke to it?"

"Cyril, you won't even try to understand me. I wanted—Oh, never mind. I'll take care of it myself." She fumbled in her purse. "Damn, I forgot my phone again. I'll need yours."

There was no point in arguing. She'd get it sooner or later. "Bring your own next time," he growled as he handed it to her. He watched as she brought up the Star News web page, clicked on 'Classifieds', and typed

Anyone who drove, heard, or saw a 2008 Chevy on Clarboy Drive last Monday at about 1 a.m., please call 854-9217.

She entered a credit card number—he was happy to see it wasn't his—and logged off.

Cyril stared at her in amazement. "Surely you don't expect an answer to that?"

"Why not? Just because you're afraid to take risks, don't expect me to wimp out."

"It's not the risk, it's the assumption. If the murderer went to the trouble of kidnapping Mad's car, he'd leave it at the zoo before he'd involve another person. You'll get nothing but crank calls."

"I don't care if I get a hundred crank calls. Cyril, I have to know I've tried."

"Okay." He didn't want to upset her. She needed her friends even if she was crazy. "If that's what you want, great. Now what?"

"Now I go home and get my phone so I won't miss the call."

"The paper won't be on the stands until evening. Unless you think the proofreader's your man."

"I suppose you're right. Let's get some more coffee and switch to polar bears. They make me laugh."

"Now there's a plan."

"You wanted to see me?" Harris asked.

The Chief looked up from under shaggy gray brows. "Sit down, John. I've been getting heat from the commissioners. They want to know why the Brooks murder is turning into a fiasco."

"I don't understand. The investigation is moving along smoothly. We have several new leads. Apparently Brooks was involved in multiple blackmail schemes—"

"I've been briefed on all that. The commissioners are more concerned about the publicity. Why all this nonsense about the zoo?"

"Well that happens to be where the body was found. But it's beginning to look like the zoo was incidental to the whole thing."

"Then why all these pictures of snakes and birds and—"

"Give me a break, Chief. The media people are having a field day. It's not my fault the murder weapon was a snake."

"But it is your fault that you let some imbecile take your picture posing with it."

"I wasn't posing. Knopstead just happened to be there."

"Then how come no one else gets in his pictures? Tell me that."

"He follows me around. I can't tell him to jump off a cliff. How would that sound in the evening edition?"

"Harris, I don't care how you get rid of Knopstead. Just do it. And what about the Rhines woman?"

"Dr. Rivers? What about her?"

"I understand there's enough evidence to convict her. What's stopping you?"

"She didn't kill him."

"Who did?"

"I'm not sure."

"Get sure. And get this straight! If you've gone soft on a pretty woman, you'll find yourself back on the street."

"Now wait just a minute. Who said I—"

"Harris, I want a full report on my desk this afternoon."

"But I'm due in Japsom City tonight. I have to speak to the—"

"I don't care if you're addressing Congress. I want that report. Now get out!"

"Yes, sir."

Harris walked slowly to his office. Someone had been talking. His phone was ringing. He grabbed It and sank into his chair.

"How was the meeting with the Chief?" Scot sounded excited—surely not about his meeting.

"Bad. Scot, who could have been leaking to the commissioners? He's been getting an earful."

"I don't know. What's he heard?"

"That Rivers is guilty. They hate all this publicity, so they're pressuring him for an arrest. He wants a full report this afternoon."

"That's going to keep you busy. I have a few things that should help."

"Shoot."

"The biggest surprise is Japsom City. We had to prod them three times to get a response. Brooks Importing is apparently hot stuff. They said it belongs to the feds and there is a high level hands-off order. I got nowhere trying to get any information beyond that."

"I'll talk to Hammond about it when I'm there tonight. We go back to college, and he's bound to give me more than that. I think we can take it they're talking DEA and that Brooks was importing something stronger than tea. What else?"

"George has been going over Brooks' bank records. Deposits correlate with the log book entries, and he's working on some of the people mentioned in the clippings. His preliminary report will be ready in the morning."

"That's too late for my report."

"But get this. A bunch of Brooks' phone calls were to Cooper's number. We haven't tied Cooper in with any of the clippings, but there must be something."

"Now we're getting somewhere. Cooper, I'd believe."

"Shall I confront him with it?"

"No. I'll do it when I get back tomorrow. We need more information first. The only way to get the truth out of Cooper is to know what it is before you start questioning him. Keep looking at the blackmail angle. Anything else?"

"Not about blackmail. But I did discover that Piper was dismissed from the Hudson Bay Zoo for unprofessional behavior. Dr. Rivers found him out. They're sending details."

"Piper, again. He keeps popping up. Check with Dr. Rivers and get back to me. Have you questioned him about blackmail?"

"No. I had arranged to talk to him this morning, but this thing with MacMillan seemed more urgent."

"Right. Maybe you should wait until you have the information on his dismissal from Hudson Bay, and cover both issues with him tomorrow. Did you talk to MacMillan?"

"Yes." McDuff was shouting into the phone. "She denied being in the zoo Monday night. Insists she was home alone. By the way, her personnel file says she worked for a small company that went bankrupt. I don't buy it, but it'll take a while to check it out."

"Did I tell you I showed Stebbins the picture of MacMillan? Says she's not sure about the face, but she'd know Brooks' girlfriend if she saw her walk. Can you arrange to get Stebbins out to the zoo?"

"Sure, John."

"What about the veterinary staff? Did you ask them what they saw Monday night?"

"Yes. They all saw Cooper. He did, in fact, visit the sick lion cubs. Aside from that, nothing unusual."

"All these fools were creeping around the zoo in the middle of the night and none of them saw anything unusual."

"That's California cool, John."

"It's also a pain in the ass. Did you assign someone other than Stevens to watch MacMillan?"

McDuff grunted. "Peterson."

"And you warned him about Stevens and the gang?"

"I told him. He didn't believe me, but I told him."

If the commissioners heard he'd let a bunch of loonies get out of control— "Scot, I want you to deliver a message to GG and her friends. Tell them to lay off. They're in over their heads. I'd tell them myself, but I don't have time."

"I'll do that with pleasure, John."

"So Brooks was a blackmailer and probably a drug dealer. Cooper was probably a blackmail victim and rarely tells the truth. Piper, who stands to lose big time if exposed, was probably being blackmailed on at least two counts. And MacMillan is conspiring with someone to do 'it' again. In addition to those potential murderers, Brooks' lifestyle makes suicide seem more likely and exposed him to large numbers of violent people we haven't even heard about. So, of course, the Chief wants me to arrest Dr. Rivers. And Scot, I want you down here at three. I'll have to leave for Japsom City by four. If I'm not finished, you'll have to take over."

"Will do."

Olaf, the male polar bear, was soaking in his icy pond.

Gertrude waved at him, and, to her delight, he waved back. His mate, Natasha, was on the other side of the grotto, entertaining the visitors on the zoo bus. She was handsome in her huge, snowy coat—

Cyril's voice cut through Gertrude's thoughts. "Now that you did something useless about your obsession with Mad's car, let's move on to the real problem."

"Which is?"

"How did the murderer get both the body and the snake into that cage?"

Olaf lumbered out of his pond and approached the window. He was green from spending so much time in his algae infested water. Gertrude wondered how Natasha felt about having a green lover.

"Hey, GG, will you stop staring at that green monster and listen to me? I want to know if it's possible to unlock the cage door while holding the snake."

"I say no. If I were holding the taipan, my hand would be shaking so hard I wouldn't be able to put the key in the lock."

"So what did the murderer do with the snake? He couldn't have set it down on the path."

"Ask Mad. She's the snake expert."

"It wouldn't be friendly to remind her of that scene. Come on. You handle snakes, too."

"A rosy boa, that's all. Still, it is an interesting question. Say I arrive at the cage door with the snake in my left hand and I'm dragging the body with my right. To get in the cage, I have to let go of the body and find my key. I open my purse—now that's interesting. A man would have an easier time than a woman. It's harder to get a key out of a purse than a pocket."

"IF she carried a purse. But you have a point. A purse would complicate the trip down the hill, too."

"Anyway, I'd get the key out, open the door, grab the body, and move everyone inside."

"You're assuming you can hold an angry eight foot snake in one hand."

"Maybe the murderer used a cage or a sack," Gertrude suggested. "No one in his right mind would wander around clutching a taipan."

"The snake must have been the best weapon he could find on the spur of the moment. Otherwise, why take it out of the Reptile House? A desperate murderer chasing his victim doesn't stop to cage the weapon."

"I wouldn't go near that weapon with a ten foot butterfly net, let alone—"

"But someone did," Cyril interrupted impatiently. "Let's stick to the facts. Someone got out the snake, dragged it down there—presumably while running after Brooks—and locked them both in the cage."

"Maybe Brooks ran in to get away and the murderer threw the snake in after him."

"Can you throw a snake?"

"Let's try it."

"With a snake? Mad would never let us use hers," Cyril objected.

"There's a lovely plush snake in the gift shop—lavender, with pink splotches and green eyes, seven feet long—almost as long as the taipan."

"You're nuts!"

"Not nuts, covetous. Let's go buy my snake."

Gertrude stood in front of the bird-of-prey cage door, holding the garish plush snake. "Here we go. We can't open the door, so we'll have to fake that part. Other than that, we can run through the whole scenario."

"Forget it. I don't enjoy making a fool of myself."

"You're the one who wanted to figure out how it was done. Besides, this spot is always deserted. Here. You take Pythagoras."

Cyril eyed the snake doubtfully. "It's so bright, it'll attract a crowd. Pilots will report it as they fly overhead. And we don't have a body. What exactly do you expect me to do?"

"I'm the body." She lowered herself carefully to the gravel pathway. "Now you drag me with one hand and hold the snake in the other."

"If you say so." Cyril gripped Gertrude by one arm and dragged her along the path toward the cage door.

"Cyril, stop! That hurts!" The snake knocked against her. She twisted her head. "His tail's caught in a bush, and the head hit me, so I've been bitten."

"Your getting bitten is okay. I'm the one who can't get bitten."

"Put me down and see if you can handle Pythagoras while unlocking the door." From the ground, she watched him approach the door, snake in hand.

Cyril stopped abruptly. "The stupid snake won't budge!" He turned to free it from the latest bush, lost his balance and fell sprawling across Gertrude who screamed in surprise. He was still grimly clutching the snake. As the dust cleared, Gertrude was horrified to see a small ring of curious spectators gathered around them.

"Cyril, you idiot! You've spoiled everything. Let's get out of here before the police show up."

To Madelyn's relief, the meeting had been mercifully short—an update on limitations imposed by the continuing investigation and a brief strategy session with the zoo's public relations man. No decision had been made on the CELEBRATE LIFE campaign, but Larry thought they'd probably proceed on schedule. In the meantime, attendance continued at an all time high. It left a bad taste in her mouth.

When the meeting broke up, she walked with Morley toward Bird Mesa. She stopped at the base of the bird-of-prey cage and turned to him.

"Morley, I have to know who killed Charles. Even if I'm never charged with the murder, that's not enough. I can't bear veiled suspicion for the rest of my life."

"John will work it out. He's already onto several leads that don't have anything to do with you. So relax. Try to think about something else."

"Ignoring problems doesn't make them go away, Morley. It just rots your spirit."

"Okay, I hear you. What can I do?"

"I need to be involved in your discussions—or investigation, or whatever it is."

"You said you didn't want to hear anything about it."

"I've changed my mind."

"But we're not really doing anything. I'm just trying to keep everybody occupied until—"

"But look what you stumbled onto last night with MacMillan."

"So you think MacMillan is our man?"

"No, I don't. The murderer hated me enough to set me up, and she hadn't even met me when Charles was killed."

"If not MacMillan, then who?"

"Charles. He's the only person I've ever known who was capable of that much hatred."

"It didn't have to be hatred. Your problems with Charles were general knowledge. And Charles apparently was involved in a risky business—"

"Yes, I've been told. Blackmail." She looked away.

"Well, an angry blackmail victim might have selected you as a matter of convenience."

"It feels like hate. Too much manufactured evidence. And a blackmail victim making trouble could have given Charles a motive for suicide."

"Okay, if it makes you happy, we'll talk suicide."

"It's so tidy. No body to carry, no worry about getting bitten—those things are all part of the grand plan. Anything else seems so impossible."

"Supposing you're right, how did he do it?"

"He could have stolen my car, driven to the zoo and done the whole number with the mud, returned the car to my garage, and then gone back to the Reptile House to steal the snake. It would have been a simple matter to carry the snake down here, unlock the gate, enter the cage, drop the pin, and annoy the snake until it bit him."

"It is remarkably straightforward. He'd have had no trouble getting the keys and your pin. But there are a couple of problems. First, according to the medical report, Brooks was dead before your car was returned. Second, he couldn't have locked the gate to the bird cage after himself."

"I hadn't heard about the medical report."

"Please don't mention it to anyone. John wouldn't appreciate my talking about it."

"I understand. So the cage remains the central problem. How did the body and the snake get locked in there?"

"How about this? The murderer chases Charles down the hill, unlocks the gate, Charles scrambles in while trying to escape, the murderer throws the snake after him and locks the door."

"No, Morley, that won't work unless the door was standing open. You need two hands for a taipan."

"Horatio says the door was closed, and I believe him. Whatever happened, he wasn't involved."

Madelyn had had enough. Maybe she could think about it later. But if she said anything, Morley would start being protective again. She needed to distract him. She was relieved to see Christine on the stairs ahead of them, staring intently at the eagle nest.

"Yo, Christine," Morley said. "Have you spotted a hatchling? They're due any minute now."

"No." She hesitated. "I was trying to find the marabou storks. They're so comical."

"Then you're looking in the wrong direction. They're both down below." Morley pointed to an ugly bird taking off from the bottom of the cage.

The undertaker bird, Madelyn thought. Oh hell!

"What's going on up there?" Morley shouted. "It looks like someone's trying to get into the cage." He dashed off.

Madelyn followed more slowly, not much caring what was happening. She wasn't prepared for what she found: Gertrude and Cyril sprawled in the dust entwined with a giant plush snake.

CHAPTER FOURTEEN

Harris grabbed the report from his printer and threw it at McDuff. "Where the hell have you been?"

"Working on that ulcer again, are we?" McDuff stooped to retrieve the papers. "Relax, John. It's only three-thirty."

"I'll be lucky to make Japsom City by seven."

"The mood you're in, you'll never make it."

Harris sighed. "I'm sorry. It's so goddamned frustrating—writing instead of doing something. And I have no idea what I'll say tonight."

"Why don't you tell them how paperwork interferes with investigations?"

"The Chief would hear about it before I finished talking. No, I'm discussing pitfalls of dependence on technology. It's easy to get lazy with all these computer hookups and lab tests, but the most important tool is still common sense." He paused. "I won't mention my own low score on that."

"Ditto," McDuff replied, "I should have been here helping you, not racing around the zoo. H.R. was useless, and I couldn't find people, not even Rivers."

"I was hoping you'd come up with some tidbit to prop up this report."

"The report's fine."

"You haven't read it," Harris said.

"You outlined the case against Rivers, right?"

"With drug dealers and blackmail victims coming out of the woodwork? Of course not."

"But that's what the Chief wants."

"I'm not going to play into his fixation—or yours. She's not the only suspect."

"But the case against her is strong," McDuff insisted.

"Brooks was a walking target. And where's Pierce? He has the report from the phone company, and I want to know who, besides Cooper, is in it."

"He'll be here in a minute. But even if it's all about blackmail, Dr. Rivers could have been involved. Why are you so sure she isn't hiding something?"

"She wouldn't lie."

"The Chief won't buy that. Let's try again. How are you presenting the facts?"

"See for yourself. It's all there." Harris looked up. "Come in, George. I read your report. Thanks for the fast work. But you concentrated on the money flow. We need to know more about the victims."

Pierce looked rueful. "That's slow going. There are a lot of people involved, but reaching them is hard. Most of the payoffs were small, but it adds up."

"I read that, yes. But you did identify Larry Cooper among the possible victims."

"Yes. But I can't tie him to any of the clippings or tapes. The phone records show calls to him, and there are a couple of entries in the spreadsheet, but no cross-references."

"Get a complete rundown on calls. Did you identify any other numbers?"

"We're still correlating them. A bunch are for take-out, repairs, that kind of thing. Brooks wasn't using apps—he had a dumb phone. Cooper's the only one we recognized."

"But you have located some of the people, haven't you?"

"Only one, a university professor. A disgruntled graduate student accused him of misappropriating federal grant money. The government auditors said there was nothing in it. But Brooks had a tape he thought was damaging. The prof said it was bull, and didn't pay. That's confirmed by the bank records and the spreadsheet. Nothing there for us."

"There's one entry in the spreadsheet that doesn't fit the pattern," McDuff said. "It's just a phone number on one of the last pages, and all by itself. We haven't been able to get through, but I checked the listing. It's an address on 15th street. I'll go by this evening."

"So we've got nothing," Harris was frustrated. "Now get this straight! Blackmail is the key, and I want the victims and their stories. That's top priority. Someone removed entries from the spreadsheet, and I think we can assume it was the murderer. Do the computer and hard copy versions of the spreadsheet match?"

"Yes."

"Maybe he couldn't find critical clippings and tapes. Do a complete check on them. And he may have deleted computer entries without really erasing them. So put your geek on that. I want victim information. Got that?"

"Yes, sir," Pierce replied.

"Is that clock right? Scot, I'm out of here. Read this stuff, correct it, add to it—anything. But have it on the Chief's desk by five. Okay?"

"No problem. Have a good trip, John. And George, thanks for your help."

"Anytime, Sergeant."

McDuff sat down heavily at Harris' computer. He brought the report up on the screen and was scanning the opening paragraph when he heard a rumble behind him.

"Where's Harris?"

"Chief! He just left. He's giving a speech in—"

"I know all about his rhetoric. I want that report."

"It's almost ready, sir."

"I didn't expect him to delegate it."

"He didn't, sir. He asked me to read it and make sure it covered all bases."

The Chief snorted. "All asses, you mean. I want that report tonight! I suppose he didn't even include the scene at Frank's. Knopstead has eyewitness accounts of Brooks threatening to kill Rivers in front of at least thirty people. I ought to hire Knopstead." He paused at the door. "Tell Harris he has one more day. I want an arrest by tomorrow night."

"Tomorrow? But Chief, we don't even know—"

"The commissioners want that Rhines woman in custody. And when they're happy, I'm happy. An arrest tomorrow, or he's off the case."

No wonder John was in such a bad mood. McDuff was feeling pretty surly himself. At least the arrest was John's problem.

Madelyn settled into the soft cushions. Her friends made her feel warm, almost cozy. Morley handed her a glass. "Here you go."

"A martini. How did you know?" She wrapped her fingers around the slender stem of the glass. It felt cool.

"It's martini time for all of us this week." His features kaleidoscoped into a wink.

Madelyn tried to relax. The room was soothing—the Navajo rugs on the walls, Kanga curled up on a pillow in front of the fire, Caruso, roosting on the drapery rod. He was a good omen. How sweet of Morley to bring her bird friend. Dear Morley. Knowing him was like owning a life-size teddy bear.

"Attention, all detectives in training. Who else needs a drink?" Morley asked. "How about you, Christine?" He walked over to her and gazed at the low cut bodice. "That's a beautiful dress. How about a matching brandy?"

She smiled and shook her head. "What I need right now is a call from Cyril. I'm worried about him."

"What's to worry? Tailing Cooper is a cinch. He's probably watching TV while Cyril sleeps in his trusty Volvo."

"Cyril won't fall asleep. He's serious about this."

"In that case he'd better paint his car. Orange is a ridiculous choice for a spook. Anyone else need a drink?"

"I can get it." Gertrude started up, but Morley pressed her firmly back into her chair. "Relax, Gert."

Madelyn smiled. Morley was trying to keep GG off her sore ankle, but she'd never put up with it. They were wonderful friends, all of them—Christine, Cyril, GG, Morley. But Larry? She needed to talk to him. If she ever made it out of this mess, she'd never take her friends for granted again.

"GG, tell me the truth." Morley was back with her martini. "Has your phone been ringing all evening?"

"If you mean the responses to my ad, things have been a little slow."

"Hah!," Morley said. "And how long do we have to wait for your mystery man? The paper's been out for several hours already."

"Let's see you put your money where your mouth is. That call is worth dinner at the Silver Fox."

"And if I'M right?" Morley asked.

"I'll—I'll take you to La Cucaracha."

"Two dinners at La Cucaracha. Fair's fair, honey. Now where the devil—" He fumbled through his pockets.

"Oh hell! Where's my pipe!" Caruso shouted.

"Thank you." Morley nodded solemnly to the bird. "Can't think without it in my hands. Now where were we? The Silver Fox. Thank heaven you haven't a chance in the world of getting a call." He retrieved the pipe and began examining it carefully.

"Think of the magnificent food," Gertrude said.

"And the stuffy waiters—"

"I think Madelyn could do without arguments tonight," Christine interrupted peevishly.

Madelyn smiled. "I don't mind. It's recreational fighting." The ad was silly, but GG was trying. She jumped at the sound of heavy footsteps in the hall.

"Cyril!" Christine was on her feet. "What are you doing here?"

Cyril's large, drooping frame was almost hidden under a black raincoat. He dragged across the room, hurled himself into the nearest chair, and stared mournfully at Christine. "And a cheerful hello to you, dear wife."

Color flooded Christine's face. "I'm sorry. You look terrible." She sat down on the footstool in front of him.

"He looks like a hound dog," Gertrude said.

"Hello to you, too."

"Are you all right?" Christine asked.

"No. I need a drink."

"We all do," Christine replied. "But why are you here? You're supposed to be watching Larry Cooper."

"This whole operation is impossible. I quit."

"No one said it was easy," Christine replied. "But you're the one who wanted to tail Larry. You can't just quit."

"I'll make some fresh coffee," Gertrude interrupted. "We have those Kenya beans you like so much, Cyril. And then you can tell us all about it."

"No you don't." Morley pushed her back into the chair.

"I do wish you would stop pushing me down. I feel like a frozen waffle."

"Cyril, what happened?" Madelyn asked.

"Drink first, then tell. Something on the order of that martini would be fine." He leaned back and shut his eyes.

"It's yours, my dear," Gertrude replied, "as soon as you tell us what you've been doing."

"Oh, all right." With a sigh, he sat up and held his head in his hands. Madelyn felt a twinge of guilt as she saw how tired he looked. They were all exhausted and on edge. By the end of the week, no one would be on speaking terms.

"Where is Larry?" Christine asked.

"If I knew that, I wouldn't be here."

"You came back here without finding him?"

"I found him and then I lost him. If I hadn't found him in the first place, I wouldn't have come back. I had to find him at least once."

Morley sucked on his pipe. "Can't fault your logic."

"So you came here while you could still find the house?" Gertrude suggested.

"I didn't realize this assignment was an IQ test. You think it's so simple, you find him." When no one responded, he continued: "I followed Cooper from the zoo to Damon's. He disappeared. In lingerie."

"You lost Cooper in lingerie?" Morley asked.

"When I realized he was gone, I went back to the car. I thought I saw him drive off, so I followed. But when the car headed straight into an apartment garage on Fifteenth Street, I knew I was in trouble. That's not where Cooper lives."

"Maybe he has a friend there," Gertrude suggested.

"No, I don't think it was Cooper."

"But Cyril, we didn't want you to follow him home," Christine insisted. "It's the rest of his life we're trying to find out about. And now we'll never know why he was in that building."

"It wasn't Cooper, Chrissy."

"Why didn't you at least follow him into the garage?"

"What a neat idea. Cooper parks, gets out and finds himself staring at me."

"Didn't you get even a glimpse of the driver?" Gertrude asked. "Larry has a hawk-like nose and thinning gray hair, and—"

"I'm quite familiar with Larry's beak. I couldn't see his car in the traffic, let alone his nose."

"You could have gotten the license number," Christine grumbled.

"Not from three cars back. Cooper probably turned off somewhere along the way—if it was Cooper in the first place. Do know how many look-alike white sedans there are in this city? Thousands and thousands. It's depressing. So I come here for some solace and a drink and get kicked in the teeth."

"Hi there! Is everybody in the living room?"

"God. It's Oliver Lake!" Morley whispered.

Oliver paused in the doorway. He was wearing a dirty white pullover, hanging about him like a lampshade. It made him look even taller and thinner than he was.

"Fine kind of friends you are, letting me hear about Brooks from my father." Oliver sounded genuinely hurt.

"We didn't send announcements," Gertrude replied.

"It's as if you didn't even think of me—"

"Wrong," Morley said.

"I told you he was no good, didn't I, Madelyn?" Oliver asked.

"If you mean Morley, we're all in agreement," Gertrude said.

"I warned you not to get involved with Brooks. But you never listen to me."

"Sorry about that, Oliver. You see, I have this urge to destroy myself." That hadn't come out right. She should ignore him like everyone else.

"When I saw it in the papers, I thought, 'It wouldn't surprise me at all if Madelyn had killed him'."

"Would you like a drink, Oliver?" Gertrude asked.

"'But whether she killed him or not, I wanted good old Madelyn to know I'm with her one hundred percent. Still, I'd kind of like an answer." He settled down next to Madelyn. "After all, I am an old friend. Which way was it? Did you kill him or not?"

"Oliver, stop that at once!" Gertrude shouted.

"It's all right. No, Oliver, I did not kill him. I was in love with him. I'm sorry he's dead." Oliver's thick glasses lent a curious owl-like intensity to his eyes. The effect was grotesque and somehow beguiling. "I know you want to help. I appreciate that."

He smiled and squeezed her hand, making her feel unaccountably sad. He was so kind, so intelligent—and so clueless.

He followed Gertrude to the bar. "I could have told you an ad like that wouldn't work."

"How do you know about my ad?"

"It's in the paper. Now what you need to do is—"

Conversation stopped abruptly when GG's phone rang. She grabbed it and answered. "What? Who? Mr. Bear? No, of course not. Idiot!"

"What was it, a kid?"

"Yes, a very funny kid."

"A lot of adults think that's funny, too," Morley said. "The zoo switchboard is swamped with calls like that every April Fool's Day."

"I wish you'd followed that car into the garage," Christine insisted. "You could at least have made sure it wasn't Cooper."

"I think he's done enough for one day," Madelyn said.

"Well, I don't. Tired or not, we don't have to be incompetent. Everything we do is so amateurish."

"We're getting professional results," Morley protested.

"That was a fluke. Sitting in MacMillan's hedge with Caruso on your head is not professional, Morley. We can't treat this like an indoor sport. We're playing for keeps."

Gertrude grabbed the phone on the first ring. "Gus? Hi. You remembered something? Great, tomorrow's fine. We'll have a nice chat. Thanks, Gus."

"Why were you sitting in a hedge?" Oliver was asking Morley.

"Just your average lurk. Now getting back to the chase, Cyril, did you try Cooper's place after you lost his clone?"

"Of course. No lights, no car."

"How about the zoo?" Gertrude asked.

"The zoo? For your information, I happen to be one of the few people in San Pablo without any zoo keys. And I wasn't about to climb the fence."

"He was following Dr. Cooper and lost him?" Oliver asked.

"Yes. He lost Cooper in lingerie," Morley explained. "How about the parking lot, Cyril?"

"Hey, I failed. I'll hand in my decoder ring. Now give me my drink and let me die."

"You could call him now," Christine suggested.

"All right, all right, I'll call him." Cyril dragged himself out of the chair. "My phone's in the car. And what, may I ask, is my excuse for calling him at this hour?"

"Ask for Mr. Rhino."

"He'll love it." Cyril buttoned up his raincoat.

"Call both his cell and his office," Christine instructed.

"How about his laundromat? Or perhaps his Aunt Tillie in Nebraska has heard from him. Okay, I'm going. But let me tell you, Gertrude baby, my martini had better be waiting for me when I come back in. It's a small thing to ask in exchange for dealing with you lunatics." He slammed the door.

The silence was broken by a sharp knock.

"How odd," Gertrude said. "No one's been knocking all week."

Madelyn stiffened as she recognized Sergeant McDuff's voice. Something must have happened. He was going to arrest her. So much for detective games.

"Ah yes, you're all here. I saw the cars in front. Good evening Dr. Rivers, Dr. Stevens, and—"

"This is Oliver Lake, Sergeant. He's come to—"

"To help." Oliver shook hands awkwardly. "I'd have been here before, only they didn't call me. And it is a disaster, what with Madelyn maybe being a murderer. She needs her friends now, even if she did kill him—"

"Oliver," Gertrude interrupted, "if you don't shut up, there will be another murder, this time with a police witness."

"Come, Oliver," Christine took him firmly by the arm and led him toward the kitchen. "Let's fix Cyril's drink. No, the bar won't do. He wants lots of ice. He said on the rocks."

"But I could help the Sergeant—" Oliver protested as the door shut behind them.

Madelyn took a deep breath and looked across at the heavy-set man in the wrinkled suit. He didn't have to dress for success. The power was his for the asking. "I'm sorry, Sergeant. He's a computer genius, but a little out of context."

McDuff nodded. "Sorry to interrupt the party. I was hoping to have a word with the group. But first I'd like to speak to you alone if I may."

"We can go in the study. Right this way, Sergeant." Madelyn switched on the light and sat down. "Have a seat. How can I help you?"

"Lieutenant Harris asked me to review a few points with you. Mostly routine. First, did you notice the mud puddle in the zoo parking lot when you left Monday?"

"I always notice and avoid that semi-permanent pond. It was relatively low Monday afternoon, but it doesn't take much to make it into a hazard."

"What time did you leave?"

"Somewhere between two and two-thirty, I think. I didn't check my watch."

"Was it raining?"

"No, just threatening."

"And you didn't notice anything unusual about the car on Tuesday morning?"

"No, I didn't."

"Moving on, did you give Brooks a key ring with a cavorting seal on it?"

"One of Christine's key rings you mean? No, Charles wasn't an animal lover."

"Finally, tell me about Ed Piper's dismissal from the Hudson Bay Zoo. I understand you were involved."

Madelyn had thought she was ready for anything, but this was a complete surprise. "I'm amazed at your thoroughness. But it's irrelevant. Ed was young and ambitious. And he was devastated to discover that his most important exhibit, a rare lizard-like reptile called the tuatara, was dead. So he had it stuffed and rigged up wires to make it move. How can it help to dredge that up? It's a breach of ethics to mislead the public, and I reported it. But it wasn't a crime."

"So why did you hire him at San Pablo?"

"I thought he deserved another chance. Bringing it up now would be destructive."

"That's generous of you. Still, you must consider your own situation. If you have any reason to believe Mr. Piper might bear you some ill will, we need to know about it."

"Ed? Certainly not!"

"I must say I find your attitude a little—"

He stopped in mid-sentence as Gertrude called out, "Mad, Cyril's back."

Madelyn looked questioningly at the Sergeant.

He nodded and rose. "We're done. Thank you, Dr. Rivers. But I do want just one word with all of you."

"Certainly, Sergeant."

When they reached the living room, Cyril was standing in the doorway, demanding his drink.

"Did you find him?" Gertrude asked.

"Where is he?" Christine joined in.

"Lost Cooper in lingerie," Caruso said. "Lost Cooper in lingerie."

For a moment no one spoke. Madelyn stifled a giggle as Christine repeated, "Well? Where is he?"

"I have no idea. He didn't answer either of his phones, and I want my drink!"

"We all had different ideas about proportions," Oliver explained, "so we ended up mixing our own for comparison."

"So I don't get one. Thanks a bunch!" Cyril walked huffily to the bar where an iced carafe of martinis awaited him. "GG, what's that stupid purple snake doing on the bar? Where do you get this compulsion to throw my failures in my face?"

"Pythagoras was not a failure," Gertrude insisted.

"I call it a failure when I can't handle a stuffed animal."

McDuff turned to Madelyn. "Why the call to Dr. Cooper?"

"You heard Caruso," Cyril replied from across the room. "I lost him in lingerie. Another example of blatant failure."

"Cyril, that's crazy. Just because the snake was plush doesn't mean it wasn't a good idea to try it, and anyone could have lost Larry—"

"Mr. Featherworth," McDuff said, "you followed Dr. Cooper through a store and lost him in the lingerie department? Is that what that crow is telling us?"

"That's about it," Cyril replied. "I thought I'd picked him up again, but when he pulled into a garage on Fifteenth Street, I figured I'd made a mistake."

"Fifteenth?" McDuff asked. "Did you notice the address?"

"It was 305."

"And when was that?"

"About eight fifteen."

"And I left there around—" McDuff started.

"What?" Madelyn asked. "You were there? At 305 Fifteenth Street?"

"Oh! You don't know who lives there?" McDuff asked.

"Sergeant, are you telling me I stumbled onto a live one and threw it back?" Cyril asked.

"Maybe."

"Who lives there?" Madelyn demanded.

"I'll have John Harris to deal with if I start giving you tips. Which reminds me. I have a message from the Lieutenant. He said to knock it off. You are in over your heads. He really means it. So listen up."

"What's wrong with telling us who lives there?" Gertrude asked.

"I'm not sure," McDuff replied. "But John doesn't trust you people. I've already talked too much, and I'd better get out of here before I trap myself again."

Madelyn watched from the window as he walked down the driveway. The others were shouting questions after him, but he waved them off.

Shutting the front door, Morley lifted the drink from Cyril's hand. "You won't be needing that. There's one little thing we'd like you to do. Get back there and find out who lives in that apartment building."

"If you're in such a hurry, go find out for yourself," Cyril replied. "I've had enough of this nonsense for one night."

"I could do it," Oliver offered.

"Cyril and McDuff may be right," Morley replied. "We're a lousy bunch of detectives and we should lay off." He winked elaborately behind Oliver's back. "Let's call it a night."

Taking his cue, the group dispersed quickly. Morley was the last to go. "I'll pass the word and get everyone here tomorrow night—everyone except Oliver."

"Great. The accomplice will have called by then, so we'll have a lot more information."

"Of course we will," he kissed her softly.

"I wish you didn't have to leave."

"I must finish reviewing those articles. They're two months late. Besides, I need to think about something else for a while.

154

And you, my dear, need to sleep. Come, Caruso." The bird flapped to Morley's shoulder and squawked loudly as they walked out the door.

Madelyn looked at Gertrude. "What in the world is Larry up to?"

"I don't know, but he's not the murderer. It couldn't be one of our friends, Mad. Don't even think it."

"Yes, of course not. Let's go to bed."

CHAPTER FIFTEEN

M cDuff stared grimly at the stack of papers on his desk. They had arrived in a dirty brown package, addressed to INSPEKTUR HARRUS. The message on top had been laboriously constructed with letters from newspaper headlines.

I THOT YOUD LIKE TO SEE WHAT WAS HID IN THE TRASH AT THE ZOO. IT CAME FROM THE SNAKE PLACE. SHE KNOWS PLENTY ON THEM TYPANGS. A WELLWISHR

He thumbed through the papers again. Lecture notes on taipans, reprints from articles, miscellaneous papers, all written by Rivers. With manufactured junk like this around, John would be even more convinced she was being framed.

But John had it backwards. That Rivers woman was much too good at playing the victim. And she'd come on too complex, even about Piper. Maybe there was something in her background—
He walked into Harris' office and was flipping through the manila folders on the desk when the phone rang.

"McDuff."

"Where's Harris?"

"Japsom City, Chief. He stayed over to try to get something out of the feds on Brooks' business."

"Bullshit! He's stalling. When he gets in, have him call me immediately."

"Yes, sir. I'll tell him." Thank God this was Harris' problem, not his.

McDuff returned to the file folders and opened the one marked RIVERS. Handwritten notes, recorded interviews with Rivers, Piper, Gypsom. This one was new. John hadn't mentioned talking to her high school friend. According to her, Rivers had been an academic whiz, quiet, hadn't dated much. She had minored in Theater Arts in college, and was good at changing her voice. Had taken men's roles in several Shakespearean productions.

McDuff reached in his pocket and pulled out a candy bar. Chewing thoughtfully, he paced back and forth in the narrow space between the desk and the window. His oversized stomach was too big for the room. Maybe his wife was right about his weight. Sighing, he threw the last of the candy into the trash, and returned to his own office.

He was close to something. But what? Rivers and Cooper. Possible murderers, unlikely stories. MacMillan. Even more unlikely. But Ms. Stebbins had squelched the idea of MacMillan as Brooks' lover. He'd taken Stebbins to the zoo entrance and waited for MacMillan to walk through the gate. Stebbins had watched her without comment. When prompted, she had replied, "That girl with the Marilyn Monroe tilt? No, that's not the one. I'd have recognized her immediately."

Another dead end. McDuff peered through the dusty Venetian blinds into the alley. It was a gray day, matching his mood. The station cat was stalking something across the way. A more successful sleuth.

Then there were the blackmail victims. His interview with Piper hadn't turned up anything new. George was interviewing the people mentioned in the clippings file, but it was slow going. And a waste of time. A blackmail victim who wanted to kill wouldn't go to the zoo looking for a weapon. Especially Cooper or Piper—that would be calling attention to themselves. But there was no convincing John—

The phone startled him. "McDuff!"

He held the telephone at arm's length as Gertrude Gypsom's voice blasted his ear. "You won't believe this, Sergeant. He called."

"A fan who caught your act with the plush snake?"

"I can explain that—"

"I think it would be better if you didn't. So you got your phone call?"

"Yes. From the ad. While I was watering the fern. That plant is lucky. It told me—"

"Ms. Gypsom, about the call?" This could take all day between what the plant said and what the man said.

"Sorry. I was sure it was him. Anyway, I remembered how upset you were when we didn't keep you informed."

Sighing, he leaned back in his chair. "Tell me about your ad."

"It was for Mad's car."

"What's that?"

"This mechanic says he unstuck Mad's car at the zoo and drove it back to the house Monday night. So she was telling the truth."

"Okay, now slow down." It must be true. Gypsom might be loopy, but she didn't lie. "How did this all come about?"

"It happened near the end of his shift. The caller claimed to be acting for a woman who was sick. He said her car was stuck at the zoo. She needed it in the morning to drive to L.A. The keys and towing charges, plus a fifty dollar tip, would be under the mat."

"What time was this?"

"The call came in about eleven-thirty, but he didn't head for the zoo until he got off work at midnight. The instructions were to bring it to my house, which was on his way home. Anyway, he towed it here, unhooked it, and drove it into Mad's garage space. Then he left the keys under the mat."

"Give me his name and phone number." McDuff jotted the information down. "Is Dr. Rivers with you now? I may want to talk to her later."

"Sorry. Your apology will have to wait. She's at the travel agent's. The Indonesia flight had to be scheduled before—Oh, but I wasn't supposed to mention that. You won't tell her I said anything, will you?"

"Mum's the word. Keep in touch, Ms. Gypsom, and thank you."

Rivers was planning a trip to Indonesia? Sounded ominous to him. Fortifying himself with another cup of coffee, McDuff called the mechanic to confirm the story.

"So you left the keys under the mat? That was it?"

"Right."

"Can you tell me anything about the man who called you?"

"Not much to say, except. . .well, the voice was a little odd."

"How so?"

"It sounded like a woman pretending to be a man, if that makes any sense."

"More than you know. I wonder if we might impose on you to stop by the station and make a statement."

"No problem, if it's really important."

"Indeed it is, sir. Thank you for your assistance."

McDuff hung up and stood staring out the window. Rivers knew how to change her voice. She could have called the mechanic herself. And now she was planning a trip to Indonesia while he twiddled his thumbs. If she got out of the country before John returned, he, Scot McDuff, would be responsible for losing her. He'd be a lot more comfortable with Rivers right here at the station where he could keep an eye on her.

McDuff escorted Rivers into an interrogation room and asked her to sit down.

"Sergeant, can't you at least tell me why you brought me here?"

"I'm sorry, that will have to wait. And I have to get a few things set up."

"I want to call a lawyer."

"Certainly." He set her phone on the table. Go ahead. I'll be back shortly."

"Don't hurry on my account." Madelyn felt numb. Maybe GG knew an attorney. She tried Gertrude's cell and then the house. After a few rings, she hung up. A message would just alarm her. Maybe Larry. She selected his zoo number.

"San Pablo Zoo, Cooper speaking."

"Larry. Thank God you're there. I've been arrested and I need a lawyer."

"Arrested? Why on earth—"

"You tell me. Sergeant McDuff isn't saying."

"But he has to tell you why. He can't hold you for no reason."

"But he is. That's why I want a lawyer."

"The zoo has a great guy. He specializes in liability, but he knows everybody. Hold on a minute."

Cooper was back on the line almost immediately. "He's in conference, but they promised me he'd call my cell within an hour. Meanwhile, I'm coming down there. I'll try to talk some sense into McDuff. Don't worry, Mad. We'll get this straightened out. See you in twenty minutes."

Madelyn sat holding the cell. She could try to call Gertrude again. Or she could just sit and stare at the wall. Maybe this was one time in her life when she didn't have to do anything except wait.

The traffic noises were in sync with the pounding in Harris' head. As he inched SNAIL toward Frank's Fish Tank, he wished he hadn't agreed to meet Scot. He wasn't hungry, he felt lousy, and there was too much to be done. The DEA agents wouldn't talk to him, so the morning had been a complete waste of time. Now he was stuck in San Pablo's noon traffic jam. At least things were looking better for Madelyn. The frame-up theory was promising. But there were still some missing pieces. Little insignificant things—like who killed Brooks. The list of candidates was too long.

He parked next to Scot's old Ford and hurried inside. His plump assistant was seated at a table by the window. He waved in greeting and knocked a glass of water onto the floor.

"John. Am I ever glad to see you."

"I'll bet. How many friends do you have who would clean up your mess?" Harris picked up the glass and handed it to the waitress.

"Thanks, Lieutenant. Now relax."

"Hi, Jess," Scot said. "Sorry about the water."

She patted his shoulder. "That's what I'm here for. You just sit and enjoy the ocean. It's special today. You'll be wanting the usual?"

"Whatever you say," Harris replied. "And an aspirin on the side."

"You have to watch those late nights at your age." She winked. "I'll have this cleaned up in no time."

"Thanks."

"So, how is everything in Japsom City?" Scot asked.

"The trip was a bummer. But at least Hammond confirmed that it's the DEA. Let's talk about you."

"I delivered your message last night." McDuff described the scene at Gertrude's.

"Scot, this has to stop! If the Chief finds out my friends have been interfering with the investigation—"

"It's mostly harmless. Do you want to hear the rest?"

"No. Yes. Go on." He listened intently to McDuff's description of the package and Gertrude's call.

"So I figured she was planning a quick trip to Indonesia, and, well, that's why I arrested her."

"You arrested Rivers? What for? She's just making travel arrangements for a pair of Komodo dragons the zoo is acquiring."

"Sure she is. But I guess it's a convenient cover for her escape—if anyone believes it."

"Must you be such a suspicious bastard—"

"I'm a detective."

"Unlike me."

"I didn't say that."

"It's written all over you."

"Well, what do you expect? All this evidence flooding in, the Chief having a conniption, and you acting like a lovesick schoolboy—"

Harris glared at McDuff. "You are way out of line."

"Sorry. I'm just trying to explain why I felt I had to take her in."

"Okay. So Rivers is cooling her heels at headquarters. Is there anything else you'd like to tell me? Like maybe you arrested Stevens' raven?"

"I talked to Piper. He came unglued. Admitted both blackmails readily enough. Begged me not to make the information public. I told him it wouldn't come out unless it was relevant. He finally calmed down enough to answer my questions about the army and the Hudson Bay Zoo. He seemed almost relieved to talk. His story matched Dr. Rivers'. It's also confirmed by Hudson Bay."

"You never told me why they fired him."

"For unprofessional behavior. His high-prestige lizard died, so he had it stuffed."

"They fired him for stuffing a lizard? It's considered bad form?"

"The problem was he didn't tell anyone it had died. By the way, Dr. Rivers says it was a tuatara and that it's not really a lizard."

"Of course not. Scot, you've been hanging around GG too much."

McDuff grimaced. "Rivers says tuataras are nearly extinct. They're protected by the Government of New Zealand, on some island. So it would have been next to impossible to get a replacement lizard."

"Okay, Then what?"

"He rigged up controls to make it move, and put it in the back of the cage, with an ordinary live lizard up front. The public couldn't tell the difference, and they were happy enough to watch the lizard in the front of the cage. Zoo people were more of a problem. Piper always told them not to get too close because it was nervous. But Rivers thought its color was bad, so she reached in to scratch its head. She said the stuffer did a remarkable job."

"A real success story."

"This isn't a joke. Piper was fired over it. Then Rivers felt sorry for him, so she hired him as her assistant. I don't think Piper likes her."

"So he killed Brooks to get even with her?"

"It doesn't seem likely. Besides, the Corbetts confirmed that he played bridge all evening the night of the murder. They don't seem to be great admirers of Piper's and I doubt they'd be able to tell a consistent lie even if they wanted to. I don't think Piper's our man."

Harris shook his head. "I don't think so either. But our behavior is even more peculiar than the suspects'. Piper's background is full of surprises. Cooper's hiding something and lying about everything. Then GG finds the man who towed Rivers' car, and you arrest Rivers."

"I told you. It was that business about Indonesia—"

"Enough said. Let's update our notes. I have an overpowering need to get organized." He pulled out his notebook. "First we have

MADELYN RIVERS

1. In love-hate relationship with the victim.
2. Had access to zoo, Reptile House, and bird cage.
3. Can handle poisonous snakes.
4. Her snake pin found near body.
5. Her car went for a jaunt Monday night.
6. Mysterious call to mechanic might have been placed by a woman.
7. No alibi for any of Monday evening.

"Has her extra set of keys turned up? You said the garage man left the ones he was using under the floor mat," Harris asked.

"Dr. Rivers called yesterday to say the extra set was missing from her desk. When we arrested her, we checked under the floor mat and found them, just like Gypsom said."

"She could have put them there herself. But she probably wouldn't have expected the mechanic to turn up." Harris looked out at the grey-blue ocean. Two gulls flew slowly past the window. "I say there'll be two sets of fingerprints on the keys, hers and the mechanic's. Whoever drove the car to the zoo Monday night surely would have worn gloves. But check, anyway. Anything else?"

"Not off the top of my head."

Harris drew a line across the page. "Next, not necessarily in order of preference, is

ED PIPER

1. Access to zoo and Reptile House
2. Can handle poisonous snakes.
3. Dislikes Rivers?
4. Was being blackmailed big time by Brooks.
5. Alibi appears sound.

"And, moving right along, we have

164

LARRY COOPER

1. Has access to zoo and Reptile House
2. Can handle poisonous snakes
3. In love with Rivers
4. Was in the zoo, near bird-of-prey cage, Monday night. No alibi.
5. Lied about what he was doing and everything else he could think of.
6. Was apparently being blackmailed by Brooks.

Harris shook his pen at McDuff. "Do you realize I heard him telling Madelyn—Dr. Rivers—to lie about her own whereabouts?"

"And speaking of Cooper— Remember I told you about that telephone number that was all by itself in Brooks' logbook? Well, I went to talk to the guy last night—B. R. Brown. Turns out he's Botticelli Brown, the animal dealer in the clipping we found in Brooks' wallet. No secret about his identity, but that's all I got from Brown. Didn't know Brooks. Couldn't imagine why Brooks was carrying the clipping around. But then, when I went to Gypsom's, I found out that Cyril Featherworth thought he had followed Cooper to Brown's apartment building last night. Tenuous, but still—"

"Scot, let me ask you one question. Why didn't you arrest Cooper this morning if you were so hot to nab someone?"

"Okay, okay. So I made a mistake. Tell it to the Chief. How about MacMillan?"

PEGGY MACMILLAN

1. Has access to the zoo.
2. Could probably nab the Reptile House key easily enough.
3. Invented ornithologist friend to get bird-of-prey cage key.

4. Can handle poisonous snakes.
5. Stevens heard her say she'd taken the zoo job for her 'assignment'
6. She and her friend are going to do 'it' again.
7. No alibi.

"Sounds like espionage," McDuff suggested

"I'm not taking that story too seriously. Morley means well, but he gets carried away. Did you identify the man he saw with MacMillan?"

"Yes. From the license plate number. He's Ted Merkle, works for an ad agency, writing scripts for TV commercials. MacMillan jumped out of her skin when I asked about him, but she won't admit she knows him. Still claiming to have spent Monday evening alone."

Harris nodded. "How about MacMillan's neighbors?"

"Three women in the block say they saw a man drive up and go into MacMillan's house Monday about seven. They were standing in a driveway talking. A Ms. Gubberidge lives directly across from MacMillan. She claims MacMillan and the man came out about eight, loaded something into the car, and drove off. Then, at—"

"What kind of something did they load into the car?"

"Gubberidge says it was a body wrapped in a sheet. She's quite positive on that point. But I don't really think—"

"No, I don't either. I can't imagine carrying the taipan out of the zoo, murdering Brooks, and then returning the body and the snake to the bird cage. Much too risky. Not to mention too early."

"Yeah. It must have been some other body. Anyway, they returned without the body about one a.m., and neither of them came out until morning. That seemed to bother Gubberidge more than the body. I guess she watched all night to be sure. She has it in for MacMillan. But it's probably true that some man, probably Merkle, arrived Monday at seven, that he and MacMillan left around eight with a large object wrapped in a sheet, and that they returned around one. Which means MacMillan's statement about what happened the night of the murder was one big lie."

"Did you confront MacMillan with Gubberidge's statement?" Harris asked.

"Yes. She denied it and said Gubberidge is 'an interfering old bitch who wouldn't know a man from a Martian, having had about equal experience with both.' I couldn't budge her on her statement."

"And then there are all of Rivers' friends. One of them might have killed Brooks to get her out of a lousy relationship. We've already covered Cooper. So we have Stevens, Gypsom, both Featherworths, and Oliver Lake, at a minimum. But only Cooper, Stevens, and possibly Ms. Featherworth have enough knowledge of the zoo. And Ms. Featherworth has a complete alibi, as does GG."

McDuff shook his head. "I can't believe it's Stevens. And no friend of Rivers' would plant all that evidence against her. That's one thing we can be sure of: if Rivers is innocent, this murderer had it in for her."

"Piper qualifies. MacMillan's a question."

"And I can't see Cooper setting her up."

"Maybe Cooper wanted to rescue her from a desperate situation," Harris suggested. "That would make him a romantic hero and get rid of the competition at the same time."

"If so, he did a lousy job of it."

"And then there are all the other blackmail victims and the drug lords. By the way, how is George coming with blackmailees?"

"He's matching up names and addresses."

"He's taking too long. I want to see that material. Set up a meeting for this afternoon."

"Okay."

Harris pushed his chair back from the table. "Let's go back to headquarters. I want to talk to Dr. Rivers. And then I'm going to find Cooper again."

CHAPTER SIXTEEN

Harris glared at his phone messages. Knopstead, the Mayor, his dentist—he'd forgotten his appointment. And the Chief. Again. Well, he'd have to wait. Harris wasn't ready to talk to him. Maybe after he'd interviewed Dr. Rivers. Moving to the window, he jammed his fists deep into his trouser pockets and stood staring at the traffic below. He was furious with Scot for arresting Rivers and with himself for letting his reaction show. But if she had killed Brooks— His muscles tensed. No, he didn't believe that. Scot had jumped to the wrong conclusion.

He wished there were some way to prove that Rivers couldn't have called the mechanic. But, regardless of what the mechanic said, Scot would argue that a real vocal chameleon could fake any number of voices. Well, he'd put it off long enough. Squaring his shoulders, he headed for the interrogation room. This time he would stick to business.

He burst into the dingy room. The barred window provided a view of the back wall and a little dreary light. Madelyn was slumped down in a straight-backed chair. A bright patchwork shirt emphasized her grey fatigue. She seemed to have wilted: her hair, her posture, her spirit. Scot would call it a plea for sympathy. And maybe he'd be right.

Taking the seat opposite her, Harris nodded with cool formality. "Dr. Rivers, Sergeant McDuff brought you down here this morning on the basis of new evidence. I would like to ask you a few questions, but first, do you know your rights? Do you want an attorney with you?"

The remaining color drained from her face, but her response was controlled. "No. I tried to get a lawyer, earlier. Larry said he'd find someone, and that was the last I heard. Larry never showed up and neither did a lawyer. But I have nothing to hide.

I wanted to talk to Sergeant McDuff this morning, but all he had on his mind was capturing me."

"He was trying to protect your rights—"

"They don't need protecting. I'm innocent."

"We have certain procedures—"

"Do they include telling me why I became an emergency when GG found the mechanic who picked up my car?"

"The mechanic says the call was made by a woman pretending to be a man."

"And if a woman was involved, it had to be me? Naturally he arrested me immediately. Anyone would have done the same."

"He had to see that as a possibility—"

"We're not talking possibilities. My arrest is an actuality. And it's based on the false assumption that I—"

"McDuff had heard about your acting experience. You used to take men's parts sometimes."

"But then, with my vast experience, I should have done well enough to fool the mechanic."

"Maybe you're rusty."

"You people have devious minds. I can't think that way."

"We look at the evidence."

"What evidence prompted my immediate arrest? I wasn't going anywhere."

"McDuff thought you were. GG mentioned Indonesia, then swore him to secrecy."

Madelyn stifled a laugh. "I was simply trying to keep the Komodo dragon trade out of the news until they arrive. I'm worried about the bad publicity the zoo is getting. Would you send your precious dragons to a Reptile House where snakes are used as murder weapons?"

She had a point. Or was it just a facile excuse? Scot was assuming she was lying. He wasn't Scot, but maybe Scot was right…He was relieved when the Sergeant stuck his head in the door.

"John, can I see you for a minute?"

"Excuse me, Dr. Rivers." He followed McDuff into the hall.

"A doctor called from the University Hospital emergency room. Cooper's there with a concussion and a broken arm. He was out cold for a long time, but the first thing he said when he came to was to demand to see you. The doctor says he'll be fine with some rest."

"What happened?"

"We're not sure, but it looks like an attempt to kill him. He was in the zoo—"

"Do we have someone on it?"

"Yes. Two men. They found a gold turtle pin with the initials MR close to the spot where the attack took place."

"Another red herring. Dare I ask why, with two men on the scene, we have to hear about the attack from a doctor in the emergency room?"

"Communications assumed we already knew."

"Remind me to have somebody's head."

"At least Cooper's in the clear. Suddenly he's a victim."

Harris hesitated. Time for caution. "He's injured, but not too injured. Maybe he fell and then decided to stage the assault."

"Why do that? This attack was supposed to implicate Rivers. He's on her side."

"He might have been trying to un-implicate her. He's one of the few people who knew Rivers was in custody."

"Guess we'll have to ask him. The doctor says he'll be able to talk to us in about thirty minutes."

"I look forward to this. Let's go." Madelyn would have to wait.

The uniformed policeman outside Cooper's room looked bored and uncomfortable, but he rose stiffly and saluted. Harris nodded as they entered the room. There was a strong smell of antiseptic in the air. Everything was white—the walls, the floor, the bed, the patient.

"Thank's for coming. I'm glad to see you." Cooper sounded dopey.

"That's a first. How are you feeling?"

"Horrible. Dizzy—headache—the whole nine yards. But this has changed everything." He winced as he tried to sit up.

Harris found the controls and raised the head of the bed. "You mean you're ready to tell us the truth?"

"I'm sorry. I know I—"

"Okay. What's on your mind." They'd get another lie, but they might learn something.

"You see, I didn't want to help you build a case against Madelyn. I was sure she'd killed Brooks."

"What made you so positive?"

"She had cause. You can't imagine what she's been up against—"

"And you can?"

"I know what it's like to be one of Brooks' victims. He's been blackmailing me for the past five months. It's a long story, but we've been trying to get a mate for our female snow leopard for several years. This is an endangered species, and we can't justify keeping a single around. But she's one of our big drawing cards—cats are favorites. And then I heard via the grapevine that Botticelli Brown, the animal dealer, had a male. Now you have to understand that we view this guy as an outlaw. The American Association of Zoological Parks and Aquariums has blacklisted him, and I'd be out of a job if anyone found out I was dealing with him. I'd be out of respect, too. On the other hand, he already had this animal in his possession, and, if I didn't take him, some bozo on one of those hunting ranches would, and he'd be hanging on a trophy wall before you could say 'endangered species.' I thought about it a long time, and I discussed it, obliquely, with Madelyn."

171

"So that's how Brooks found out about it?"

"I don't know. She may have mentioned that I was considering it. She thought it was a lousy idea, and I never told her I'd actually made a deal. Anyway, I took a chance, and Brooks took me. I know, I should have gone to the police, but I kept thinking I'd find a way out of it." He grimaced. "All I did was delay the inevitable."

"It may not be necessary for this to become public. Not if you cooperate with us now."

"I'd be grateful."

"Just out of curiosity, was it you Cyril Featherworth followed to Brown's house last night?" McDuff asked.

"Cyril was following me? Yes. I guess so. I went there to be sure Brown would keep quiet about our deal. He agreed, readily enough."

"But getting back to the murder, your deal with Brown doesn't explain why you thought Dr. Rivers had killed Brooks."

"I was in Frank's when she had her famous fight with Brooks. After she stormed out, he came over to my table. He said Mad wasn't any use to him now, and that he was going to ask her for 'support' payments in return for keeping quiet about Brown. He thought she was in on it. That night I couldn't sleep, so I went back to the zoo to think it over. I saw Mad's car outside the service gate, and that upset me. She'd canceled out on dinner saying she was sick. I walked up to the Reptile House, intending to confront her, but then I changed my mind. It wasn't the right time to start something."

"So what did you do?"

"Wandered around aimlessly. The zoo is soothing at night. I started down the steps by the bird-of-prey cage and, about halfway down I stumbled over Brooks' body. The whole thing came together. Mad had lied to me about dinner because she was planning to murder Brooks. Not that I blamed her for wanting him dead, but it was still hard to believe. I was standing there, trying to decide what to do, when I thought I heard someone coming."

"Did you see who it was?"

"No. I heard footsteps down at the bottom of the cage. I thought he was coming up the stairs."

"And you didn't want to have to explain the body?"

"Exactly. And I wanted to delay the discovery until Mad was gone. I was hoping she could work out an alibi. Anyway, I unlocked the door and dragged Brooks under that bush. That took forever. Dead bodies turn out to be heavy."

"You must have made a lot of noise. Didn't the person on the stairs come to check?"

"No one came up the stairs while I was there."

"So you locked the door, and then?"

"I was afraid he might have spotted the body and was calling the police. So I went to my office and waited. Nothing happened. It must have been one when I left. It was a relief to see that Mad's car was gone."

Harris let his breath out slowly. "So it was you who put the body in the cage. Do you realize we've been spinning our wheels over who had access to the Reptile House and the bird cage? You've really screwed up the investigation."

"Sorry. I thought I was doing the right thing. For her."

"Did it ever occur to you that the right thing might have been to believe her?" Harris stopped as he felt Scot's eyes boring into him. "Well, we're on the right track now. Unless you have something else you'd like to tell us?"

"I'm sure it's hard for you to accept, but it's all true."

"Just one more thing," Harris said. "Did you move the snake?"

"I didn't know there was a snake. It must have slithered in on its own. Something moved on the ground just inside the cage as I was locking up. We probably almost met in the doorway. That could have been the end of me."

"I can see it now. Your body, Brooks' body, the taipan, all intertwined at the entrance to the bird-of-prey cage."

Cooper squirmed uncomfortably. "I'd rather not dwell on that."

"Getting back to the incident this afternoon, did you see anyone before you were attacked?"

"No. I was going to the police station. I wanted to help Madelyn. I walked past the bird-of-prey cage, hoping to jog my memory about Monday night, and headed for the parking lot. That's when it happened. I woke up here."

"Look, Dr. Cooper, we'll want to talk to you again about all this. But the doctor said not to tire you, and we need some time to restructure our thinking."

"Yes. Now that I know Mad's innocent, I have a lot of my own restructuring to do."

Harris and McDuff drove to the station in silence. Cooper's story changed everything. Harris parked SNAIL and was about to get out when McDuff stopped him.

"So what do you make of it, John? Is he telling the truth?"

"Yes. It's incredible, in a way. He gave us his motive, opportunity, the whole bit. No one but an imbecile would do that. And this time, his story checks out with our other information. I believed him."

"So did I," McDuff agreed. "But where are we now?"

Harris watched the recruits drilling at the Police Academy across the way. What energy. It was all downhill after forty. That's what his wife had always said— Ex-wife. Why did pain last so long?

"More to the point, where are YOU now?" Scot asked.

"Sorry. I'm back. So now Cooper is the injured party. Unless he or Rivers have staged this to throw us off."

"I doubt it."

"But it's possible. Or Cooper could have had an enemy who wanted us to think there was only one perpetrator. That one works even if the attacker knew Rivers was in custody."

"I don't see that."

"If he didn't know she'd been arrested, it was a direct attempt to implicate her in the attack. And, if he did know, he wanted us to believe Brooks' murderer was setting her up."

"I see what you're saying. But it seems more likely that the attack was for real. Brooks' murderer wanted Cooper dead, for whatever reason, and implicating Rivers was icing on the cake."

"For that matter, the attack could simply have been a way of strengthening the case against her. That's elegantly straightforward. I'll go with that for now."

"But it wouldn't implicate Rivers unless she had a credible motive for killing Cooper." McDuff mopped his face with an enormous handkerchief.

"Oh, that's easy. Cooper knew something incriminating. I'd buy that. And, as a matter of fact, he did."

"You're right. So, returning now to the real world, what do we do with Dr. Rivers?"

"We let her go and tell everyone she's cleared. Regardless of what's going on, that seems like our best strategy with the murderer."

McDuff nodded. "Okay, but things are getting stickier. Mind if I arrest the amateurs before one of them gets killed?"

"They'll be all right. But we need to get this settled, and fast."

"That's what the Chief wants. Did you talk to him?"

"I'll tell him we're close. But close to what? If not Rivers or Cooper, then who?"

"My favorite is MacMillan. Her behavior has been so consistently bizarre."

"I suspect we're too caught up with all the amateurs. It's probably a professional job, with some connection to blackmail or drugs. Let's get out of this sun."

Harris felt better about the case than he had since that lunch with Scot on Tuesday. They were in agreement again. Together they'd get to the bottom of it. He climbed out of SNAIL and headed for the interrogation room, Scot close behind.

CHAPTER SEVENTEEN

"Oh hell! Where's my pipe!"

Caruso's rasping voice was uncannily clear through the closed bedroom door. Madelyn smiled. She would enjoy seeing the bird. Still, she wasn't so sure about the party—or whatever it was. But it was time to join them.

She paused at the entrance to the living room. The setting was perfect—friends, a blazing fire, a vivid bouquet on the table—yet nothing was happening.

"Hey, what is this?" she asked. "A wake?"

"Madelyn, welcome!" Morley set his pipe on the mantel and strode toward her.

Christine gave her a hug. "Are you OK? It's been a terrible week."

"It's just plain weird. I get arrested because my story about the car is true. I'm cleared because someone tried to implicate me. We have a party to celebrate my release and you all act like you've lost your last friend."

"We're battle weary," Morley explained.

"I suppose that's why Cyril is lying face down on the couch. Is he asleep?"

"I say asleep," Christine replied. "That or dead, and he's not the type to get himself killed."

"Oliver, can you stop working on that puzzle long enough to say hello?"

"Madelyn! It's you and you didn't do it!" Oliver jumped up and enveloped her in an enormous bear hug.

"I didn't do it just for you."

He returned to his cross-legged perch in front of the coffee table.

"Do you realize your tie is sweeping the pieces onto the floor?" Madelyn asked.

"I still have enough pieces here."

"Let me get you a drink, Mad." Morley offered. "A martini?"

"Yes, please. But I'm still concerned about the group mood. Have you heard bad news?"

"We haven't heard anything," GG replied. "That's the problem."

"Only part of it," Christine added. "Your desperate plight isn't so desperate anymore. Some of us are missing the excitement."

Morley's face flushed. "I resent that. We're not in this for cheap thrills."

"And you're not feeling let down because I didn't kill him?" Madelyn asked.

"Of course not! And for your information, Christine," Morley waved his pipe viciously, "the excitement is still with us. There's a desperate murderer on the loose. The real work has just begun."

"You expect more violence?"

"Yes. There'll probably be another attack like the one on Larry. Mad, you and Larry are in danger."

"Will the police provide protection?" Christine asked.

"I doubt it. And I'm not willing to sit around waiting for Harris to get his act together."

"Morley's right." Cyril's voice floated up from the depths of the couch. "If the murderer is frightened, he'll come after them. Mad, you need a watchdog."

"Are you applying for the job? I'd feel ever so safe knowing you were here, sleeping on the rug."

"I'm serious. Most people won't tangle with a big dog unless they've been formally introduced."

"Cyril, be practical. By the time we got a puppy and trained it to bark at the right people—"

"The wrong people."

"—the murderer could have killed me a hundred times over."

"I was talking in general. You need a watchdog!"

"To protect me every time someone kills my lover and tries to frame me? You do understand that is not my choice of lifestyle?"

"There's no point talking to you."

"Mad, look! I finished the tiger."

She leaned over Oliver's shoulder. "That blue piece doesn't belong in the tiger. You can't jam it together like that."

"It doesn't have to fit perfectly. The point is the color. See how beautiful the tan fur is next to the rocks?"

"Oliver, that's a zebra. Please put on your glasses. You're ruining my favorite puzzle."

"Well, I'm sorry. I didn't mean to hurt your precious puzzle." Pulling his glasses from his pocket, he stuck them on his prominent nose and stalked to the bar.

Madelyn collected pillows and settled into them. Her friends seemed at odds with each other, and she was feeling distant, herself. Or maybe just exhausted. John had said he might stop by to call off the amateur detectives. She had hoped he would come, but now she wasn't sure. She couldn't really trust him.

"Look out, Oliver!" Cyril yelled. "You spilled my drink!"

"Well, I'm sorry. You were standing on my foot."

"It's time to get organized," Christine said, raising her voice. "We're understaffed, anyway, and now Larry's been injured. Tomorrow, he's being released from the hospital. We'll have to protect him and Mad. That means two people—"

"I'll take care of Mad," Gertrude said. "I won't let her out of my sight."

"Please don't do that to me," Madelyn pleaded.

Morley answered Gertrude's phone, which was sitting on the bar. "Gert, it's Gus."

"Oh dear. I forgot him this afternoon."

"He noticed."

"Tell him tomorrow for sure. If I'm not here, he can get in through the back to pick up his tools."

"He already did that. He says one of the tools isn't his. He doesn't even know what it's for."

"Tell him it's a bonus."

"He really wants to talk to you."

"He can stop by tomorrow. I'll be here all day."

Morley relayed the message and hung up.

"They're still mad about the overtime, aren't they? But it was their own fault. I didn't spill the paint and I had to replace the rug—"

"Gert, forget the paint. Where were you this afternoon?"

"At END."

"You went to work?" Morley asked.

"You traitor!" Cyril croaked.

"I thought the murder was over when the mechanic called, so I dropped in at the office. We have a new project."

"Just what I wanted to hear," Cyril said.

"The kickoff lunch is Monday."

"Monday? There's no way I'll be ready to—"

"Can't you discuss that later?" Christine asked.

"Sorry. GG, tell them we're busy playing detective from now until—whenever. I'm going to stick with Larry. You say he's being released at eleven-thirty? Are you picking him up, Mad?"

"Yes."

"I'll drive. Then I'll stay at his place for the weekend."

"Maybe with his cooperation you can keep track of him."

"Hey, Chrissy, that was my first try."

"Aside from Larry and Mad," Morley said, "I don't think anyone is in immediate danger. Our real priority is to catch the murderer. I'm going after some new leads."

"I thought you were hot for MacMillan," Christine said.

"She's in this up to her frosted eyebrows."

"Are they really? Isn't she worried about getting dye in her eyes?"

"Gert, if you'd shut your beak for five seconds, we might get through this."

"Sorry, Morley. Where were we?"

"We were talking about MacMillan. I say Harris will take care of her. I say we concentrate on finding out what Brown's up to."

"Who?" Gertrude asked.

"B. R. Brown? The man Cooper went to see on Fifteenth Street?" Christine asked. "We don't know anything except his name, and we aren't even sure he knew Charles Brooks."

"But we know Sergeant McDuff went to that apartment," Gertrude said. "There's got to be some connection with Charles."

"What makes you think this case has McDuff's undivided attention?" Cyril asked.

"I refuse to believe Cooper and McDuff visited him for unrelated reasons," Morley said. "And I intend to find out what's going on."

"So you're going to go sit in his hedge?" Gertrude asked.

"Laugh if you want. That hedge got results. Someone has to find out who that guy is, and I'm the only volunteer."

"I'll do it, Morley," Christine said. "I want to help."

"But, Chrissy," Cyril objected, "your art show is coming up. You have to get your paintings together."

"They're all set. And this is more important."

"Why don't we just ask Larry? Anyway, I don't like the sound of it."

"So now we get the male chauvinist ploy. Listen, my dear hubby, you aren't in any position to talk. You didn't exactly cover yourself with glory."

"And you're not about to let me forget it."

"Lost Cooper in lingerie, Lost Cooper in lingerie," Caruso commented.

Madelyn let the conversation flow over her. She could tell them who B.R. Brown was, but it didn't matter. They weren't really going to do anything with the information, anyway.

"Could we please stick to the subject?" Morley yelled. Here's the plan. Cyril's with Larry, Christine's following our mystery man, I'm going after MacMillan. Maybe I'll get lucky and she'll drop my loafers in a Goodwill pickup box."

"Your loafers?"

"The ones I lost in the hedge."

"Forget the shoes, Morley. You ruined them when you stepped in McDuff's plaster casts."

"They were the most comfortable shoes I ever had."

"Morley! You're the one who wanted to stay on track."

"Right. You, Gert, have basic responsibility for Mad. And if we're all going to be out in the field, we must have some way to stay in touch."

"That would be GG," Cyril said.

"And just exactly what does that mean?" Gertrude asked.

"Merely taking advantage of a natural resource."

"Okay. I'll be sure my cell's on. Gypsom Detectives, at your service. Christine, we need a bald eagle logo."

"How about a clever monkey?"

"I prefer the intensity of the eagle eye, the ferocious talons—"

"We get the picture, GG." Cyril interrupted, looking pointedly at the phone on the bar. "Just promise me one thing. Carry your cell and leave it on. I don't want to be talking to your voice mail."

"No problem. But I might need some help corralling Mad."

"Look, guys, I'll make sure I'm not alone. Trust me."

"What about me?" Oliver asked.

"You are responsible for. . .the puzzle," Morley replied. "It has to be finished by Monday. And I must say you're doing a terrific job."

"But I want to help find—"

"Forget it."

"Something's burning! The chicken!" Gertrude's wail cut across Oliver's reply. "Come on, everyone. Dinner is practically served. Or at least, it will be when we save it."

Madelyn settled back against the cushions and enjoyed the scene. It had been a good party, after all. Once they had a plan, her friends had become their usual impossible selves. Morley had moved to his spot in front of the fire and was holding forth on breeding lammergeyers.

Across the room, Cyril and Gertrude were arguing about their new programming project. Christine was talking to Oliver, who knew about what. Yes, they were back to normal. In another week or two, they would have forgotten Charles had been murdered. But she wouldn't forget. She'd have to live with that ugly truth.

"Fire! Fire!" Caruso shouted.

"Wishful thinking, old fellow." Morley handed the bird a slice of apple. "This has been a dull party for you."

Madelyn laughed with the others and tried to lose herself in the cross conversations. But it didn't work. John hadn't come. He would have understood that the case was far from over for her. That the biggest question still remained unanswered. Until she knew who had killed Charles, she couldn't get on with her life.

"You're working late."

Harris turned in his chair. "You too, Chief."

"A couple of the commissioners wanted to talk."

Harris grimaced. "I'm sorry about—"

"I can handle them. Arresting Dr. Rhines turned out to be a good thing."

"You heard about that?"

"Some members of my staff think I should be kept informed."

"I was going to call—"

"No you weren't. You're a stubborn, independent wise-ass just like I was at your age. I'll forget it this time. But I don't like to be ignored."

"I have that straight, sir."

"About the commissioners— I was able to convince them that we're on the right track." He paused. "Are we?"

"I'm not sure. This blackmail angle is driving me nuts."

"I thought by now you'd have learned to delegate."

"I did. Pierce has been through it. I'm double checking. But I suppose the commissioners—-"

"You're in luck there. We have two days to make an arrest as long as you keep your picture off the front page. No more funny photos at the zoo. Got it?"

"Right, Chief."

"Two days, max. I suggest you get some sleep and let someone else do your clerical work."

"Yes, sir. See you in the morning."

Harris turned back to his computer. The Chief had a point. But, half an hour later, he was still at his desk, scrolling through reports. He was overlooking something. What really happened Monday night? All that activity in the zoo, hordes of people wandering in and out, the guard making his rounds, yet no one heard a commotion in the Reptile House, or Brooks' run down the hill— Wasn't he screaming? No one saw the mechanic hitching up Madelyn's car? There had to be something. He found his notes from the first interview with Stevens.

MORLEY STEVENS

1. Walked to dinner at the pizza place
2. Returned via the front gate. Let in by Horatio Jones

3. Spotted a man dressed in a suit and carrying a white trash can (?)
4. Worked until eleven and went home.

Nothing new there. What about the guard?

HORATIO JONES
1. Saw Cooper walking in zoo
2. Did rounds every ninety minutes
3. Checked service gates
4. Let Stevens in and saw him later in his office

And then there was Cooper. He had probably told them the truth in the hospital, but it wouldn't hurt to review all the notes.

Tuesday's version didn't help—his story had been that he had gone home to bed early. On Wednesday, he'd said he'd looked in on sick lion cubs, (verified by vet staff), and had seen Stevens, Horatio, and four people from the vet center. Finally, after the attack on Friday, he'd said he'd seen Rivers' car, stumbled over Brooks' body, moved it to protect Rivers, waited in his office in case of trouble, and left about one, noticing that Rivers' car was gone.

And that was it. But wait. What about Botticelli Brown? Scot must have followed up on that— Harris pulled up notes from the interview at 305 Fifteenth.

BOTICELLI BROWN
1. Exotic animal dealer
2. Has worked with Cooper in the past, but not since the ruckus with the Zoological Association.
3. Hasn't seen Cooper in months.
4. Knows nothing about Brooks

Scot had been puzzled by him. He had been totally uncooperative at first and defensive when he did start to talk. Lying? Or just uncomfortable with policemen?

Another dead end. Maybe they should find out a little more about this guy. He'd talk to Scot in the morning.

So what did they really know? Brooks had been bitten by the taipan between eight and midnight. It probably wasn't suicide, but it could have been. And Cooper had probably moved the body into the cage around midnight, but he might be lying. If it was murder and Cooper's story was true, the murder occurred no later than 11. Three days and that's all they had. That and a lot of noise.

At least Madelyn was no longer chief suspect. But she wouldn't be safe until the murderer was in custody. The Chief was right. It was time to get some rest.

CHAPTER EIGHTEEN

Gertrude stood uncertainly in the doorway watching Cyril and Madelyn get into his car. "You're sure I shouldn't come along?"

Cyril stuck his head out the window. "Don't worry, we've got her surrounded. Larry and I will drop her at Frank's, and Harris guarantees her safety after that."

"Now listen to me, Cyril. Go into Frank's with her and wait until you've found John. He might be late."

"GG, no one's going to shoot me in the middle of a crowded restaurant."

"Can't be too careful. Now promise you'll both call when you change position. And Mad, you call me immediately if you find yourself alone."

Gertrude watched the car disappear with a feeling of disquiet. How silly! Madelyn was in good hands.

She had just walked into the house when her phone rang. It had to be Oliver. He was the only one she hadn't heard from recently.

"Oliver?"

A confused splutter hit her ear.

"Listen, I don't have time for anything but your location. And please stop shouting."

"Lady, do you want the Porsche or not?"

"My Porsche? The blue one?"

"It's blue, but it ain't yours."

"I'll take it. When can I pick it up?"

"I can't hold it past two-thirty."

"I'll be there in twenty minutes."

The timing could not have been worse. Still, Cyril, Madelyn and Larry were tied up for several hours, Morley was following

MacMillan on a shopping expedition, and Christine was parked on a street in Westdale. She had no idea where Oliver was, but that didn't matter. Her cell phone was in her pocket. So no one would miss her. She rushed out the door.

Madelyn paused inside Frank's. It had only been five days since she'd met Charles here. But this restaurant was too much a part of the zoo routine to avoid. Best to get it over with.

John hadn't arrived. She requested a table next to the largest aquarium, well away from the windows. It would be relaxing to watch Octo in his tank. Charles had always avoided the small octopus. Octo came close to the glass and seemed to be grinning at her. She ordered white wine for herself and some bits of crab for him, and spent several minutes feeding him. He held each tidbit with his suction disks before finally transferring it to his mouth. She enjoyed the clinging feel of the disks as they brushed her hand.

When the crab meat was gone, she settled back with her wine. It was all so confusing. Larry had lied to the police, to everyone, because he had believed she'd killed Charles. He had assumed it was self-defense, but was worried that a jury might convict her. That easy acceptance of her guilt hurt. Obviously, she didn't really know him.

Still, she had to admit she had wondered if Larry might have murdered Charles. Was that so different? Maybe the normal rules of friendship didn't apply to murder.

"Am I interrupting something?"

"John. You startled me."

"Sorry."

"Don't be. You saved me from talking myself into a bad mood."

"Something happened?" He sat down opposite her and motioned to the waitress for coffee.

"Larry's lies got to me. I thought he was my friend."

"Don't take anything Cooper says too seriously. He may have a different explanation tomorrow. Besides, we all get in strange places."

"Like me at the police station."

"You were a bit cool."

"I was simply responding to your stuffy speech."

"And you made your point." He grinned. "It took me a while to decide to call you this morning. Will you accept my apology?"

"Now, yes. I'm not sure why, but everything seems different today."

"I'm worried about your friends. Are they serious about giving up their detective games?"

"Did you ask me here to find out what my friends are doing?"

"Oh, that wonderful element of trust. Listen, Madelyn, you don't have to tell me if you don't want to. But they could be in a lot of trouble."

"It may be hard to believe, John, but when you get right down to it, they've got more common sense than most."

His laughter rippled across the restaurant chatter. "I must be thinking of some other set of people."

"Believe what you like, Lieutenant. They're as reliable as you get." She ignored his incredulous expression and changed the subject. "You missed a funny scene last night. Taffy, our rosy boa, escaped from her cage and climbed onto the shelf over the bar. Poor old Oliver was fixing a drink when she landed on his shoulders. You should have heard him scream."

"I can just see Oliver with a snake for a neckpiece. I'm sorry I didn't drop by."

"I'm sorry, too."

"Look, Madelyn, what are your plans this afternoon? I have the strictest orders to keep an eye on you."

"Everyone's being over-protective. But you must have work to do."

"Work? What's that? The fact that the Chief's ready to fire me for incompetence is not preying on my mind."

"Is he really upset?"

"Yes. But I need some perspective, a fresh angle. So what's your plan?"

"I'm going to my office. The mail's been piling up all week."

"Mind if I tag along? The snakes might inspire me."

"You're afraid to leave me alone."

"That's part of it. But I do want to spend some time thinking about snakes. Honest."

"This case is affecting your brain, Lieutenant." She laughed, toasting him.

"I see nothing's changed. Same papers in the same stacks on the floor."

"If it changed, I'd never find anything in this office."

"It has a certain homey feel."

"Do I detect a note of sarcasm? Excuse me for a moment. I promised GG I'd stay in touch."

She felt John's eyes on her and looked away self-consciously as she counted the rings. "She's not answering. That's strange, after all the talk—"

"All what talk?"

"Oh, nothing. I just expected her phone to be on."

John was browsing through the books that lined the wall. "Where should I look for a description of the taipan?"

"Try Kingshorn's SNAKES OF AUSTRALIA."

When she glanced up a few minutes later, he was gazing intently at a picture of the snake.

"That's it!" He jumped up and slammed the book shut.

"What's what, John?"

"I— But Ed told me— Look, Madelyn, I've got to find Markleson. That bump on the head—and the alibis—and all this chaos—" He paused. "But what about you? I shouldn't leave you here alone."

"Don't be ridiculous. I'll finish up the mail and take a cab home. No one's going to attack me in my own office."

"Well—"

"I'll be fine."

He rushed out. Surely there was nothing in the book. She glanced idly at the picture. It wasn't even a good photo. Must have been something else. Sighing, she returned to her work.

Madelyn paid the cab driver and walked to the front door.

Someone was sitting on the step. Startled, she jumped back, ready to flee. Then the figure moved and she recognized Oliver.

"Where's Gertrude?" they asked each other in chorus.

A phone was ringing. "It's the landline." Madelyn unlocked the door and ran inside. "Hello?"

"Where's Gertrude?" Cyril shouted.

"I don't know. I just walked in."

"Madelyn, is that you? Larry's looking for you. There's a real mess at the zoo. We need you. I'll put him on."

"Mad? Is that you?"

"Of course it's me. What's going on down there?"

"Half the animals are loose and Piper says some of the poisonous snakes are missing."

"What happened?"

"We don't know. Cyril and I were here and Piper comes running in yelling about being chased by a white tiger. He said the cage doors were open."

"Do you know how many animals are loose?"

"No. It seems like all of them. We've just cleared out all the last of the visitors. Now I'm trying to organize a roundup."

"Eiiii!"

"What is it, Larry?" He didn't answer. She heard nothing but the sound of furniture falling. "Larry! What is it? Cyril! Someone answer me! What's going on?" She listened intently. "Larry?" Still nothing. Maybe she should call the police.

"Mad, it's OK." Relief flooded through her at the sound of Larry's voice. He was panting. "I felt something cross my foot, and my first thought was poisonous snake. But it was one of your tegu lizards."

"So the outdoor terrarium is open."

"Piper's in the Reptile House, checking. We need you down here. I'm calling all the curators."

"Why don't you get Ms. MacMillan to do that for you?"

"I couldn't find her. We have security people on the gates. What a mess. The art show's tonight, and the big high mucky-mucks will be coming any minute."

She had forgotten the art show. Charles and the opera and the art show. Tonight.

"Some of the animals can climb the fence." Larry sounded frantic. "It'll be hours before we can do a complete inventory, and we'll never be able to find the small creatures after dark. That gives us about forty minutes. . . Oh no!"

"What is it? Larry—" She winced at the unmistakable sound of his receiver hitting the floor.

After a moment, Cyril said, "Mad? You still there?"

"Cyril? What's going on?"

"Larry went to help Piper." He sounded remarkably calm. "The white tiger IS chasing him."

"If you say so. Tell Larry I'm on my way."

She tried calling Gertrude again, with no luck, so she left her a hurried note. "Come on, Oliver, let's go," she yelled, as she ran to the car.

CHAPTER NINETEEN

Gertrude turned into the driveway, reveling in the Porsche's tight cornering. This had been a great day! She had the car and two puppies. What a stroke of luck that the car's owner had a litter of St. Bernards. He'd been weird about selling one to her, but she'd finally convinced him it was the perfect present for Mad. The animal shelter was probably a mistake. But the Saint needed a playmate, and Falstaff was the dog she had always wanted. His mother was a German shepherd and they said his father came from a good neighborhood.

"Welcome home, kids." The sleeping puppies didn't respond. "And there's one of your new friends on the doorstep. Oh, oh. It's almost five. We don't want to hear about it, do we? Now you sit here quietly while I—"

"Gert, is that you?"

"Morley. Why are you outside? Where's Mad?"

"How should I know? I thought you were in charge of communication?"

"I—I've been busy. But my phone's been with me the whole time. Have you tried calling?"

"Repeatedly. I suppose the crisis is over. You wouldn't have gone car shopping otherwise."

"I wasn't shopping. I just went to pick it up."

"Where was it? Florida? Gee, Gert, you could have brought me some key lime pie."

"Morley, be serious." She unlocked the front door and walked into the entryway. "Have you talked to Larry? And what have you done with MacMillan?"

"She lost me. I followed her through endless department stores—her taste is abominable—and on to Merkle's apartment where I sat for three hours before thinking to check behind the

193

building. They'd gone out through the alley. Larry wasn't home, so I came here. I was, I might add, kind of surprised that I couldn't reach you after all that talk about being our call center."

"I had to run an errand, and I didn't promise to stay home. Just to keep the phone with me. I wonder where Cyril is. Let me give him a quick call." She pulled out her phone and punched his number. "It's not working." She peered at the phone. "Morley, I hope you have your cell. Mine's dead and I can't reach Cyril."

"Of course I don't. I told you Caruso threw it in the toilet ages ago. But forget Cyril. There's a note from Mad here on the table." Morley handed it to her.

She threw her cell phone across the room and read: "Larry called. Animals are loose at the zoo. He needs help with the snakes. Funny business. I'll call you later.'"

Morley ran his hand over his thick, grey hair. "We'd better get the hell over there."

He followed her to the car, but stopped abruptly, staring into the back seat.

"What are you waiting for?" she asked. "Get in."

"There's a—a thing with a huge head in there."

"We don't have time to discuss the dogs. Just get in the car."

Madelyn and Oliver parked next to the service gate and hurried toward the Reptile House.

"Gosh, Mad, it's almost dark. What are you going to do?"

"Check the reptiles. That's my first responsibility."

"Bet you never had anything this exciting happen in the zoo before. I'm sure glad you asked me to help. I—"

"Oliver, I'm sorry. I really can't let you help. The snakes are dangerous and you don't have any experience with them. I'd never forgive myself if you were bitten." Worse yet, he might step on one of them.

"I can do it, Mad. I held a snake once when I was a kid, and he wrapped around my arm. It was a gopher snake, I think."

"If you really want to help, go find Larry." She stopped to retrieve a baby Galapagos Island tortoise from the day lilies beside the path. "Tell him I'm here."

"Well, if you insist—"

"He's in Administration. This road will take you to the front door."

"You're sure you don't need me?"

"I'm sure."

Oliver hesitated before heading uncertainly down the road.

She smiled at his retreating form. He looked absurd in his black trench coat. Now maybe she could corral her wandering snakes before they'd gone too far astray. There was that pregnant rattlesnake—

She was relieved to find the Reptile House door firmly closed with a rag blocking the crack underneath. That was the only opening in the building large enough to allow a snake to escape. Ed must have fixed it before going to find Larry.

Opening the door cautiously, she stepped inside and switched on the lights. No snakes were in sight. She placed the tortoise in a makeshift pen and stood listening. The building was quiet. Unnerved, she tiptoed down the familiar corridor toward her office.

"Ed? Are you here?" Silence greeted her. She shivered.

She wasn't afraid, but— the important thing was to be careful where she put her feet. Snakes didn't like to be stepped on any more than people did.

What was that? Something had moved, next to the file cabinet. It was slithering toward her. The taipan! Not six feet from her, coiled and ready to strike. So close…she must back away slowly… a sudden movement could trigger the strike…she was still within easy range. She felt sweat on her face and hands, a tight knot in her stomach as she watched the forked tongue tasting the air. She fought the hypnotic power of the vibrating coils, beautiful in the dim glow.

She was almost out of range— she had made it. Gasping for breath, she ran for the door and turned the handle. It was sticking again. She tried once more, but it wouldn't budge. What if the snake was pursuing her? With the strength of terror, she pulled the door open, slammed it shut behind her, and collapsed against the outside wall, sliding down onto the tile floor of the gallery.

For a moment she concentrated on the cool surface of the tile, the security of being safe on the ground. She'd never been afraid of a snake before. But even in his cage, the taipan had been making her queasy. She had a sudden vision of Charles, running down the hill pursued by the snake. Now it was after her.

Nonsense. Struggling to her feet, she had to acknowledge that she, Madelyn Rivers, Curator of Reptiles, had actually run away from a snake. And she was still shaking.

She was startled to see a young bear cub lumbering toward her. He had to be from the Children's Zoo. The poor baby must be frightened. Madelyn approached him slowly, enjoying the determined way he was proceeding down the walk, his roly-poly body shifting at each step. Perhaps she could finesse him into going home. But when he caught sight of her, he turned and dashed off. He was not about to give up this first taste of freedom.

She smiled. He'd find his way home when it was time to eat.

The lights flickered— then went dark. A power failure seemed unlikely in this weather. She shivered violently. It had to be deliberate. Nothing else would explain the loose animals, the lights going out. But who?

Larry? Could Larry have staged his injury to divert suspicion? She'd never believe that. But she couldn't stop the images— Larry hitting himself on the head, Larry opening the cages, Larry picking up the phone to ask for help—

Maybe he hadn't made any other calls. She hadn't seen anyone since she arrived. And she had sent Oliver to Larry's office. He would know she was alone. She felt her way to the side of the path and stood still. Where should she go? Suddenly she felt something slithering across her foot. Jumping back, she choked off a scream. The taipan? It was too dark to see what it was or where it had gone.

The cold feel of the unseen creature lingered. She crept forward slowly. Larry could have set this up to get her back to the zoo. And now she was alone. Maybe he was coming for her. No, that was impossible. Not Larry! Besides, Cyril was with him. But Cyril had lost Larry the last time he'd tried to follow him. She had to get out of here. But she'd left her purse and keys in the Reptile House. She couldn't open the service gate.

She brushed against a shrub at the side of the path and drew in her breath. This was ridiculous. She had to think rationally. She would find her way to the main gate and ask the guard to call John. He'd know what to do.

Having a plan helped. She could sense animals all around her, but they stayed out of her way and she was nearing the main gate. And then she heard footsteps ahead of her. She froze as a flashlight beam focused directly on her.

"Mad, is that you? It's me, Larry."

She turned and walked away from him.

"Hey, wait for me!" He caught up with her in two strides. "How long have you been here?"

"Oh, a few minutes." She didn't want him to know she'd encountered the loose taipan.

"What a mess! I feel so powerless. Here," he gestured toward the stone bench at the side of the path. "Let's sit for a minute. Help me figure out if I've forgotten anything important."

"You're the one who set up the procedures."

"I didn't have this kind of crisis in mind. I may trash the

Procedures Manual. At least the phone routine worked pretty well. Except for Wellman."

"The chimp keeper? What happened to him?"

"His daughter told me her folks had gone out to dinner. She didn't know where. I called six restaurants before I found him. He was furious. He said he was enjoying the best steak he'd ever eaten, and he wasn't about to leave his wife in the middle of their anniversary dinner even if an army of chimps had invaded the zoo."

"It sounds like leaving the steak was the real problem," Madelyn said.

"Yeah. I told him to bring it along if it was so damned important to him, but to get his ass down here."

"Did you reach all the curators?"

"Except for Morley. And they called in most of the other keepers. So now what? Should I call the bomb squad? Are we up against terrorists? Animal haters? Zoo haters? Who's the enemy? I've never been at such a loss."

"You're doing everything you can."

"I didn't plan for so many disasters at once. I even had Morley's teacher—what's her name? Suttersby—demanding to see him. She didn't want to leave." He sounded frustrated.

"I know it's a real mess. But not having lights makes it all so much worse. Why hasn't the backup generator kicked in?"

"I don't know. Fortunately, the electrician who installed it was here working on the lights for the art show. One of the policemen is driving him down to the plant to have a look."

"Did Cyril go with him? I thought he'd be with you."

"No, I managed to lose him. I was getting bored with being followed."

That was a strange comment. Was Larry planning something? She felt beads of perspiration breaking out on her forehead as he shined his light on her face.

"What's the matter, Mad? You look frightened."

"It's—it's nothing."

"But something's wrong. You're white as a ghost. Here, put my jacket around you. Better?" She nodded, unable to speak. "Now tell me what frightened you."

"It's—it's the snake, Larry. The taipan. It's loose in the Reptile House. I thought it was chasing me." Even thinking about her encounter made her hands shake. Clasping them together, she looked at him. "I didn't think I'd ever be afraid of a snake."

"That was a terrible experience. Of course it scared you. But you mustn't let it stop you. It's like falling off a bicycle and getting right back on. Look, let's you and me go catch it. Once it's back in its cage, you'll feel better. And that'll keep us occupied until the electrician fixes the lights." He handed her his flashlight and helped her stand up. Putting his good arm around her, he guided her toward the Reptile House.

"I'd go after the taipan myself if it weren't for this sling. And, truthfully, I'm still not at my best. It must have been that blow on the head—"

Blow on the head. That was what John had said, just before he rushed off. There must have been something fishy about that attack on Larry—and about Larry. Larry had murdered Charles.

And now—

"Larry, I…I forgot to…I left—" Unable to think of a credible lie, she tore herself free. She must get away. What if he had a gun? She must run—

"Mad!" His shout sounded distant. "Where are you going?" She heard his footsteps falling behind and was dimly aware of a light and Larry's angry voice shouting, "Who's in that bush?"

She was running in the dark, but she knew the path like the back of her hand. His shouts grew fainter. She kept running. Finally, she realized she had left him far behind. It was time to stop and check her position. She turned on the flashlight and caught a glimpse of a fox disappearing up the walk. She started to chase it, but stopped short. There were more important problems—like getting out of there alive. She had to catch her breath. Sinking onto a bench, she huddled in Larry's jacket.

Oliver didn't take the road to the Administration Building. He knew it was shorter to go by path, through Bird Mesa. But the twilight confused him and he soon found himself back on the maintenance road. Strange, the way they were always changing the paths. It was almost as if they wanted you to get lost. Well, he'd fool them. He'd stay on the perimeter road. It would take him to the entrance even if he'd started in the wrong direction.

It was only after he had trudged along for more than fifteen minutes that Oliver remembered what an enormous place the zoo was. Madelyn had told him they had over two hundred and fifty acres. It would take him forever to walk all the way around. He'd have to find one of the paths through the center. This was promising. A wide road leading down the hill. He'd be back at Administration in no time.

After a few more minutes, Oliver stopped and looked around again. He'd never seen the rest area ahead. He must have walked to Los Angeles. Well, wherever he was, he was lost. Slumping down on the nearest bench, he tried to orient himself. There had to be signs somewhere.

What had happened to the lights? This was no time for a power failure. He'd never find a sign in the dark. Maybe he should try the footpath to the right—that side was usually north.

A man's voice startled him. It seemed to be behind him, in the bushes. Stooping, he listened intently.

"Come on, Sarah, please." It was almost a whisper. "I can't carry you. Please, will you stand up?"

Oliver waited impatiently as the voice grew louder.

"Poor baby, I'm sorry. I don't know who's responsible for this, but whoever it is will have me to deal with. Come on, sweetheart, you're going to be all right."

Sarah. Who was Sarah? And why didn't she want to stand up? That could have been Stevens back there. The voice was too soft to be positive, and he couldn't see a thing in the bushes. He would sneak up on them. No noise. Crawling slowly under the shrub behind the bench, he barely stifled a scream when his hand encountered a woman's shoe.

"Oliver, get your hand off my foot."

Even through the whisper, he could sense her fury.

"Must you foul everything up?"

"Christine! Why are you—"

"Hush! He'll hear you!"

"But I want to know what's going on—"

"Later, you idiot. Get out of here or I'll never forgive you."

"Who is it back there? At least give me a clue." What was that? He could hear the crashing of a heavy weight through the nearby branches. Must be an elephant.

"Out! Now!"

He started to refuse, but this was not the time to argue. Not with an elephant two feet away. He would leave quietly. Mustering as much dignity as he could in his awkward position on the ground, Oliver edged himself back toward the path. Why did they all want to get rid of him, anyway? He could be every bit as clever as the rest of them. Never mind. He'd show them. That was probably MacMillan in the bushes. And Christine was trying to keep up with her. But Sarah? He'd never heard of a Sarah. Still, it wasn't worth worrying about. MacMillan wasn't the murderer. If Christine wanted to waste her time, that was her problem. Besides, they'd all respect him after he'd nabbed the real killer. Even Lieutenant Harris would have to thank him. Yes, he'd get the murderer, that dirty skunk. Tonight.

A brilliant flash startled him as he emerged from the bushes. Good. The photographers were already following him. His triumph would be in the news. Back on the path, he hurried off in search of the villain.

Morley sighed with relief as Gertrude parked by the front gate. What a ride. She'd been bad enough with the old Buick. The zoo was totally dark. Not a light anywhere.

"Morley!" Gertrude sounded scared. "It must be a trap. Mad's in there being murdered. Hurry."

Trap, indeed. Count on Gert to make a big deal out of a power failure. Still, it was odd about Larry's message— "It's probably temporary. Come on—"

They were locking the car doors when a howl erupted from inside. "What the devil is that noise?"

"The puppies must be awake." Gertrude stuck her head in the car and switched on the overhead light. She wrapped a large beach towel around the St. Bernard and picked her up. "Is the baby unhappy? Morley's going to take good care of you, sweetie. Don't you worry your pretty little head." She handed the heavy, warm bundle to him.

"Are you crazy?" He was not going to go along with this nonsense. "What am I supposed to do with this young horse?"

"Be gentle with her, won't you, darling. She doesn't even have a name yet, poor baby." She leaned over and kissed the big head. "Look at those eyes. Won't Mad be pleased?"

"Gert, we have an emergency on our hands. This is no time for puppies."

But she wasn't listening. Picking up the second dog, she hurried toward the gate.

"Hold on here, Gert!" He followed her, clutching the puppy to his bosom. When the policeman at the entrance caught them in the circle of his flashlight beam, Morley assumed he had an ally. Surely they wouldn't be allowed inside with the dogs.

To his annoyance, the sight of two distraught individuals carrying animals wrapped in blankets was adequate identification. The man didn't even ask what they had captured.

"The lights went out about five minutes ago," he said, opening the gate. "Should be back on right away. But in case they aren't, I have some extra flashlights."

"Thanks. We had no idea we'd need them."

Morley recognized the large flashlights as part of the zoo emergency kit. So Cooper was getting things organized.

"There are a lot of people wandering around in there without lights," the policeman was saying. "It must be kind of spooky. I just heard a woman scream. Probably someone stepped out of the shadows and scared her."

"More likely, Mad's been killed."

"Pardon me, ma'am?"

"She was agreeing with you. Thanks." Morley turned on his flash and followed Gertrude past the Administration Building.

"Morley," she whispered, "I meant what I said. The murderer could have attacked Mad and no one would have noticed. We've got to find her."

"Calm down. It's important to think this through carefully. This looks like Peggy MacMillan's work to me. Who else was going around collecting zoo keys, I ask you? I'm going to concentrate on finding her."

"Morley, you're knee-jerking, not thinking. We can't do anything until we find Mad—"

"Look, Gert, we are here to practice preventive homicide, and that means we must find Peggy—"

"—and kill her?" Gertrude drew in her breath.

"No, no, we want to disarm her. Nothing more." The puppy licked his face. He had to find some safe place for this bundle of love. If he could get away from Gert, he'd lock the dog in his office. Caruso could entertain her. "You go find Mad and look after her while I track down Peggy. That way we can get everything under control."

"That sounds reasonable. She must be in the Reptile House, looking for her snakes. I'll go help her."

"She may not want a dog—" It was too late. Gert had disappeared, and she was headed for the Children's Zoo. She'd be safe there. Pulling the blanket tight around the puppy, he hurried toward his office.

The path was deserted, and Morley made good time. He stopped at the door and fumbled for his key ring. It was difficult, reaching in his pocket while holding the enormous animal with the other arm. Ah. He had it. Now to open the door. On the third try, the key turned in the lock and he was in the outer office. He gave the door a shove and heard it click against the frame. But had it latched? He'd check in a minute. The first order of business was shutting the Saint into his office.

He felt his way down the hall. It was easier than fumbling for the flashlight in his pocket. When he reached his door, it was locked. He forgot to lock it half the time. Why not today?

He fumbled again, managed the lock and stepped in, shutting the door behind him. Moving forward, he stumbled and almost fell. What had hit him in the shins? His briefcase. Someone had left it right in front of the door.

Well, at least he could relax in here. Gratefully, he set the dog down, letting the keys fall. He used his flashlight to make a quick check of the floor. He'd better pick up the stray books. He didn't want them chewed up.

He was interrupted by a whir of wings. Caruso landed on the back of the desk chair.

"Some broad, some broad."

"No, Caruso. You're to forget that one. Meet your new friend, the Saint. Nice puppy, nice puppy."

"Nice puppy," Caruso responded obediently.

"Good. Now if you two will settle down, I'll be on my way."

The dog was already curled up in the corner. Now was the time to escape. Flashlight in hand, Morley opened the door and stepped out. But something had preceded him into the hall.

"Nice puppy," Caruso remarked from the end of the corridor.

Had he closed the outer door when he came in? He turned the light beam on it in time to see Caruso swagger through. Morley ran down the hall in hot pursuit, but Caruso was already outside, perched in a nearby tree.

"Some broad, some broad."

"Caruso, come back here this minute!"

"Nice puppy," Caruso replied as the Saint galloped into the back of Morley's knees.

"Rest, rest, perturbed spirit," proclaimed the bird.

Moonlight peeked through the clouds long enough for Morley to see Caruso flap toward the bird-of-prey cage and perch halfway up the structure. Oh well. The bird would return. He'd rather not have him loose in this loony bin, but he'd be okay. And the dog showed no inclination to run off. She was licking his face enthusiastically. He'd put her back in the office and get on with it.

Gathering her up, he tried to open the door. It had latched this time. He felt for his keys, then remembered. They were on the floor by his desk. He was locked out.

"Nice puppy, nice puppy."

Looking up, he saw Caruso, silhouetted against the sky, headed toward the top of Cat Canyon. What a mess. He had let Caruso out, he was locked out of his own office, and he was still saddled with the dog. Exhausted, he sank down on the step, holding the puppy tightly to his chest.

CHAPTER TWENTY

Gertrude knew she was lost. But each new trail looked familiar, and she kept hoping this time she was headed for the Reptile House. If only Morley had stayed with her. He knew his way around the zoo. And Falstaff was getting heavy.

"Morley's impossible. Did you know that, Falstaff?"

He didn't respond. She tucked him securely under her arm and started off again in what must surely be the right direction. The moon was behind a heavy bank of clouds and the flashlight did little to dispel the sea of blackness that surrounded her. The huge eucalyptus trees lining the pathway rustled in the wind, compressing the night.

"Good thing I don't scare easily," she whispered in the puppy's ear.

She was walking resolutely when she tripped over something that slid off into the underbrush. It felt like a snake. But even if the snakes had escaped from the Reptile House, they wouldn't be lying about on the path. Her imagination was out of control. All the same, it had felt like a snake.

Well, let someone else worry about the animals. Her problem was Mad. The murderer might have captured her by now. Maybe he was torturing her. Gertrude tried to walk faster.

"Hello, Kanga," she said as a cat rubbed against her ankle. "You do pick the damndest times— Oh no! You can't be Kanga!"

"Grrrrrrr!" It was a lion. Lioness. No mane.

"What a nice voice you have." She backed away, flashlight trained on the enormous animal. Maybe she should turn it off. No, lions were afraid of light. No need to panic. "Stay calm, Falstaff. We're fine. I'll just back up and turn slowly—"

The lion lifted one paw and reached out toward her.

Frightened, Gertrude jumped out of range and fled. As she ran, she tried to keep the light on the path ahead.

And then her foot hit a root and she stumbled forward, breaking her fall with the flashlight. She tried the light: nothing. The bulb must be broken. As her eyes grew accustomed to the dark, she became aware of an outline in the path. She reached out gingerly and touched the cold, smooth skin. It was like a—a boulder. Someone must have let out the pet rocks. Well, at least she'd made it away from the lion.

She'd sit on the boulder and rest. Falstaff was small, but he was getting heavier by the minute. Gratefully, she arranged the sleeping puppy in her lap. He didn't seem at all concerned by the strange smells. He was going to be a sensational dog.

But she was too wound up to sit still. She set Falstaff on the ground and stretched her arms over her head. It was time to find Mad. Taking a deep breath, she felt the boulder move and slid onto the ground. The rock was alive? Reaching out, she encountered a large, scaly foot. Of course. A giant tortoise. The tortoise, glad to be rid of his burden, shifted his position and settled back to sleep. Gertrude had just leaned against him when she felt a movement next to her. It was probably something small and cuddly from the Children's Zoo.

Slowly, she moved her hand in the direction of the intruder, expecting fur or feathers. Instead, small, sharp teeth came down hard on her fingers. Leaping up, she let out a muffled scream and, clutching Falstaff who was working up to a ferocious puppy growl, she started running blindly down the path. She mustn't scream. There was a murderer loose in the zoo, and she didn't need his attention.

Someone was coming, flashlight in hand. She pulled up short and hid in the bushes next to the path. She wanted to ask for help, but this person was stopping every few feet to attack what appeared to be a giant hunk of meat. Not reassuring. She'd had enough surprises for one night. She was persuading herself to get up when she heard a familiar voice:

"Oh hell! Where's my pipe?"

"Morley! What a relief. Forget the pipe. You're supposed to be catching the murderer."

She heard the flapping of wings and felt a bird swoop past her head to perch on the back of the bench. Caruso! She laughed shakily. "Okay, old friend. With you here, I have the courage to move on."

Tucking Falstaff under one arm, she started off again.

Caruso kept pace, bouncing cheerily from bush to tree to bench along the way. By the time she had reached the refreshment stand at the bottom of the hill, she was exhausted. She had to rest.

It was open. She herded Caruso inside and closed the door.

The bird quickly found himself a comfortable roosting place on the counter while Gertrude collapsed on the floor with Falstaff.

She couldn't carry the puppy another step, and it was dangerous for Caruso to be wandering around the zoo. But she had a plan. When they fell asleep, she would go find Mad. As if in tune with her thoughts, Caruso said:

"An hour of quiet shortly shall we see

Till then, in patience our proceeding be."

She smiled. "So tell me, Caruso, how do you think Morley is getting along with the St. Bernard? Falstaff, do you realize she's about ten times bigger than you already?" The puppy seemed pleased by this, and she felt him stand and wag his tail. After a brief tour of their new quarters, he settled down in some packing material in the corner and fell asleep.

Gertrude sat quietly for a few minutes before creeping to the door and pulling on the handle. It wouldn't turn. It must have locked automatically. She pushed and shoved and kicked, but to no avail. There had to be a way out. The serving window wouldn't budge. It was secured with a heavy bar and two padlocks. No hope there. She tried shaking the door as hard as she could, hoping to knock something free. No luck. Forgetting her sleeping dog, she used the broken flashlight to hammer at the lock. She had to get out of there, fast. She'd never forgive herself if Mad was murdered while she was locked in the refreshment stand. Falstaff, frightened by her sudden outburst, began to howl.

Morley staggered down the hill toward the refreshment stand. He should investigate that racket, but he'd have to rest first. The weight of the puppy was too much. He collapsed gratefully onto a bench and buried his head in the soft fur. He couldn't tail the murderer like this. And now someone was coming. He'd better hide. He didn't want to chance a confrontation with the murderer—not with a young horse to protect.

But the lanky figure moving down the stairs past the bird-of-prey cage wasn't looking for confrontation. Cyril was freezing. And he wasn't at all sure what he was supposed to be doing. This had to be the silliest exercise Gertrude had ever involved him in, and that was saying a lot. He knew nothing about animals, and the roars and growls he had been hearing were much too close for comfort. And then there was all that banging at the foot of the stairs. Well, he'd had enough. He was going to find out what was happening.

He was starting purposefully toward the gate when a heavyset figure emerged from the bushes directly in front of him. Jumping back, Cyril focused his flashlight on the brown and white features of a huge, shaggy head. It was too much. Letting out a blood curdling scream, he dropped the light and turned to flee.

But before he had gone two steps, he felt a firm hand on his shoulder.

"Calm down. It's me, Morley."

"Morley? Then who's that?" Cyril stooped to retrieve his light and shined it on the strange object. "It's a dog! Why?"

"I've been asking myself that same question. It's a present for Mad—"

"And you wanted to give it to her before the murderer does her in?"

"Yeah, sure." Morley paused. "Sorry. The puppy is making me crazy and Caruso is loose. I don't even know what I'm supposed to be doing."

"Same here. Who am I following? Do you remember?"

"I have a list. Here, you take her for a minute. She's extremely affectionate." He shoved the puppy, blanket and all, into Cyril's unresponsive arms. "Wait— Wasn't that MacMillan?"

"What? Where?" Cyril hadn't seen anything.

"She's going up those stairs," Morley whispered as he moved away.

"Wait! Where are you going?"

"I'll be right back," he hissed, hurrying off.

Great, really great. The puppy licked Cyril's face. "Oh, quit it." Well, there was nothing else to do but wait for Morley to come back. Sitting down under the bushes at the side of the path, he wondered once more what made him consider these people his friends.

But Morley wasn't worrying about Cyril. He had found MacMillan. He'd spotted her earlier in the evening, creeping around the service road with her boyfriend and the white trash can they'd had the night of the murder. And here they were again. They were going to do it—whatever IT was— And IT was obviously connected with Brooks' murder. Cyril would have to wait. Morley was going to find out what these two were up to—and put a stop to it!

Morley's pursuit of MacMillan had not gone unobserved. In his black coat and bowler hat, Oliver Lake faded from shadow to shadow in the eucalyptus grove. He paused in front of the refreshment stand, torn between the desire to follow his prey and his curiosity about the frantic shouts coming from inside. But he couldn't stop now. He had lost Stevens once, and he wasn't about to lose him again. He could check out the noise later. Hurrying to catch up, he didn't notice that the stocky figure had stopped moving until they almost collided. Turning off his flashlight, Oliver dodged under the nearest bush. To his consternation, his hand touched something warm and furry.

"For Christ's sake, Oliver, can't you look where you're sitting?"

"For Christ's sake, yourself, Cyril." What was Cyril doing in a fur coat, anyway? "How was I to know you were lurking under this particular bush? I've got more important things on my mind. I'm following the murderer."

"Glad someone thought of that."

"Keep your voice down."

"Get a grip, Oliver. You could set off a keg of dynamite here and no one would notice."

Morley had started up the stairs. "There he goes. I must catch him in the act. Check out that noise in the refreshment stand, will you?"

As Cyril watched him depart, the moon came out from behind the clouds. The black-clad figure was sneaking along behind Morley. Oliver thought Morley was the murderer? Cyril shook his head in disbelief. Well, he had enough problems of his own. Forget Oliver and forget the mysterious noises in the refreshment stand. It was probably a sympathetic vibration from Oliver's brain. He had to find a place to stow the dog. Wearily, Cyril picked her up, wrapped the towel around her, and trudged off down the path.

Madelyn heard an animal in the bushes behind her bench. Even with her flashlight, she couldn't see anything. Then she heard a man's voice nearby.

"Let's have some of that light over this way," he said.

"Just a minute," she replied. As she turned the flashlight, Madelyn spotted a man in a keeper's jumpsuit bending over something in the brush.

"Come give me a hand, will you? Sarah won't get up."

Sarah. . .Who could that be? Another body? "Who are you?" she asked.

"We can introduce ourselves after we get Sarah out of here. Hurry up, We don't have all day."

It could be a trap. Maybe that was the murderer…She shined the light on his hands. He was holding a coil of rope…"I'm sorry. …I must go…" She was running now. "Take good care of Sarah."

Now run. No light. The path turns right, then left. "Ouch!" The rose thorns had ripped her sleeve. Stay alert. Maybe no one is coming— Risking the light briefly, she spotted a bench. She would sit and catch her breath. There had to be other people around, but the murderer—Larry—or that man with the rope— might get here first. She sat up sharply. Something was moving in the bushes behind her.

"Can't you make less noise with that?" It was a woman.

"I can't help it. The stupid thing keeps getting caught in the shrubbery. Let's get on the path," a man's voice replied.

"And run into the photographer again? That's all we need, a nice closeup. Tell me once more. Why cardboard?"

"Paper's not sturdy enough. We didn't have a choice. But I admit it's awkward."

They were gone. At least they hadn't seen her. The woman's voice was familiar. If she followed them she'd have company. But she too tired.

Madelyn watched the white tiger stalk by, with two shadowy figures close behind. That was the second time she'd seen them in the last half hour. At least those keepers were trying to do their jobs. She was shirking hers. She'd actually let a snake frighten her. Well, that was one thing she could control. She'd go check on all the snakes. She'd probably be safer in her office than here, anyway. She knew her way around in there.

But as she started toward the Reptile House, she realized someone was coming up the hill, flashlight in hand. Stepping into the shadows, she waited. Larry. She held her breath as he approached. He was stopping. The beam of light was moving from tree to tree. She froze. He mustn't see her. He was muttering to himself. She strained to hear, but couldn't understand what he was saying.

Finally, he continued on and she moved back onto the path. Something hissed. Her flash picked out the tail of some unidentified creature, disappearing into the undergrowth. As she straightened up, a brilliant flash confused her and she fell, sprawling ignominiously on the path.

"That you, Dr. Rivers?"

It was the red-headed photographer who had been in the zoo the day of the murder. If only she could stay with him, maybe she'd feel safe.

"Wait! I want—"

"Sorry, ma'am. This picture's too good to give up."

"But I need help. Please—"

He was gone. She would have to make it on her own. Anyway, for all she knew, he was the murderer. Madelyn tried unsuccessfully to laugh as she turned into the covered gallery.

The Reptile House door stuck. She'd get that fixed on Monday. It finally yielded and she stood for a long moment, sweeping the light back and forth over the entryway, before stepping in. No snakes were visible. She closed the heavy door and continued down the passage. Her flashlight beam jerked from floor to ceiling, from shelf to window as she searched for reptiles. She was near the taipan's cage. Maybe Ed had captured the snake. Or was it still loose?

Carefully she approached the cage, her cone of light a tunnel in the dark interior. She tried several different angles, but couldn't spot the snake. There were more flashlights in the storeroom. She could go find a couple of them— They were in a box right in the middle, surrounded by crates— Crates that could be full of snakes. The entire collection could be hiding out there, all of them angry, all of them ready to strike—

Well, if they were, she'd simply have to catch them and put them back in their cages. She couldn't proceed without more light.

She turned the handle on the storeroom door and opened it cautiously. For a moment she couldn't see anything. And then her flashlight picked out the king cobra, coiled loosely in the middle of the room. She flung the door shut and shoved a cage against it.

"Mad, are you here? Do you need some help?"

"Christine!" At last! Someone she could trust. Christine could help check the snakes. And her large electric lantern was perfect. "Be careful! I don't know who's loose. But why are you here? I thought you were tailing B. R. Brown tonight."

"I lost him hours ago. Cyril called me at home and asked me to come down. But now I can't find him."

"Well, I'm glad you're here. I need help taking inventory. The taipan was loose earlier, so I want to check all the snakes."

"You worry too much. Whoever let the taipan out was probably making a symbolic gesture."

"No. The king cobra's out. I met him in the supply room."

"We can manage him, can't we? He's not even full grown."

"They're tricky. I'd rather wait until Ed's here."

"Oh, come on. Let's try."

"You've got to be kidding. You don't 'try' with a king cobra."

"Whatever you say. So how do we count snakes?"

"You go out front. I'll shine my flashlight into the cage from this side, through the peep hole. I want you to check on the position of the snake. If he's well away from the inside door, I'll open up and have a good look. We'll start with the venomous ones."

"What's the signal?"

"Thumbs up when there's no snake near the door, otherwise down."

While Christine moved outside, Madelyn probed the space under the cages with her light. That area was empty. The lantern appeared in front of the boomslang's cage. Madelyn focused on Christine's hand. Thumbs up. Good. Opening the door, she spotted the boomslang pair, hanging in their usual tree.

Madelyn checked off the rhinoceros viper, the gaboon vipers, and the krait— All safely in their cages. The black mamba was next. He was a particularly nasty character, and fast. She would have to work quickly. At the thumbs up sign, she pulled open the door and—

She heard her scream before she knew what was happening. As the dark, sinuous body hit her shoulder, she jumped aside automatically. Where was it? She backed away from the cages, toward the sink. Her light was feeble in the black void. Then she spotted him near the wall. He was moving away from her. That was good luck. She grabbed the long hook from beside the sink and had him back in his cage almost before she realized what she'd done.

Her heart was pounding. She shut the cage door and pushed the lock in place.

"Mad! Are you all right? Did he bite you?"

"No. Why, Christine? Why thumbs up?"

"I didn't see him until he was on you. I—I'm sorry."

Christine looked pale and shaken. "Well, forget it. He didn't get me and he's back in his cage. He just scared me half to death." Her wobbling knees gave way and she sat down in the middle of the floor, well away from potential snake hiding places.

"I can imagine. I've never been more frightened myself."

Christine was fumbling around by the sink. "Christine, get out here in the middle of the room. A snake could be hiding in those shelves. I need a couple of minutes and then you can help me round up the loose creatures in the hallway. Christine?" She turned to see her picking up a large mallet. What on earth was she doing with that?

"You're right, Mad. I need to sit a moment, myself."

She was still moving. She was. . .

"Mad? Are you in here?"

Ed, at last. What a relief. "Yes, Ed. Come in carefully. Some of the snakes are still out."

His enormous lantern cast a warm glow on the corridor walls. "I caught the taipan earlier," he announced.

"He's in his cage?"

"Yes. Then Cooper needed help with the alligators. We just finished rounding them up."

"You have a professional now, Mad, so I'll go on. I was a rather doubtful addition, anyway." Christine started for the door.

"Why the mallet?"

"Protection." She raised it in farewell.

Madelyn stood up. She must be flipping out. She'd thought for a moment that Christine was planning to hit her over the head. Uncertainty had a way of eroding reality. She couldn't go on like this. She had to know who had killed Charles so she could stop suspecting her friends.

Madelyn took Ed's hand. "I'm really glad to see you. I was starting to feel crazy."

"It's not just you, Madelyn. The whole zoo's gone haywire. And the people are worse than the animals. I saw that friend of yours run past here like the devil was after her."

"GG? What's she doing here?"

"I assumed she had come with you."

"No. I'm here alone. The murderer must be responsible for all this."

"You may be right." Ed poured coffee from a thermos into an ancient cup and handed it to her.

"I don't trust anyone anymore. I got scared talking to Larry, and I actually ran from one of the keepers. I was even getting spooked about Christine when you came in." She laughed weakly. "I suppose you're next. I don't understand myself. You people are my friends. This murder has given me a severe case of paranoia."

"Well, they might be afraid of you, too."

"Me? Oh, you mean because I might be the murderer?"

"There has been some discussion of that." Ed smiled.

"I've been cleared. The police know I didn't do it."

The smile faded. "But the evidence. It all pointed to you. The police must think you're the murderer."

"In the beginning, yes. That's all changed now. What's the matter?"

"You killed him. Everyone knows you killed him."

"Ed! You're talking nonsense "Madelyn backed away from him. Ed. Of course. "I—I'm sorry. I—there's something I must do."

She dashed for the door, slammed it shut and ran into the road. A truck engine started behind her. Ed? She ran faster, hoping to reach the main gate before he caught up with her. Someone was gunning the engine. He was picking up speed, coming toward her. No lights. Why no lights? It was going to hit her!

Desperately, she dove for the side of the road. If she could roll down the hill, out of sight—

A wrenching pain in her shoulder slowed her. There was a sickening crunch in the road and an object flew through the air toward her. What— A log. The truck passed. She lay there— motionless, breathless, terrified. Finally, she heard it turn down the hill toward Cat Canyon.

Madelyn was shaking violently. Someone had tried to kill her—and almost succeeded. A zoo cart passed slowly along the road, lights on, spotlight scanning the hillside. She tried to move, but her injured shoulder made it difficult. The light caught her.

"Madelyn! Are you all right?"

"John!" At least she knew he wasn't the murderer. Yes, I'll be just fine now."

Gertrude heard a truck stop. A zoo official? Surely he'd rescue her. Still, all kinds of people had passed by and managed to ignore her. She'd even heard Cyril. Maybe she hadn't made enough noise. "Help! I'm locked in here!" she yelled.

"Some broad! Some broad!" Caruso exclaimed.

"This is bad enough without your insults."

"Oh, hell! Where's my pipe?" His tone was conciliatory.

Not to be outdone, Falstaff started to howl again. She searched for a window, or a viable crack. The only possibility was a crooked knothole in the wall that gave her a view of the high end of the bird-of-prey cage. That was not going to help. Wherever Cyril was, he wasn't there.

She peered through it once more, hoping to find a way to enlarge her view. The moon was brighter now. The cage looked cold and stark against the charcoal sky. Still, something was happening. Yes. Someone was on the cage, on the outside, climbing the wire.

The peephole restricted her view to a circle of wire a few feet across. The climbing figure was already out of range. Maybe he'd come back the same way. She was transfixed, watching the lifeless cage. Here he came. But he was going up, not down.

And there was a second figure climbing with him. They were pulling a huge white cylinder. Now they were gone, too. And here was another one. She'd know that bulky outline anywhere. It was Morley. And close behind him, two more figures.

"Morley, have you lost your mind? Get off the bird cage!" she yelled. He didn't respond.

A second vehicle was arriving. She could see the glow of its lights through the cracks. Did that mean that the first one didn't have lights? Odd. She started banging on the door again.

Harris braked sharply at the bottom of the hill and pulled up next to the zoo truck. That was the truck, but where was the attacker? The bird-of-prey cage loomed ahead. They had come full circle.

"Mad, are you all right back there?"

"I'm a little stiff, otherwise okay. If you don't mind, I'll stick close to you. I've had enough confrontations for one night."

"I don't know about that. I'm hoping to confront the murderer."

Grabbing a pair of binoculars from the floor, he jumped out of the cab. The truck was empty. What was that scraping? He turned the truck's powerful spot on the bird cage.

"Who turned on that light?"

The voice was coming from above. Looking up, Harris saw Stevens, hanging on the side of the cage. What the—

"The jig's up, Stevens."

That sounded like Oliver Lake's voice. Yes. There he was, hanging from the cage a few feet from Stevens. And below him was Harley Knopstead.

"What's going on up there?" Harris shouted. "Come down right now, all of you. That's an order."

"What happened—!" The voice came from the shadows. Shifting his flashlight, Harris spotted Cooper, eyes wide with astonishment. For once he seemed to be at a loss for words.

"Who's there? Oh!" A zookeeper in a jumpsuit ran up, out of breath. "Is one of them—"

"No," Harris replied.

"But who—"

"Wait a moment. You up there. Get your asses down here and then stay put. All of you."

Morley started talking before he touched the ground.

"Anyone—"

"No," Harris said.

"What are those people doing on my cage?"

"I was about to ask you the same thing. Where's Scot?"

"Right behind you, John."

"Good. Go check out that noise coming from the refreshment stand, will you?"

McDuff forced the door open and Gertrude emerged, with Caruso on her shoulder. She was carrying something in a blanket.

"Mad, are you all right?" she asked. "I was so worried—"

"That you locked yourself into a nice safe hiding place?"

"Larry, this is no time for sarcasm," Madelyn said.

"That was an accident. I was looking for a safe place for Caruso and the puppy. Morley, where is Mad's?"

"Mad's what?" Madelyn asked.

"Your dog. Morley has it."

"GG, you know I don't have a dog."

"But of course you do. You just haven't met her yet. And now Morley's lost her."

"Cyril has her," Morley said. "Where did he disappear to?"

"Over here." The voice seemed to come from a great distance. Harris shifted the spot again and picked up a lanky figure struggling up the walk with a St. Bernard puppy asleep in his arms. This was crazy. He was pursuing a murderer, not running an animal shelter. But before he could object, Cyril offered the dog to Madelyn. "She's all yours."

"Why, GG? Why now?"

"She's to go with Falstaff."

"Falstaff?"

She was interrupted by a stocky man leading a large chimp in one hand and eating a baked potato from the other. The chimp was chewing on an ear of corn. Silence fell.

"As soon as Jake smelled my dinner, he came running."

Wellman patted the chimp on the shoulder. "What's going on around here, anyway? I've never had to eat a steak dinner on the run before."

"Get that chimp away from my cage," Stevens shouted. "The birds are frightened enough without primate intervention."

"Stevens," Harris said, "simmer down. What were you doing up there?"

"I honestly don't know, John. I was trying to keep up with the others." He pointed to the top of the cage. A gasp arose from the group as the spot picked out an enormous sheet of cardboard. In large letters over a picture of birds were the words

CONDOR CIGARETTES

Condor cigarettes? Harris moved the beam higher. Beyond the sign, near the eagle's nest at the top of the cage, were two small figures. Harris adjusted the binoculars on them.

"MacMillan and Merkle!"

"There's someone else up there," Gertrude said. "I saw him go up ahead of those two."

221

Harris turned the beam even higher. She was right. Someone was clinging to the wire just outside the eagle's nest. As he raised the binoculars, something glittering fell through the heavy beam of light. Focusing the spot on the figure, Harris looked through the glasses to be sure. Yes. Thank God!

"Christine Featherworth, I have a warrant for your arrest," he shouted. "You will be charged with the murder of Charles Brooks and with the attempted murder of Madelyn Rivers. Come down at once."

For a long moment, she didn't move. Then slowly, deliberately, she pushed off from the wire. Helplessly, Harris watched as she fell, tumbling through the air. He tried to follow with the spot, but lost her. There was a dull thud as her body hit the road below the cage.

He moved toward the sound. She couldn't have survived that fall. Now where— He stumbled on the step. Better get a flash. There would be one in the truck.

He had just reached the vehicles when the lights came on, revealing the stricken group. Cyril was sitting on the ground, his face buried in the puppy. Gertrude was moving uncertainly toward him. The others looked stunned. Harris picked up the tape cassette lying on the ground. That was what had fallen. It was unlabeled. And there was the body.

Harris looked up at the whir of wings above. Caruso had perched overhead on a cross beam of the cage.

"Some broad killed her lover! Some broad!"

CHAPTER TWENTY-ONE

"Just one more, Dr. Rivers," Knopstead pleaded. "I'll never get shots like this again."

"Sorry. I've had it." Madelyn moved away from the grinning Komodo dragons and sank onto a nearby bench. The new arrivals were getting good publicity, but she was too tired to pose any longer. She'd been at the zoo until three a.m., collecting stray animals, and then found Gertrude's house full of people who wanted to talk. Poised between horror and curiosity, they needed their friends.

The drive to the airport to meet the dragons had been a relief. Now they were safely installed in their new enclosure. And the whole process, from the removal of the first nail in the crates to the emergence of the dragons, had been dutifully recorded by Knopstead. He seemed to have declared himself official zoo photographer.

"Got it! Terrific, Lieutenant."

Madelyn laughed. Knopstead had caught John and the larger dragon peering intently at each other over the low wall. "Hi, John," she said. "I didn't expect to see you here."

He sat down with a sigh. "And I didn't expect Knopstead. Between the bird cage last night and the dragons today, the Chief's going to kill me."

"Has he no sense of humor at all?"

"None. Are you about finished here? I told GG and Morley we'd meet them at Frank's."

"Good. The dragons are all set." She stood up stiffly, and he reached out to steady her.

"What is it?"

"I'm a little sore. But what really hurts is I know I'll never trust my judgment again. About anyone."

His blue eyes were dark with concern. "Give it some time."

She nodded. "Let's go eat. I'm starved."

Madelyn smiled across the table at John. "I'm glad to see you're not on duty. That must mean I'm no longer official business."

John clinked his martini glass against hers. "Give it some time."

"To the passage of time," she said. "Logic tells me you are right."

"You've been something more than official business almost from the beginning." He paused. "But tell me, how is Cyril? That must have been a terrible blow for him last night."

"He's as confused as the rest of us. I think he talked all night. Gertrude and Oliver stayed with him. He was asleep when I left. Oliver is still there, and GG and Morley are picking up Cyril's sister at the airport. She's flying in from San Francisco."

"Yes, Morley told me they might be slightly late—but here they come."

"We dropped his sister off at home," Gertrude told them. "Cyril's still asleep. And Oliver has a question: who is Sarah? Apparently he almost met her in the bushes—"

"Sarah's a sea lion. But we missed it, didn't we?" Morley interrupted. "You've already explained everything."

"I told Madelyn you'd be doing the explaining."

"Stuck, are you?" Morley pulled out a chair for Gertrude with one hand and signaled the waitress to bring drinks with the other. "Sure I can explain it," he said. "GG was attacked by a lion, and Oliver followed the sea lion around the zoo because he thought she was me. Then I climbed the bird cage because Peggy was unveiling a condor. But anyone could have told you Christine was the murderer."

"Three questions, Morley. Why did she do it, how did she do it, and how did you know?'

"Christine!" Gertrude repeated. "I still can't believe it. I spent hours talking to Cyril. He's devastated, and he doesn't understand. Why did she do this, John? Why kill Charles?"

"Caruso said it all. Some broad did kill her lover. That's what made his announcement so chilling."

"Charles was Christine's lover?" Madeline asked.

"She'd been meeting him at his apartment for a long time. From what Ms. Stebbins tells us—"

"Ms. Stebbins?" Gertrude asked.

"—Brooks' neighbor. She says it started before you met him, Madelyn. The tape Christine was trying to retrieve from the top of the cage contained an emotional appeal to Brooks, pleading with him not to end their relationship. He must have taped it, then used it to blackmail her. He probably figured that was the fastest way to get rid of her. She wouldn't have wanted anyone to hear it. But I think she killed out of jealousy. She couldn't stand to lose Brooks—especially not to Madelyn."

Gertrude looked bewildered. "All of this was going on and no one had a clue? Even Cyril? It doesn't seem possible."

Morley put his hand on Gertrude's arm. "We didn't really know her. But how did you figure it out, John?"

"We'd been concentrating on the people with no alibis for the critical period—eight to midnight. People like Cooper. And we'd thought the murderer had moved the body into the cage, but that turned out to be Cooper. So when I realized that the murderer hadn't necessarily attended the murder, I started considering people with good alibis."

"Vulture droppings! Explain yourself."

"After lunch yesterday, I went with Madelyn to her office. While I was waiting for her, I read a description of the taipan. Turns out they're short-fanged snakes. When they bite, the venom is injected into the wound inefficiently. To compensate for that, the taipan has developed an unusual mode of attack. It wraps itself around the victim, hangs on tight, and keeps biting for a long time. That way the snake can be damned sure the victim gets a full dose of venom."

Madelyn shook her head. "I knew that, but I didn't think of the implications."

"Ugh!" Gertrude shivered. "Brooks must have run all the way down to the bird-of-prey cage with the snake wrapped around him like a tourniquet."

"But how did that point to Christine?" Madelyn asked.

"The people with good alibis were Christine, Cyril, Gertrude and Piper. We never seriously considered Gertrude, and Cyril seemed unlikely. He didn't know much about the Reptile House. Of course we couldn't be sure that the murderer was one of the people on that list. But I reviewed the cases against Christine and Piper. Piper's resentment of Madelyn was clear enough, and his alibi was excellent. He'd played bridge through the whole period. But somehow I couldn't buy him as the murderer. And once I started putting things together, Christine seemed a lot more probable. Jealousy is a powerful motive. After I had verified a few points, I was almost sure she'd done it."

"So Cooper pulled both Brooks and the snake into the cage. But John, how did Christine engineer all that while she was driving around the city with Gert and Cyril?" Morley asked.

"She set up a booby trap. She put the taipan in a small, light-weight cage, and balanced it on the ledge above the front door of the Reptile House. Her phone records show she called Brooks late in the afternoon, so I assume she made an appointment to meet him there Monday evening. The idea was for the cage to break apart on the victim's head—"

"That mysterious blow to the head—" Madelyn spoke softly. "That was what you were talking about when you left."

"Right. We should have paid more attention to that part of the autopsy report. But getting back to what happened, Christine correctly assumed that the taipan would react to all this by attacking the nearest warm body. She was lucky. It was Brooks. But she wouldn't have been devastated if it had been Madelyn. She wasn't taking too great a chance by leaving the baited trap."

"She might have killed Ed," Madelyn said.

"True. I wonder if she would have cared," John replied.

"She knew someone was going to walk in that door and be attacked by the taipan. How could she act so casual all through our dinner?" Gertrude asked.

"As Morley said, none of you really knew her," John responded.

"Going to the zoo Tuesday morning must have been tough for her. She couldn't have known what had happened." Madelyn swirled her drink in the glass, watching the colors change. "And then somebody told her the body was in the bird-of-prey cage."

"Yes, that must have been a bad moment. She knew she hadn't put Brooks in the bird cage."

"If I'd been paying attention that morning," John turned to Madelyn, "I'd have asked you a few more questions about that battered cage sitting in the middle of the Reptile House entry. Not to mention the stepladder I almost broke my neck on. I must have bumped into it six times, and all I did was apologize."

"All very well, John," Morley said, "but don't tell me you put this whole thing together from reading the description of the taipan in a book."

"That, and something Madelyn told me yesterday. She gave me a vivid description of Taffy, the rosy boa, dropping onto Oliver's shoulders. That reminded me of the autopsy report and the comment about a blow on the head. I thought I'd found the answer and, like an idiot, I went dashing off to talk to Markleson and Stebbins, leaving Madelyn alone. That was the stupidest thing I've ever done."

"I can take care of myself," Madelyn insisted.

"Sure you can." He smiled at her. "Anyway, Markleson agreed that the blow on the head was consistent with my description of the cage, and I remembered the seal key ring that had turned up in Brooks' pocket. The fact that you hadn't given it to him didn't prove it was from Christine, but it was suggestive. Then Stebbins looked at Christine's picture and immediately identified her as the woman who'd been visiting Brooks. And she'd described a tan Volvo earlier."

"Their car is orange—" Gertrude said.

"Have you ever noticed how that color of orange looks tan under artificial light? Anyway, it all fell into place. By the time it finally dawned on me that I'd better get back to the zoo, it had become a war zone. That really scared me because I was almost certain Christine would go for Madelyn next."

"And to think I had no idea—" Madelyn leaned back in her chair.

"Mad, when you make an enemy, you do it right," Gertrude said. "Tell us, John, how did Christine manage the car?"

"That was simple. She swiped Madelyn's spare keys ahead of time. She left the zoo, probably around five, and took the bus to your place. She assumed Mad was with Larry, and that could have fouled her up. Fortunately for her, Mad was asleep and didn't hear the car being backed out of the driveway. Christine drove back to the zoo, apparently arriving after the heavy rain had started. She'd probably planned to let the air out of a tire—anything that would require assistance. But the fresh mud was tempting. That way, there'd be new tire tracks near the reptile house service gate. With the car thoroughly stuck, she was all set. She set her trap, left via the back door, and went on to her class, intending to go out for beer afterwards. Then you people arrived, thereby providing her with an ironclad alibi. She must have excused herself during dinner to place the call to the mechanic."

"Yes, I remember her doing that," Gertrude agreed. "But she was just gone a few minutes."

"It was a good alibi. But, fortunately for us, she made too many other mistakes. Someone ransacked Brooks' apartment early Tuesday morning. She probably went there to search for the tape."

"Cyril would have noticed she was gone," Morley protested.

"I don't think so," John replied. "He told me he was out like a light that night. She probably drugged him, but there's no way of proving it now."

Madelyn had a sudden image of Cyril stretched out on the couch, saying how tired he was. "I teased him about it." Gertrude looked stricken.

"Anyway, the tape must have fallen from Brooks' pocket when he was being dragged into the cage, and, in the morning, one of the birds picked it up. My guess is that Christine spotted it in the nest and was looking for an opportunity to retrieve it. She decided to finish off Madelyn at the same time."

"I saw what must have been the tape twice, myself." Morley sighed. "I meant to retrieve whatever it was before it harmed the birds, but then something came up."

"I noticed it, too, Morley, and I'm a detective. Don't blame yourself."

"So did she open the cages?" Gertrude asked.

"Her prints are all over the locks. She probably thought the general confusion would cover for her while she took care of Madelyn and the tape."

"That makes sense. But why didn't she wear gloves?"

"Good question. Maybe she was getting rattled, or maybe it was overconfidence. She'd been very careful about fingerprints until then."

"But why did she attack Larry?"

"I can only guess. She probably wanted to strengthen the case against Madelyn, but also, she may have figured out that Larry had moved the body, and been concerned that he knew something."

Madelyn nodded slowly. "So I had good reason to be paranoid. There was such an eerie feeling about the zoo. No lights, the animals wandering around in the shadows— I was imagining all kinds of things. I even hid from Larry. Christine frightened me, but actually Ed scared me even more. There was something about the way he was talking— I started running, looking for the nearest exit. Thank heaven you turned up when you did, John."

He smiled.

"I have to know about the CONDOR CIGARETTE sign," Morley said. "It almost makes you think the murder was a publicity stunt."

"The murder was the last thing they wanted. MacMillan works for an ad agency, and CONDOR CIGARETTES is their new account. They were hired to introduce the product and make CONDOR a household word. Since they can't use TV or radio commercials for tobacco ads, they wanted media attention, so they were planning to run the campaign from inside the zoo. Signs would appear mysteriously in and around the bird-of-prey cage and, with luck, they'd end up on the six o'clock news."

"They went to so much trouble. Imagine Peggy taking a job in the zoo—"

"They had to have access to the zoo to put up the signs. This was a nationwide campaign. They were planning to distribute free packages of cigarettes outside all the major zoos. The packs would have contained endangered species cards. You know, like baseball cards. It might have been effective."

"But it did work, didn't it?" Gertrude asked.

Harris nodded. "You have a point, GG. Their sign will certainly be on the evening news. I'm not sure Peggy thinks they succeeded, though. The zoo may want to press charges."

"How did they get the sign into the zoo without being noticed?"

"They rolled it up."

"My trash can!" Morley said. "It was a rolled up sign."

"Right. That's what you saw the night of the murder. Apparently there were so many people skulking around that they lost their nerve. And it was quite a crowd: Morley, Horatio, the vets, Christine, Larry—not to mention Brooks and the taipan. Anyway, they claim that hearing the cage door clang shut was the final straw. They decided to try again later."

"I wasted a lot of energy following MacMillan," Morley said. "I didn't even consider Christine. And there we were, telling her everything we knew."

"We were all following red herrings," Gertrude said. "And all the time, Gus could have straightened us out if I'd only listened to him. But no, I was too busy with my own schemes."

"What did Gus know?"

"He'd seen Christine crawling into the house through a window last week."

"That must have been when she took my pin."

"Probably. Gus knew she was a friend, but he didn't think it was right for her to force her way in. And, believe it or not, that tool he said wasn't his, the one I found under the stairs, turns out to be one of Christine's palette knives. She must have used it to force the catch on the window. So I had two chances to find out Christine had been sneaking around."

"All the players in this case were connected to one another, but the connections turned out to be unrelated to the murder. Somehow you don't expect a guy involved in as many shady deals as Brooks to be killed by a jealous woman."

"Where did all those photographers come from?" Morley asked.

"They were everywhere," Gertrude said. "When I was running away from that rock—"

"It's called a tortoise, Gert. A Galapagos Island tortoise—"

"—I was fleeing from the rock when I tripped. Then a flash went off in my face. It scared Falstaff half to death."

"The same thing happened to me," Madelyn added. "I actually tried to stay with Knopstead for company, but he had his own agenda."

"It was all Knopstead," Harris said. "He had come early for the art show. Then, when he realized the animals were loose, he was in his glory."

"The art show!" Madelyn had forgotten it. "What happened to the art show?"

"Postponed until next month," Morley replied. "Cooper had a guard and the PR guy stationed at the main gate to keep the guests out, while apologizing appropriately. Did you talk to Knopstead last night, John?"

"Yes. He was there almost as late as I was, checking and uploading his shots. And he was back this morning to get the Komodo dragons. He figures this case has everything: wild animals, a murderer skulking around the zoo in the dark, even a weird group of people hiding from one another in the shrubbery."

"And a raven acting as Greek chorus," Gertrude said.

Morley nodded, fumbling in his pockets. "Oh hell! Where's pipe!"

CPSIA information can be obtained at www.ICGtesting.com
Printed in the USA
LVOW10s1806220714

R8632000001B/R86320PG395347LVX2B/1/P